CONQUEST

THE POWER TRILOGY
BOOK 3

A WORLD OF DREJON NOVEL
DOT CAFFREY

Conquest: The Power Trilogy Book 3
Copyright © 2017 Dot Caffrey

This novel is an updated edition of Conquest of Power: The Trilogy of Power Book 3
Copyright © 2017 by Dot Caffrey

Cover design by eBook Launch
https://www.ebooklaunch.com

ISBN-13: 978-1-947392-34-2

First Printing: 2019

For my Dad.

CHAPTER ONE

"AND JUST WHERE do you think you are going?" Neshya asked.

Regnaryn turned, surprised anyone else was out at such an early hour.

"Um, I was just going for a walk."

"Bah!" the cat-like yekcal said. "First of all, it is far too early for you to be up and about. And, more importantly, if you were just going for a walk, why would you be carrying a pack?"

"Please tell me you were not trying to leave me again," Graeden said as he approached from behind. "Do you not remember what happened the last time we were separated?"

Regnaryn turned to her mate, surprised by the expression of intense hurt on his face. "I am sorry. I was not thinking about that."

"Why do you continue to feel you have to leave, sister?"

Neshya asked.

"You know why. It was all my fault. All the death. All the suffering. All of it because of me," she said, turning back to the yekcal with whom she had been raised. "Look at yourself, even after all these months since the attack, you are not fully healed and Immic is still unable to fly. And, what of Mama and Papa and all of the others here in Reissem Grove who continue to mourn the loss of their children or siblings or mates. I cannot bear to think that if the Master returns, he will rain down even worse horrors upon us."

Graeden put his arm around her and she pulled away.

"I am the reason that Reissem Grove was attacked. Had I not returned, none of this would have occurred. If I am gone, you will all be safe."

"Perhaps," Neshya said.

Graeden glared at him.

"But you are the only one who sees it that way," Neshya continued. "No one else blames you. Surely you must know that."

"So they say, but how can they not?"

"Because we know you. Know you and love you," Neshya said. "There is no reason for you to run away."

"I am not running away, I am merely leaving. To protect you."

Neshya shook his head.

"But what if he comes back?"

"We will be ready for him," Neshya said.

Regnaryn just looked at the yekcal.

"So, now that we have settled that, let us head home. I am starving and Mama will have enough food for you two as well."

Neshya turned and walked down the path toward home. Regnaryn and Graeden followed.

CHAPTER TWO

"WHY ARE YOU WAKING me so early?" Graeden asked. "The sun has barely risen, unless..."

He reached for her and tried to pull her back into bed with him.

Regnaryn laughed. "Sorry, my love, but now is not the time for that. Do you not remember that we are to meet with the others this morning?"

Graeden sat up and ran his fingers through his sleep matted hair. "Why does everyone insist on being up at the crack of dawn around here?"

"Just hurry up and get ready. You do not want to make Papa and the others wait, do you?"

She turned and left the room, calling over her shoulder. "The tea is almost ready."

Graeden got up and dressed, happy to see she was content in her life in Reissem Grove again.

#

"Good morning," Regnaryn called as she and Graeden entered her parents' house.

"Morning? It is closer to evening than morning," Ayirak grumbled.

"Oh, stop being dramatic, it is no such thing," Trebeh replied. "Come through to the garden, children. Everyone is here and we were just about to get started. Can I get you something?"

Before they could reply, she handed them cups of tea and gave Graeden a plate of meat-filled pies.

"Really, Mama? You feed him and not me," Neshya said, throwing his hands up in the air in mock dismay.

"You, young man, have already eaten two, or was it three, helpings. I think you have been well-fed," Trebeh replied.

"Overfed, if you ask me," Immic added.

"I do not recall anyone asking you, feather-brain," Neshya said trying to be serious but unable to pull it off.

"Enough!" Ayirak snapped. "We are not here to listen to you two play games. We have serious matters to discuss, and if you two younglings wish to be part of this…"

The elder yekcal did not need to finish.

"Sorry," both replied.

Regnaryn and Graeden nodded greetings to all and sat down beside Ellyss.

"Now, on to the business at hand," Varlama said in her usual matter of fact tone. "We need to find the Master. Find him and end him."

"That is just like a tazzamira to state the obvious and do so as if it was as simple as breathing. If it were that easy, we would have already done it," Phrynia replied shaking her head.

"And leave it to a drageal to jump to that conclusion," Varlama chuckled. "I did not say it was easy. But look at the talent we have assembled here. There are few who can match the feline ferocity of the yekcal or deal with an aerial attack from the drageals, the most feared of all the dragons. Add to that the tenacity of humans and there is no way we will not be able to accomplish our task."

"And even one tazzamira in battle is a force to be reckoned with," Phrynia added.

Varlama nodded.

"Be that as it may, before we can find him, we need to know who he is," Ellyss said. "Surely the 'Master' is not his given name."

"I agree," Varlama said. "But we know little of him other than that name."

"I am not sure that is so," Phrynia said. "He may have given us more clues than he meant to."

"You might have a point there. I think we know more than we realize, we just need to put it all together," Trebeh said

"Then, that is where we need to begin," Ayirak said, "although I think most of us here in Reissem Grove know nothing more of him than the sound of his voice before the last of those vile beasts died."

"I believe Trebeh and I heard his voice before that," Phrynia said. "During the incident when he tried to take over Regnaryn's mind and body. Remember, Trebeh?"

"Now that you mention it, yes, I do recall a voice. From its tone it seemed to be cursing, but I did not recognize the tongue," Trebeh replied.

"Nor did I. Though, even at the time, I thought it sounded vaguely familiar. Since his attack I have been thinking more about it and I believe that once, long ago, I heard similar sounding words spoken by Grenwald."

"My father?" Regnaryn sputtered, nearly spitting out the tea she had just sipped.

"Yes," Phrynia replied.

"Surely you cannot believe my father and the Master are connected. Can you?"

"It would make sense," Graeden added. "Think about how many times he mentioned your father's death to you. Why would he do that if there was no connection between them?"

"He attacked you as well, Graeden," Regnaryn snapped. "Does that mean he is connected to your family?"

"That is not what we are saying, child," Trebeh replied. "But you must admit he did speak of your father a great deal and his tone seems to suggest a personal relationship of some sort. As if he knew him."

"And we must explore every possibility. We know so little, even the tiniest morsel of information could be key," Phrynia added.

"Graeden, what do you recall about your encounter with the Master at the inn?" Varlama asked.

"Pain. A great deal of pain. And an overwhelming feeling that I was losing myself, that my essence was being devoured." Graeden squirmed in his seat and looked down at his hands. "That voice...it badgered and belittled me with every phrase...every word...as if I were less than nothing."

Regnaryn squeezed his hand.

"Do you remember the exact words?" Varlama continued.

He took a deep breath. "All I can recall is he kept demanding to know why I was going to *her*." Graeden looked at the tazzamira and then at the others. "I had no idea what he meant. No idea who he was talking about. I mean I did not have a destination in mind when I left home, but every time I told him that, he called me a liar and..." He faltered, remembering the pain that followed.

"Did he ever call you by name? Seem to know who you were? Where you came from?" Phrynia asked.

Graeden looked into the drageal's face and thought a moment. "No. Come to think of it, he never did. He never addressed me at all, just demanded answers to his questions, questions that made no sense."

"So, he may not actually know who you are," Phrynia said.

"But then how did he know where he was and where he was going?" Ayirak asked.

"And of his relation to Regnaryn?" Neshya added.

"If he is a seer, or employs the services of one, he could have become aware that a person would be at a place on his way to a destination. If that was the case, that may be all he knows of Graeden," Trebeh said.

"The way Jucara knew to send Aloysius and myself to aid him," Ellyss said.

"But you knew who I was," Graeden said to Ellyss.

"Yes," Phrynia said, "because you had contact with Jucara before that, did you not?"

Graeden smiled. "Yes, though at the time I thought her merely a childhood dream. It was not until I met her in the flesh, so to speak, after Regnaryn's return, that I realized she was real."

"And she did tell us to keep an eye on you because there was more to you than we thought," Trebeh added.

"So you are saying, if Jucara knew me—who I was, where I came from—the Master could know the same," Graeden said.

"Did you not say that the glass window in Hammarsh Keep has a likeness of Jucara along with your ancestor and a golden drageal?" Regnaryn asked.

Graeden nodded.

"She may have known your family, so, it could still be possible that the Master has no idea who you really are," Phrynia said.

"Even if he does not know who I am, what of the people at the inn," Graeden said. "I made no secret of my identity to them. And since he took over their minds, would he not find out the information in that way?"

"Maybe, but, I doubt he cares who you are, only what you can do for him," Regnaryn replied. "In all the times I encountered him, my feeling was he considers everyone beneath him, only he is of any consequence. The rest of us are of no value."

"Yes, from all we have seen of him so far, I am of the same mind as Regnaryn," Varlama added.

"Can we afford to assume that?" Ellyss asked.

"Do we have a choice?" Phrynia said.

"If we are wrong in our assessment of the Master and he does know who Graeden is," Ellyss said, "and where he came from, that could be a problem for his family."

Graeden paled. "I had not thought of my family. How would

they cope with that monster?" He jumped up. "I must go to them immediately. Warn them. Protect them."

"Just wait a moment, son," Ayirak said as he gently grabbed Graeden's arm to stop him. "First of all, we do not know if they are in danger. And, secondly, and I mean no disrespect, but what will you be able to do to defend them. Your newly acquired skill summoning fireballs is erratic at best, and..."

Graeden pulled free and glared at the massive yekcal. "I do not care. I will do whatever I can to protect them, be it by fireball or arrow or anything else. I will not leave them to him."

"We are not saying that you should," Trebeh replied.

"Then what are you saying?" Graeden snapped.

"If I may," Ellyss said, "I believe I have a solution. Allow me to go to Hammarsh Keep. I am already known to your family, at least your parents, so I am sure they will accept me into their home and heed my warning."

"I was thinking the same thing," Phrynia added.

"Just a moment," Neshya began, "while it may be all well and good for someone, be it Ellyss or Graeden or any of us to travel to Graeden's homeland, what good will that do? The distance between here and there is too great for us to communicate. And even if they could, how long would it take for any of us to get there? And what can you as one man do anyway? Or are we going to send an army?"

Immic chuckled. "I do not mean to make light of the situation, I am only thinking of how Graeden's kin would react to the sight of us arriving on their doorstep."

The others smiled at the thought.

"No, an army would not do," Ellyss replied. "And you make some very good points, Neshya. However, I do have some skills both in physical and magical combat..."

Ayirak snickered, and some of the others smiled at their friend's words.

:Some skills, eh? Since when did modesty become part of your character?: Ayirak mindspoke to Ellyss.

"As I was saying," Ellyss continued, ignoring the outward reactions and the words in his head, "if worse comes to worse, I think the people of Hammarsh Keep and I will be able to fend off the enemy."

"Even if that is so, it will take you months to get there," Graeden cried. "What are they to do in the meantime?"

"He can leave at dawn and be there within three days," Phrynia said. "Maybe sooner."

Everyone, save Ellyss and Varlama, turned towards the drageal, surprised at her remark.

"I did not think it my place to ask for such a privilege, Phrynia," Ellyss replied.

"What are you two talking about?" Graeden asked. "How can he get there in three days?"

"He will fly."

The drageal's matter of fact statement was met with shock around the garden.

"Do not act so surprised, there was a time, long ago when man and drageal flew together," Phrynia added.

"Then I will take my leave to prepare," Ellyss said, leaving the others still pondering Phrynia's remarks.

#

"So, back to what we know about the Master," Varlama said. "It seems to me there is a link between him and Grenwald. Finding it will be the key to figuring out who and where the Master is."

"And how do we do that?" Trebeh asked.

"I am afraid I have spent far too much time isolated on my mountain, taking no notice of what was developing in the world outside," Varlama replied, "to be of much assistance in that."

"As have we," Ayirak added.

"Well, we can no longer remain isolated. We must go out and find him or else who knows what havoc he might rain down on others," Phrynia said.

"Grenwald was a Prince, was he not?" Graeden asked.

"Yes, before he went to Karaleena's homeland he was, though he never said the name of his kingdom," Ayirak replied.

"He rarely spoke of his past and, when he did, he always seemed sad. No, not sad, troubled. Almost as if he harbored some deep regret or guilt," Trebeh added. "Why do you ask?"

"I am far from being a royal and just barely considered a noble, and I am not sure if the same would hold true for Grenwald's homeland..." Graeden hesitated.

"Get to the point, boy," Ayirak interrupted.

"Sorry," Graeden said, his face reddening. "Where I come from the higher nobility, and especially the royals, are encouraged to keep journals documenting their daily lives—what they do, what they think, everything. So, I was wondering if perhaps Grenwald followed the same practice."

"I never heard him speak of nor saw any such things," Ayirak said.

"He might not be open with them. They are probably hidden somewhere."

"The house you are living in was his and Karaleena's," Trebeh said. "And after their deaths nothing was touched until you moved in. Did you find any such journals?"

"No, but they still may be there, possibly in a hidden alcove or such."

"If there were such a thing, I am sure we would have found it by now," Ayirak said. "No, I do not believe you will find any such hidden areas in that house."

:*I do not think we should be so quick to dismiss your idea, love,*: Regnaryn mindspoke to Graeden. :*Regardless of what Papa says, I think we should explore the house more thoroughly.*:

Graeden nodded and squeezed her hand.

"Shall we move on?" Ayirak asked.

#

"There is something about the Master that does not seem quite right," Varlama said.

"Oh, so you are saying there are things that seem right about him?" Neshya said with a laugh.

The tazzamira paid no attention to the young yekcal's snide remark and continued. "If the Master is so powerful and so evil, why have we not heard about him before?"

"Our first encounter with him was Regnaryn's first dream," Trebeh replied.

"But at that time we did not know it was him, we thought it was just a bad dream," Regnaryn added.

"The people at the inn called him by that name," Graeden said, shuddering at the memory of his ordeal.

"There was of course, the next dream, where he tried to take over Regnaryn's mind and body," Phrynia said.

"And the battle outside Reissem Grove," Ayirak added.

"There were a few others," Regnaryn said.

"Others?" Trebeh asked.

Regnaryn nodded.

"There was another dream, on the road, before I met Jucara," Regnaryn said and then lowered both her eyes and her voice. "And those vile, lizard-like gawara. They spoke of him as the Master as well."

"Has anyone considered that the Master may have been involved in the illness that befell the humans here in Reissem Grove?" Varlama asked.

A look of shock and disbelief crossed the faces of all those gathered.

"That sounds a bit far-fetched. Why would you think that?" Phrynia asked.

"I am merely stating a possibility. Think about it, we have heard of no other such plague or illness anywhere else in the world. Do you not find that to be the least bit odd?"

"And," Graeden added, "he continually refers to Grenwald's death."

"Exactly," Varlama said.

"Do you really think he has that kind of power, that reach?" Ayirak asked.

Varlama shook her head, "I am not sure. But I think we need to consider it, to keep an open mind to anything that might be his work."

"Even if he was responsible for that tragedy," Ayirak said, "does knowing that bring us any closer to him? We still do not have any idea who he is, or for that matter, what he is. Is he human or some other race of being?"

"I know you disagree, Ayirak," Graeden began, "but I still feel there is some merit in trying to discover if there were any journals left by Grenwald, especially with as many references as the Master made to him."

"And the level of hatred in his voice when he did," Regnaryn added.

Graeden nodded and continued, "Surely, there must be some connection between the two."

"Has anyone considered the possibility that Karaleena may have seen something in one of her readings?" Trebeh asked. "Grenwald was a major part of her life, after all."

"Also, we cannot forget the prophecy she made concerning Regnaryn," Phrynia added. "I am sure she saw more than she revealed to us."

"And any seer worth her salt, and Karaleena was well worth that and more," Trebeh said, "always keeps a log of her readings. Wherever her books are, Grenwald's are likely in the same place, if they exist."

Ayirak shook his head. "I see I am outnumbered in the thought that there are secret journals and writings hidden somewhere in the house. We shall mount a search tomorrow."

CHAPTER THREE

SEVERAL MONTHS AFTER the last encounter with his niece, Jurcheval remained incensed by it and repeatedly railed against her and what she had done. Anyone within earshot of his tirades to an empty room were both frightened and confused. But none dared question Jurcheval's erratic behavior.

"How does she continue to best me?" Jurcheval roared yet again. Still, the thought of the power she displayed thrilled him, making his imagination run wild with the possibilities it presented once he wrested it from her. "Oh, how sweet the taste of revenge will be on the day I destroy you, niece. Not only will I slay my brother's child, but the acquisition of your power will make me truly invincible. My only regret is that my dearest brother," he snickered, "will not be there to witness my final victory."

He took another sip of wine and pondered the one problem that stood between him and her power. As long as she stayed within the boundaries of that wretched sanctuary, he knew he could not reach her. He could not breach that place's barrier and he had long since lost the ability to enter her dreams. Still, he would not give up.

What he needed was a way to lure her away from that place, to get her to come to him. That would, of course, require finding the right bait.

The boy! Surely, if his kin were found and threatened, that would bring them out. After all, she is her father's child and can likely not bear to see innocents hurt. Then again, he thought as he smiled, she does have a touch of me in her as well. Look what she did to the gawara.

But, how to find the boy's kin? He knew nothing of him, not even his name.

This is all the fault of that inept seer and wizard, Drakorem, Jurcheval seethed. *He should have insisted on following the boy when he left that damned place. But that is all water under the bridge. I cannot bring him nor those idiots at the inn that let the boy escape back from the dead...or can I?* He contemplated that idea for a moment, and then shook his head. *No, even if I could find a wizard, or whatever, who could summon the dead, that is still not an option I am willing to pursue, at least not until all other possibilities have been exhausted.*

"What I must do," he said, "is determine what I do know of him."

#

"Gentlemen," Jurcheval said as he entered the Council Chamber, "I am sure you are wondering why I have summoned you after all this time. It has been well over a year since the last meeting, has it not?"

The king's cordial demeanor did nothing to quell the fear the three Council members felt since receiving the summons. Undell, the eldest member of the Council, rubbed the scar on his forearm, a reminder of a time when he mistook the king's pleasantness for something other than a mask to conceal his evil.

"It has indeed been quite a while since we have had the honor of being in your company, Sire," the second man, Ilyan, said

"How can we be of service to you, Majesty?" Undell asked.

"I need you to assemble a force, spies of a sort, to find someone, or rather, his family," Jurcheval said.

"Of course, Majesty," Orem, the youngest of the men, said.

Undell was not so quick to agree. "I sense there is more to this than just a simple search, Sire."

"Always the wary one, eh?" Jurcheval said. "Yes, there is one little problem. I neither know his name nor where he came from."

The three men looked at each other and then at the king.

"That will indeed make it a more difficult task. Is there anything you do know about them?" Ilyan asked, trying hard not to sound insolent.

Before the man had finished his sentence, the young page who had been silently standing in the corner approached the table and laid a large scroll before Jurcheval, then quickly receded back to his corner.

The king unrolled the paper to reveal a map. The men moved closer to get a better look.

"I know he headed south from the place he is now, which is here," Jurcheval said and pointed to Reissem Grove on the map. "If we blanket the land with spies, surely they will be able to uncover something of his origin."

The men looked at each other, each waiting for someone else to be the first to comment on the infeasibility of the plan.

"That is a great distance to cover, Sire. Where would we get that kind of manpower to conduct such a search?" Undell asked.

"Not to mention, we really do not have any idea what we are looking for," Orem added. "Would it not be better to seek the advice of a seer? Perhaps they could find something of the boy's family to aid us in the search."

Jurcheval's displeasure at the suggestion was immediately visible, and all three men feared what might follow.

"I have yet to find a seer who could deliver what I needed," Jurcheval said. "No, it will be up to you three to find the resources."

"Is there no way you can narrow the search area? Even a little would help, I am sure," Ilyan said.

"I have been giving this matter a great deal of thought and have recalled several things about where I first found the boy and where he might have come from."

The Council members drew in closer.

"The inn where the boy was captured was in this area," Jurcheval said, drawing a fairly large circle with his finger. "And I believe he came from this direction," he added drawing an even larger circle. "This would make sense since he headed south when he left that wretched sanctuary. I suggest we search villages and so on where he may have come from, likely this direction," he said, waving his hand over the map in another wide sweeping motion.

The men looked at each other.

"Sire, though you have given us a direction to follow, that is still quite an expansive area to cover," Undell said.

"Even if we find twenty people, which will not be an easy task, I doubt if we will be able to adequately search that much land," Orem said.

"Not to mention, it is quite a distance from here," Ilyan added. "How will we keep in contact with them?"

Jurcheval smiled. "Let me worry about that. Your job is to find the right people."

Before the men could say anything more, the king departed.

#

The king looked up as the nervous young wizard entered. "Worrelk. So good of you to come."

"The honor is all mine, Sire," the young man said, wondering why he had been summoned.

"I have a task for you."

"Of course, Majesty."

Jurcheval explained to the magicker what he needed.

As he listened, Worrelk drew in a breath, an action that did not escape Jurcheval's notice.

"Is there a problem with my request?"

The young man took another deep breath. "Seeing stones have not been constructed in quite some time, Sire. And to create twenty or more…"

"Did you not learn the technique from your father? And he from the seer that found the spell?"

"Yes and no, Sire."

Jurcheval glared at Worrelk.

"Neither of us ever actually created the stones, although my father assisted his predecessor, Drakorem."

Jurcheval growled under his breath at the mention of his former seer.

"Did I not just use them a year or so ago? Who made those? Bring me that person," Jurcheval growled.

"Those stones were the last of the ones Drakorem created before his death." Worrelk reddened, afraid his words might further anger the king.

"Death? You mean execution," Jurcheval snapped. "I know very well both how and why he died. Make sure you do not follow in his footsteps."

Worrelk had all he could do to keep himself from visibly shaking in fear at the threat.

"As for the stones, if there are no more of Drakorem's, you will just have to make more."

The wizard swallowed hard. "In all honesty, Sire, I am not certain I can. My father said it was a very complicated process." Worrelk saw the displeasure on Jurcheval's face and quickly continued. "The first thing I must do is find the spell book among my father's things. Once I do that, I will have a better idea of the feasibility of completing the task."

"Yes, yes," Jurcheval said, not hiding his displeasure. "Be quick about it. If I remember correctly, it takes several days for the potion to mature and I need them as soon as possible."

The young man nodded and turned for the door.

"And, do not even think about trying to flee," Jurcheval said as the young man's fingers touched the door knob.

"Never, Majesty," he said and left the room. Once outside, he added, "Where would I go?"

CHAPTER FOUR

ELLYSS AND THE YOUNG drageal, Curme, arrived outside the walls of Hammarsh Keep several hours before sunrise.

"What will you do now?" the drageal asked. "I fear it would not be polite to attempt to gain entry to the Keep at this hour."

"Neither polite nor safe," Ellyss replied. "Perhaps I can contact Graeden's sister, Taaryn."

"Mindspeak to her? Do you think that will work?"

Ellyss shrugged. "I am not sure. Her brother is quite talented, so perhaps."

"Why his sister and not his parents?"

"Graeden asked me to find her first. He fears she is angry with him because he left without telling her. He thinks if she is the first to hear he is well, her anger will subside."

"Siblings," the drageal said with a chuckle and then waited.

"I do not think I reached her. Oh well, it was worth a try. And now, my friend, it is time for me to thank you for your services on the journey and bid you farewell. Soon enough many in the Keep will be astir and, well… I will wait here for a more civil hour before I approach the gates."

"I think not my friend," Curme replied, pointing at the sight of a figure peering out an upper window.

Ellyss looked just as the figure retreated back inside. "Ah. Now to see if that was more than mere coincidence."

It did not take long before a young woman exited a side gate of the Keep and crossed the grounds toward them. Curme slipped into the shadows.

The young woman slowed her pace as she approached Ellyss, and stopped just beyond a sword's length from him.

"I am not sure why I have come here to meet you, a complete stranger. Yet…" she said.

He noticed that while she did have a weapon on her belt, she was neither covering nor drawing it.

"I am sorry to call you out like this, young miss…"

"Yes, yes. I know. You have word from my brother."

The look on Ellyss' face made Taaryn laugh.

"You heard my words?" he asked.

"Of course, why else would I leave the warmth of my bed at this hour? Are you the one he left with?"

"Yes."

He reached into his tunic, withdrew a folded note and handed it to her. "From Graeden."

He watched a smile develop on her face at the sight of the cryptic symbols scribbled across the back of the paper.

"Yes, this is truly from Graeden," she said and unfolded it. "Does your friend want to come out, or am I such a fright at this hour he wishes to hide in the shadows?"

"Friend?" Ellyss asked.

Her face blanched as she began to read her brother's words. Ellyss surmised Graeden had written something of the battle and the threat.

She carefully folded the letter and looked back at Ellyss. Her eyes widened, and she drew in a breath at the sight of the drageal standing beside him.

"Fear not, Taaryn, he will not harm you."

She stood silent another moment and shook her head. "You misunderstand, sir. I am not afraid, rather, I stand in awe. My brother's description did not do you justice," she answered unable to take her eyes off Curme.

"I am flattered, young miss," the drageal said. "Your brother was also remiss in his details of your beauty."

She flushed slightly at the compliment and then turned back to Ellyss. "Sirs, I fear you have me at the disadvantage for you both seem to know much of me, while I know nothing of you, not even your names."

Ellyss coughed nervously. "Forgive my lack of manners, dear lady. I am Ellyss, and this is Curme. As you know, we were sent by your brother."

"Oh, yes. The letter. We must let Father and Mother know of this immediately," she said.

"I will take my leave now and return to Reissem Grove," Curme said.

"Thank you, friend," Ellyss answered.

:I will tell the others all is well here,: Curme mindspoke to

Ellyss.

Before Taaryn could bid him farewell, Curme was gone with only the faintest breeze and no sound at all. She stood staring skyward but could see no sign of the drageal in the night sky. She shuddered slightly as a cool night breeze wafted over her.

"Dear lady, you will catch your death standing here in the chill air," Ellyss said as he wrapped her in his cloak.

Taaryn thought to protest, but there was something in the genuine concerned look in his eyes that stopped her.

"Thank you. Now, let us get inside before you, too, catch a chill."

#

The couple approached the gate and Ellyss saw the guard shoot a questioning glance at the young woman. Taaryn nodded and the pair entered.

"Is it not too early to disturb your parents?" Ellyss asked as Taaryn led him up a winding stairwell.

"No, they are very early risers," she said and then laughed. "With all the children in the family, I think this is one of the few times of day when they can enjoy some peaceful time alone."

"Then, perhaps, we should wait."

"No. I am sure they will want to hear the news of Graeden immediately. I do hope none of the others are with them."

"I sense they are alone," Ellyss said.

"You can tell who is in a room?"

He nodded. "And sometimes I can tell what they are doing if there are no shielding barriers in place."

She looked at him and grinned. "I will have to remember that."

He was about to explain when they reached the door to the sitting room. Taaryn rapped gently, announced herself and waited for a response.

"Come in, child," Emmaus answered.

The young girl opened the door and took a step inside. "Mother. Father. You remember Ellyss, I am sure. He brings news from Graeden. Grave news."

Emmaus and Prescia looked up at the pair.

Before they could speak, Ellyss said, "Fear not, he is well."

"Child, you nearly took the life from me, saying such things," Prescia chided her daughter as she motioned the two to join them. "And, as for you, sir, I see you continue to enjoy arriving at the oddest of hours."

Ellyss smiled. "My apologies for the hour, Lady. I had intended to wait, but…"

Prescia laughed. "So, it was my impatient daughter who dragged you in here?"

Taaryn blushed. "I dragged no one. I just thought you would want to hear the news of Graeden as soon as possible."

"I understand," Prescia replied. "Now, Ellyss, do tell us of my son."

"Though Graeden is well, or was when last we parted, Taaryn was correct in saying I do bear grave tidings."

Ellyss handed Emmaus the second letter from Graeden and waited while the pair read the words from their son.

"He says you will answer our questions," Emmaus said as Prescia took the letter and reread it.

Over the next hour, Ellyss recounted the occurrences outside Reissem Grove. The others listened intently with only an occasional gasp interrupting his tale. The mention of Graeden casting fireballs during the battle caused them to shake their heads in disbelief.

"Graeden?" Emmaus asked. "Do you really expect us to believe my son could do such a thing?"

Ellyss nodded and continued, finishing his tale by quoting the words that came from nowhere and everywhere at the same time. Words that threatened both Regnaryn and Graeden and all they held dear.

"And you think this Master might attack us to get to Graeden and Regnaryn?" Emmaus asked.

"We are not sure. But that is the manner in which the Master acts—with intimidation and sideways threats to those who may not be as able to defend themselves as his main target. That is often the way of such evil beings."

"How will we stand a chance against them if they come?" Taaryn asked. "We have no magic. We cannot create barriers like Regnaryn did."

"Perhaps not," Ellyss said, "but we do not believe the attack will come as a magical one. The one aimed at Reissem Grove was of physical force and we have no reason to believe the Master will change his tactics here. Although I cannot create a physical barrier like the one that protects Reissem Grove, I am able to create a deception barrier."

"A what?" Taaryn asked.

"A shielding that will hide the Keep from the sight of the Master."

"And that will protect us?" Emmaus asked.

"It is not infallible, but it will help to keep those not aware of this place from finding it."

Emmaus' response was interrupted by a knock on the door. Taaryn opened it to find her brother, Matteus.

"I am sorry to disturb you," Matteus said. "I was informed Taaryn had brought a stranger into the Keep, but I see you are already aware of his presence."

"This is Ellyss and he is not really a stranger. He is the one who accompanied Graeden on his journey," Prescia said.

"Sir," Matteus said and bowed to the stranger.

"He brings us word from Graeden," Prescia said.

"Oh, do tell," Matteus replied.

"Your sister can tell you all you need to know. Your mother and I wish to talk to our guest alone," Emmaus said to his children.

The siblings knew better than to protest their dismissal, and left the room without further discussion.

#

"Tell us more of Graeden," Emmaus began after Taaryn and Matteus departed.

"What do you wish to hear, Sir?"

"Emmaus, where are your manners? Our guest has had a long journey and is likely parched. Surely, whatever he has to tell us can wait until he has something to drink."

"A drink would be most appreciated," Ellyss answered.

Prescia nodded and walked to the sideboard and poured three glasses of tea.

"I understand," Prescia said as she sat beside Emmaus, "you are the one who rescued my son from that cursed inn, are you not?"

Ellyss nearly choked on the tea.

"I was not aware Graeden..." Ellyss sputtered.

"Remembered? Or told me?" Prescia finished his thought.

"Both, My Lady," Ellyss answered. "You are even more remarkable than your son believes. It is not often anyone can fluster

27

me but ..."

Emmaus laughed. "Yes, my dear wife is able to disquiet most people when she wants to."

Prescia shook her head at his remark and continued. "About the inn. I am curious, sir, how did you know Graeden was in danger there before anything transpired?"

Ellyss noticed that while Prescia's tone was pleasant, it held a distinct edge of anger.

"Why did you not make your warnings more straightforward?" she continued. "And, even more baffling to me, why did you not help him before those monsters hurt him so?"

"Sadly, nothing I could have done would have altered what happened at the inn."

"What?" Emmaus asked. "How could you know that?"

"As unbelievable as it might seem, that incident, with all its pain, was written into his fate and no one, save Graeden himself, could have changed it. Sometimes, there is little we can do to alter another's destiny."

"Bah," Emmaus grumbled. "I do not believe that our lives are preordained by anyone or anything."

"Perhaps, you are right, sir," Ellyss replied, his gaze drifting far from where he sat.

"Enough about fate and destiny," Prescia said, realizing her guest would reveal no more of the incident. "Tell us about these fireballs you say Graeden created."

"Yet another thing you speak of that sounds impossible," Emmaus added. "He never did any such thing while he was here."

"No, I am sure he did not," Ellyss said, stifling a chuckle, "but here in Hammarsh Keep, his love was not under threat of mortal attack."

"Ah," Prescia said, "that makes sense, although I do find it hard to believe he had such a talent hidden within himself."

"Will he be able to do it again?" Emmaus asked.

"I do not know. When I left Reissem Grove, he still felt the incident was merely an accident, brought on by circumstance—the heat of the moment, you might say. He is of the mind that it will never happen again."

"But," Prescia interrupted, "you disagree."

Ellyss nodded. "Yes, as do the others in Reissem Grove. They are working with him to determine for certain if it is something more than just a freak battle occurrence. And, if so, they will be able to train him in both its use and, more importantly, its control."

Prescia shook her head and sighed. It all seemed so bizarre, Graeden, her most sensitive child, taking on the role of monster slayer.

CHAPTER FIVE

"TELL ME, LITTLE SISTER, what is going on here?" Matteus asked when they were in the hall.

"All I know, Graeden is safe," she said, trying to look innocent.

"Do not give me that look. I know you, and if you were in that room, you know what is going on."

"Fine, but let us go somewhere else to talk."

"No one will be in the library at this hour," Matteus said.

I wonder how much I should tell him, she thought as they headed for the library.

:You can tell him everything you know, Taaryn.:

Ellyss' voice in her head caused her to stumble on the stair.

"Are you all right, Taaryn?" Matteus asked, catching her

before she fell.

"Yes, I am fine. I just had an annoying thought jump into my head," she answered, continuing down the stairs.

Ellyss laughed into her mind and was gone without another word.

#

The two reached the library, empty as expected, and sat in two overstuffed chairs in a corner.

"Tell me the news of Graeden," Matteus said. "And of this Ellyss fellow. There is something about him that I do not trust."

"Why not?"

"To begin with, look at the hour he arrived and not only burst into the castle, but disturbed Mother and Father."

"He did not burst in," she said with a laugh. "I brought him to them. He thought he should wait for a more civil hour."

"How do you know him well enough to do such a thing?"

"I do not. This is the first time I met the man. I saw him from my window and went down to see who he was."

"What were you doing up at such an hour?"

She looked away. "Actually, I was asleep. Somehow his presence woke me," she said, choosing not to tell him of Ellyss' voice in her mind.

Matteus looked as if he was going to explode. "His presence? That is insane."

Taaryn did not reply.

"What is even more inexplicable is that you went outside the castle walls...in the middle of the night...alone...to meet a stranger lurking there. Have you totally lost your mind? Why would you do such a thing? Why did the guard not stop you or at least accompany you?"

Taaryn shrugged her shoulders and allowed her older brother to continue his rant.

"Who is this stranger? And how do we know he tells the truth?"

"To begin with, he is the one who travelled with Graeden when he last left the Keep. More importantly, there is something about him. Something that tells me this is a man of honor and he speaks the truth."

Matteus shook his head. "Do not tell me you are going to be like Mother, always finding truth in people's eyes."

"Whether I am or not is not the point here. You asked and I gave you my answer."

He was surprised at her reply. "Still, you should not have gone outside the walls unescorted. After all, you had yet to know who he was."

"Be that as it may, I just knew this man did not pose any threat to me nor anyone else here."

"You truly are sounding more like Mother," he replied. "But..."

She cut him off. "Do you wish to hear the news of Graeden or would you prefer to continue scolding me?"

Matteus shook his head. "Go on then, tell me of Graeden, since my warnings are obviously falling on deaf ears."

"I am not sure you will believe even half of what I am about to say, but it is all true," she began. "And I am certain there is more that I, we, have yet to learn."

"That sounds both mysterious and ominous," Matteus said.

She nodded.

"But how do you know this news truly comes from Graeden?

I am still not sure I believe what this stranger tells us."

Taaryn reached into her pocket and pulled out the note Ellyss had given her earlier.

"This is why," she said, pointing to the symbols on the paper.

"What? Someone scribbles something on a note and you think it is from Graeden? Anyone could have done that."

She glared at him. "No, this is most definitely from Graeden. These are not mere scribblings, this is the sign we use, have used for years, to ensure notes were from us and not from one of you trying to have us do something that would get us in trouble."

Matteus' face broke into a wide grin. "So, that is how you two did that. We had always wondered."

Taaryn did not respond.

"May I read it?"

"No. The letter is for me."

He chuckled. "Why does that not surprise me? But do tell me more."

"What do you know of the reason Graeden left?" she asked.

Matteus thought a moment. "We were told he had fallen in love with someone from a distant land. I guess we assumed that is where he went off to."

"That is true. He did go back to Regnaryn. But did you ever wonder why he left so quickly and without even bidding anyone farewell?"

He scratched his chin. "Now that you mention it, it is odd that none of us ever asked."

"Oh, no, do not include me in your ignorance."

Matteus smiled at her indignation. "And just how did you gain this knowledge?"

"I asked."

"All right then, we have established the fact that I am an uncaring oaf of a brother, who thinks of nothing but his own comfort," he replied.

"No, that is Gantell," she said and both laughed. "But, remember, Graeden and I are twins. Even if he wanted to, he cannot keep anything from me for very long."

"And does Mother know of this as well?"

Taaryn rolled her eyes. "Oh, come now, Matteus. Can any of us, most of all Graeden, keep anything from Mother?"

Matteus laughed. "True. So tell me of this place that took Graeden from us."

Taaryn drew in a deep breath and began the tale of what she knew of Reissem Grove. She started with the mundane. Where it was. What it looked like. Of the people there, at first revealing only names that meant nothing more than possibly a people of a different land.

Matteus listened in silence until she spoke of the drageals.

"Do you take me for a fool, little sister? How can you speak of such things as drageals as being real? They are just fables," Matteus said.

"They are real," she answered so quietly that Matteus had to lean toward her just to hear. "And just this night I met one."

Her statement, so calm and matter of fact, caught Matteus off guard.

"You what?" he asked.

"There was a drageal with Ellyss outside the Keep's walls."

Matteus jumped up. "Take me to him."

Taaryn took his hand. "Curme has already departed."

The disappointed look on her brother's face told her he believed her. And she continued, telling him all she knew of Graeden's new life and abilities.

Matteus listened in silence, hanging on her every word until she was done.

"All of this, these beings you speak of, Graeden and magic and all the rest, sound too fantastical to be true."

"I felt the same when first I heard of these things."

"You have yet to explain why this man has come."

She nodded and told him what Graeden had written to her and what Ellyss had added.

"You think there is more to this than what you have been told?" Matteus asked when she finished.

"I am sure of it. And I fear whatever it is will be far from pleasant."

"I agree, sister, but we can do nothing at this time on that subject," Matteus said and then his face lit up. "Now tell me more about the drageal you met. Did he look like the one in the window?"

She smiled at his childish excitement. "Yes and no."

"Bah, that is no answer."

"As a matter of fact, it is. He resembled the rendition in the window but was far more beautiful. More magnificent. And he was not golden."

Matteus grinned. "Go on."

She nodded and told him all that had occurred and answered all of his questions about the magnificent creature they had previously thought imaginary.

#

The siblings did not stop talking until they were interrupted by the sounds of the librarian's footsteps arriving to start his day.

"Oh, forgive me, young ones," the old man said, "I did not expect to find anyone here so early in the day. Should you not be in the dining hall for morning meal?"

It was only at that point, the two realized how long they had been talking.

"Perhaps you both should go join the others," the librarian said as he looked them over, "once you are properly attired, of course."

The siblings looked at each other and giggled.

"Of course," Matteus said.

They left the library and headed toward their rooms.

"I do not believe we should tell the others of Curme or the rest of what we spoke of here just yet," Taaryn said as she started up the stairs.

"I agree."

CHAPTER SIX

"WHAT IS THE MEANING of this? Where is the meal?" Gantell grumbled as he paced around the dining table. "I have duties to attend to. Where are Mother and Father? It is rude of them to be late with no explanation."

The clearing of a throat behind him silenced the angry young man. He turned and saw his parents and a stranger. Emmaus glared at his son, but he said nothing.

"As soon as Taaryn and Matteus arrive…" Prescia began, then saw the pair at the door. "Ah, there they are now."

The servants entered, and the morning meal began. As the family ate, the normal conversations ensued, as well as hushed questions about the stranger.

At the completion of the meal, the youngest siblings left to attend their lessons, but Emmaus motioned for the others to remain.

"What is going on?" Gantell grumbled again. "I am already late for my duties."

"We have news of your brother," Emmaus said as the last plate was removed.

Everyone sat back down, looking to their father with anticipation.

"Allow me to introduce Ellyss. He is a friend of Graeden."

Ellyss nodded. "First let me assure you all, Graeden is well."

"And why should he be anything else?" Gantell interrupted.

"Because the world outside of your sheltered walls is far more dangerous than any of you could ever imagine," Ellyss replied.

The tone of his voice quieted Gantell.

"Shall our guest go on? Or do the lot of you intend to continue embarrassing me with your rudeness?" Prescia said when it appeared there might be further protest.

"I was sent here for several reasons. To tell you of Graeden but also, and more importantly, to warn you of a possible impending threat."

"Threat?" Gantell shouted and jumped to his feet "What kind of threat? If we are threatened, why are we sitting around talking. We should be arming ourselves, preparing to meet it."

Ellyss grinned, infuriating Gantell and some of the others. Only Matteus and Taaryn sat in silence.

"In good time, young sir, in good time," Ellyss said. "But do you not think it wiser to hear who and what the threat is before you go running off to confront it?"

Matteus unsuccessfully stifled a laugh, which enraged his brother.

"That sounds reasonable to me," Matteus said. "Perhaps you

should let the man speak."

Gantell sat down, his face red with anger.

"Please, do go on, Ellyss," Prescia said. "I am sure there will be no more outbursts from my children."

Gantell snorted, but said nothing.

"While your brother is well, I do have some disturbing news. The tale I am about to tell you," Ellyss began, "will be hard for you to believe. But I assure you, every word is true."

Ellyss turned to Gantell. "I meant no insult by calling your life sheltered. In the scope of all there is, it is just that. There are things in the world that you could not imagine in your wildest dreams. Things you think fable and myth are, in many cases, fact."

"This is nonsense," Gantell grumbled. His sentiment found allies among some of his siblings. No one seemed to notice their parents, as well as Taaryn and Matteus, did not protest. "Seriously, Father, surely you cannot believe this mad man?"

"Ah, but I do, son. I do," Emmaus replied.

"As do I," Taaryn added.

"What has poisoned your minds to believe such tall tales?"

"If truth be poison, then let us all be tainted," Prescia said.

Gantell and the others, shocked by her words, fell silent.

"Please continue, Ellyss," Emmaus said.

Ellyss nodded. "I know not why, but magic has been suppressed in this land, not just here in Hammarsh Keep but all throughout this kingdom. It was not always so, and is not the case elsewhere in the world. You laugh at the old one who tells you of the future. Even if it comes to pass, you still do not believe or if you do, you hide those beliefs away."

There was no response.

"That is a discussion for another day. For now, I need you to believe me, believe every word I say, for it is, indeed, the truth."

Though there were still a few hushed words, all in the room, including Gantell, nodded.

Ellyss told the family about the incident at the inn. And while some gasped and other shook their heads, no one interrupted.

"And when he returned here, a broken man, only some of you," he said and looked at Taaryn, "saw through his insistence that all was well. You not only sought out the truth, but you believed his tale of the magical place he had been and the beings he had met."

"I do not care what you say, sir," Gantell snapped. "I, for one, do not believe in either magic nor these mythical creatures you speak of."

Yes, Graeden said you would be the one that would be the most argumentative, Ellyss thought.

Emmaus handed Gantell the letter. As he read his brother's words, Gantell's face changed from scorn to disbelief to awe.

"I apologize, sir." Gantell handed the letter to Matteus.

"I understand." Ellyss waited as the letter made its way around the table.

After the last one read the letter, they looked at each other in astonishment, then directed their attention to Ellyss, who said nothing.

Gantell spoke first. "How do you propose we defend ourselves against this person? We have no magic."

Ellyss smiled. "That is the same question posed by your sister and parents. And, as I told them, our hope is that it will not come to that. We might get lucky. The evil we face, the one called the Master, might never even think to look for you."

"And if he does?" another sibling asked.

"I will surround the Keep with a barrier of sorts, a magical glamour that will hide it from the eyes of anyone who does not already know of it."

The room erupted into chatter, ranging from questions to utter disbelief.

"That sounds a bit far-fetched," Matteus said. "But then so did most of what you have told us this day. But if Graeden trusts you, then so will I."

Everyone in the room agreed.

"We cannot rely solely on the shield," Ellyss said. "We must also prepare ourselves for attack, one that will likely be as physical as it was in Reissem Grove."

"We will be ready," Gantell said.

Your brother knows you well, Gantell, Ellyss thought. *He said, once you believed, you would be my staunchest ally.*

"Perhaps, later today," Gantell said, "we could meet to discuss how we will defend ourselves against this potential threat."

Ellyss nodded. "Yes. That is a good idea."

"Good. Now that is settled," Prescia said, "it is time for all of you to get on with your day."

The siblings rose from the table, departing in a flurry of hushed conversations. Only Taaryn remained.

"I think they will be hard pressed to concentrate on their normal routine after hearing Ellyss' news," Emmaus said.

Prescia nodded, then turned to Taaryn. "Have you no duties to attend to, child?"

Taaryn nodded. "I do, but I thought I might show our guest around the Keep. I do not think he saw much of it on his last visit and he might need to get an idea of what we already have in place defense-wise."

"Good idea," Emmaus said.

Prescia eyed her daughter with a bit of suspicion but she did not respond.

CHAPTER SEVEN

ELLYSS FOLLOWED Taaryn into the hall.

"What do you wish to show me first, Taaryn?" Ellyss asked.

She did not reply, merely nodding for him to follow her.

Once outside of the castle, out of earshot of everyone else, she stopped and turned to him. "What are you not telling us?" she asked.

"I am not sure what you mean," he began, ready to assure her she was mistaken. "I have told you all I know of the situation at hand."

"So you say, but I sense there is something more. Something you do not want us to know."

"I assure you, my lady, I have told you all I know of both Graeden and the Master."

Before she could protest, he put his finger to her lips and felt a swelling in his heart the likes of which he had never before experienced.

She wanted to argue with him, wanted to demand that he tell her now. Instead, she nodded her agreement. He took his finger from her lips and she felt a strange sensation, but the feeling disappeared in an instant.

"Come then," she said when she had regained her composure. "Allow me to show you my favorite place in the Keep."

Taaryn led Ellyss to a secluded garden behind the castle. When she reached the destination she sought, she turned to him. Whether it was the way the sunlight danced off the small stream that flowed through the garden or the fact this was the first time he had truly looked at her, Ellyss felt awestruck by her beauty.

She sat on the bench overlooking the water. She motioned him to sit beside her. He obeyed without question, compelled for some unexplained reason to do whatever she asked of him. He could not say what made him feel so biddable. Whatever it was, he knew it was unlike anything he had ever before encountered. Not in this life, nor in any other.

"Now," Taaryn said as he sat beside her, "tell me what is really happening. What you are hiding?"

"As I have already said, I am not withholding anything from you."

"But you are. I can feel it." She thought for a moment.

He shook his head. "In all honesty, I really have no idea how the Master might show himself, though I do have some guesses based on what I have already seen. I suppose I thought I was shielding you from the fear of knowing what might happen."

The expression on her face told him she found that insulting rather than comforting,

"I am sorry. I was wrong," he said quickly before she could

respond to his previous statements. "There is a strength in you, as there is in Graeden. Please forgive me."

He took her hand in his, surprised that, rather than pull away, she smiled and looked into his eyes. In the next moment, her eyelids fluttered, her breath grew shallow and she slumped against him.

#

Taaryn was assaulted by a barrage of images in the depths of Ellyss' eyes. Some recognizable, others seemingly from times long past.

The images flew by so fast, she could not focus on one before the next one appeared. The only thing that remained clear in her mind was a profound sense of pain—physical pain, both delivered and received.

Along with the pain was an even deeper sense of sorrow. A sorrow that could not be lifted. She sensed all of these images and sensations had actually happened, and for some reason, Ellyss accepted them.

In the next moment, she was no longer an onlooker. Both the sorrow and the pain thrived within her. She felt overwhelmed. When the pain became unbearable, she screamed in agony.

#

She opened her eyes and saw Ellyss. He cradled her in his arms, speaking in a tongue she did not understand. When he realized she had come to, he stopped talking and tightly hugged her.

"Thank the stars you are all right," he said as he released his hold on her.

"What happened?" she asked. "What were those things I saw? Those feelings? The pain?"

Ellyss shook his head, but he would not look at her. "I am sorry. It is all my fault. I... I do not know how that happened. I... you..."

His voice trailed off.

"Ellyss, you must tell me. What were those things?"

He stood and walked slowly to the nearby tree. He leaned against it, his back to her. "What you saw are the sins of my life. I do not know how you were able to so easily enter the inner depths of my mind." He turned and looked at her, "No one has ever been able to get that deeply inside me to see them. I am sorry. Sorry for what you saw. For what you felt. Sorry I did not realize sooner and prevent it."

She felt, as well as saw, the sorrow in his eyes.

"I will not allow it to happen again," he vowed.

She stood, went to him and put her hand on his shoulder.

"But how could those be the sins of your life? Some of those images seemed ancient. You cannot be telling me you are hundreds of years old, can you?"

"No, in this lifetime I am but a few years older than you."

"I do not understand."

He forced a smile. "No, I am sure you do not. There is no reason you should. It is a long tale, one I have not told for many years. It is not a happy one, and I am sure you would not enjoy it. So, let us put it off for another time—perhaps on a cold, moonless night in front of a blazing fire with a jug of ale when the likes of tales of this ilk are best told," he said, trying to make light of the moment.

She tugged at his arm, forcing him to face her. "No. Tell me now."

The look of determination in her eyes told him there would be no avoiding or delaying the explanation.

"If you insist, but I do not think you will savor it."

He took her hand and led her back to the bench.

"What you glimpsed within my mind or my soul, if you wish to call it that, is the curse I have lived with for many eons," he began.

"Curse? You mean like some sort of spell?" Taaryn asked.

He smiled. "Ah, if it were only as paltry as that. No, this is a curse—cruel and unbending. It is my punishment for sins committed in a distant time. Sins so heinous that I have not, even after so many lifetimes, fully atoned for them. The curse is in the memory of those sins. The memory and the experience of them, not as the perpetrator, but as the victim."

As he spoke, she saw he showed no malice toward anyone except himself.

"I do not understand," she said. "How could you have committed these acts ages ago? You are barely older than me."

"Ah, yes. I had forgotten your people do not subscribe to the belief of rebirth. That is of little consequence whether you believe or not. In my case, it occurred with the twist that I recall all of my past, especially my crimes."

Taaryn said nothing, though he could see in her eyes that her mind raced.

"It was a very long time ago, when gods and demons walked the land alongside mortal creatures. I was what you might call a demon, a low ranking one as demons go. For, even then there was a hierarchy, a class system—haves and have nots. But I desired greatness and power and I had a penchant for blood. I reveled in the pain I inflicted on others, fed on it like sustenance."

Her eyes widened at his revelation, but she said nothing.

"I was merciless. I gained power by destroying those of similar and lesser rank, be they god or demon. I tortured and slaughtered mortal creatures. I thought them inferior, their lives of no consequence, and delighted in their suffering. I plotted against those gods and demons who outranked me, and I succeeded in destroying some of them. The lands ran red with the blood of my victims and the fires of my destruction decimated the world. I thought myself invincible."

"Like the Master?" she asked.

He looked at her with sorrow in his eyes. "Far worse than he will ever be, even if all his plans come to fruition."

Taaryn gasped.

He looked away.

"Yet, in reality, I was no more than a brute, a drunken oaf in a tavern. It did not take long for the remaining gods and demons to band together and put a stop to my reign of violence and terror. I, in my vanity, continued to believe myself both superior and unbeatable." He shook his head and grimaced. "But I was quickly shown my own weakness. They defeated me as easily as one would stamp out a small bug on the ground."

"Why did they not destroy you?" Taaryn asked.

"That would have been too easy, too humane an end for me. They chose a punishment befitting my heinous crimes. My punishment was for my essence, my soul, to survive through the ages, occupying one mortal shell after another until I atoned for all of my sins. I have lived through uncountable lives and have barely removed a drop of water from the ocean of sins I committed against others."

He turned to Taaryn, surprised to see a tear running down her cheek. He wiped it away.

"Do not shed a tear for me, my lady. My punishment was, and is, just."

"But you are no longer that thing, that demon. Why should you continue to carry the curse?"

"The debt has yet to be paid, Taaryn. I know that and I accept it." He gently brushed the hair from her face. "But just hearing you say those words has made my burden a little lighter today."

"No one else has ever told you that?"

He shook his head. "You, my dear girl, are the first in all of my lifetimes to ever hear the story. As I said before, there has never been anyone who has touched me as you have. Even the drageals, known for their ability to find the truth no matter how deep one tries to hide it, have never been able to glean the true nature of my being."

She smiled and pressed her lips softly to his cheek. She wrapped her arms around him and whispered in his ear. "You are a good man, Ellyss. I know it. I can feel it."

He embraced her, and a tear trickled down his cheek. The couple sat, neither one wanting to release the other until a noise behind them broke the silence. They released their hold on each other and looked around to see Gantell.

"So, this is where you two ran off to," Gantell said as he strode up to the bench.

If he had seen them embracing, he made no mention of it. Neither did they.

"Were you looking for us for something specific," Taaryn began, "or are you just shirking your responsibilities again, big brother?"

"First of all, you know I take my responsibilities very seriously, and I am hurt and insulted that you could say such a thing in front of our guest."

"Bah, nothing hurts your feelings."

"You may be right," Gantell replied with a deep laugh.

"And the reason you sought us out?" she asked.

"Oh, yes, of course. I want to talk to Ellyss about some ideas I have for our defense of the Keep," Gantell answered. "Unless, I am interrupting something."

"No, we were just talking," Taaryn replied almost too quickly.

"Good." Gantell sat on the grass in front of the bench.

CHAPTER EIGHT

WORRELK ENTERED his rooms and frantically began to search amongst the many piles of his father's papers and books for the spell book in question. He knew failure to find it was not an option. While neither he nor his father had ever suffered the wrath of the king, he remembered horrific tales of what happened to those who failed to satisfy Jurcheval's wishes.

He searched through the various stacks of papers and books. While he found both his father's and Drakorem's notes, the book they referred to was not among them. He slumped to the floor in defeat. What would he do? Running away, as the king had already reminded him, was not an option. Even if it were, where would he go? He had spent his entire life in and around the confines of the castle, rarely venturing further than an hour's walk from its gates.

He lay back on the floor and stared at the ceiling. The damned book must be here somewhere. He never discarded anything of his father's that had to do with magic and the like, so where was it? He closed his eyes, trying to remember what it looked like and the last time he had seen it, but to no avail. All he recalled was watching his father gingerly hold the book. Again, he racked his brain to remember what his father told him about the book. But the harder he thought about it, the more fleeting the memory became until it was gone.

He reached up, covered his eyes with his hands, and then pulled at his hair as if the pain might release that which he needed to recall. It did not.

He lay there several moments in silence, then opened his eyes and shook his head. This was not doing him any good. He rolled onto his side, facing the wall. There, wedged between two bookshelves, was the small clothbound book.

He crawled over to the shelves and reached for it. As soon as his fingers got close to it, he felt a sharp pain in his hand. He drew back.

Seated, he looked skyward. "Father, is this your doing? Do you have some reason why I should not read this little book?"

He waited a moment, not sure if he really expected a reply from his long-passed father or not.

"It is a matter of life and death, my death, that I find the spell contained in that book," he continued.

Still nothing. He reached for the book again with the same results.

"Please, Father. I beg of you. If this is your doing, please release it," he pled to his surroundings.

Again, nothing happened. He put his head in his hands and sobbed. "If you will not help, dear Father, you have condemned me to what will likely be a most heinous death at the hands of our king."

He sat and shook his head for a few moments, trying to think what he would tell the king. The book was here, but unattainable. That would not go over well. But, neither would not having found it at all. No, he needed to come up with a way to remove the book. If he could not, he would throw himself from the tower, a far less painful end than what the king would have in store for him.

He opened his eyes and moved to his knees to rise. Just then, he was shocked to see the little book lying on the floor in front of the bookshelves.

He raised his eyes to the heavens. "Thank you, Father."

Worrelk reached for the book, half expecting to feel the sharp pain again. This time, he picked it up without any consequence. He thumbed through it until he found the spell he sought, the Eye of Control.

"You did not lie, Father. This is by far the most complicated spell and potion I have ever seen," he said as he reread the spell for the third time. He shook his head. "Be that as it may, I must do it. The king is not a patient man."

He read the spell again, this time jotting down the needed components. As he perused the list, he shook his head. "This is not good."

#

"As I recall it takes near on a week to create the seeing stones. So why are you here?" Jurcheval asked.

Worrelk steeled himself against his fear. "Unfortunately, Sire, there is more than just timing."

Jurcheval glared at him.

The wizard took a deep breath. "I have encountered several

obstacles in the creation of the potion. In fact, I am not so sure it can be done."

Jurcheval raised an eyebrow. "Why is that?"

"It is a matter of resources."

"Bah, I used them just a few years ago."

"That is true, Sire. Unfortunately, since Drakorem created those, most of the resources for the required ingredients have been all but exhausted in these parts."

"Then, search for them elsewhere. I must have those stones." Jurcheval said.

"Even if I find the resources for the potion, Sire, I do not have the correct base stones. Drakorem used something he called listening stones. I can find no mention of how to make those in any of the papers of either my father or Drakorem. And, though the potion does not specifically cite the use of them, Drakorem indicates those stones added an additional level of power to the items."

"Do not worry about the listening stones, I will ensure you have as many of those as you need."

Worrelk tried to hide his surprise.

"How long do you think it will take to gather the other required ingredients?"

"I am not sure, Sire. I may need to travel quite the distance to acquire them in the quantities we need."

Jurcheval walked closer to Worrelk and moved his hand toward the wizard. Worrelk recoiled. The king smiled as he lightly brushed something off the young man's shoulder.

"Well then, you had better be off." Jurcheval walked away. As he left the room, he called back, "I need not remind you the price of failure, do I?"

CHAPTER NINE

ALTHOUGH SEVERAL MONTHS since the attack, Immic still could not fly. His other injuries had healed quickly, but the damage to his wings had been quite severe.

"At least you know you will be able to fly again," Graeden said. "Once your wings have fully healed, you will be soaring high above and looking down on the rest of us just like you always have. And now that Neshya's burns and broken arm are healed, he will be able to do... well, whatever it is he does."

Neshya feigned hurt at his friend's remark. Immic did not respond.

"Everyone is expecting me to not only explain how I made those fireballs, but to repeat it," Graeden continued, shaking his head in frustration. "Damn it! I keep telling them I have no idea how I did it. They just happened."

"Graeden, I am sure they only expect that of you because they think you can do it," Neshya replied with an uncharacteristic seriousness.

"That is my point, I cannot!"

Immic and Neshya looked at each other, trying to decide what, if anything, they could say to help their friend.

"I am sorry." Graeden looked away. "I should not be bothering you with this."

"I understand your fear and frustration," Immic said. "I, too, harbor doubts of my abilities. And my future."

Neshya and Graeden looked at the drageal in amazement. Never had they heard anything but confidence, usually bordering on bravado, from their friend.

Immic saw this and chuckled.

"Wings are far more delicate and complicated than one might imagine. What happens if they do not heal perfectly? If I am never able to fly again?" The drageal continued in a thoughtful tone, "What would I do then? Without flight, I would lose my life's meaning. I would lose me."

"But the healers said you would be fine, did they not?" Graeden asked.

"Yes, they did. And your teachers said you can create fireballs at will."

"That is not the same thing," Graeden responded sharply.

"Really? We both fear we will be unable to once again do things that are expected of us. Is that not so, little brother?"

"Looks like he has called your bluff," Neshya said with a laugh.

Graeden glared at his friends.

Neshya laughed again. "If I were you, Graeden, I would give up. I have known this drageal for many more years than you and have never seen anyone win an argument when he thinks he is right. And…"

"He always thinks he is right," Graeden finished his friend's thought.

Immic nodded.

"And I agree with him. Maybe, you are just trying too hard," Neshya said.

"Like when you were trying to learn to mindspeak," Immic added.

"Well, I think that was due to an entirely different problem." Neshya snickered.

Graeden's face reddened.

"Why not lighten up, try to have some fun with the training," Neshya continued.

"Fun?" Graeden asked.

"Yes, fun. Instead of thinking about how to do it, imagine yourself setting fire to Phrynia's feathers or Varlama's hair?" Neshya continued with a grin that revealed the yekcal's large, sharp teeth. "That just might be the key to it. If it works and you do singe them once or twice, I bet they would let up on you."

Immic grunted. "If you set my mother on fire, you will have to deal with me."

"Hold on, Immic," Graeden tried to sound afraid, aware that Immic was teasing him as much as Neshya. "I do not even know how to create fireballs, never mind setting anyone on fire."

Immic did not respond.

"Great, Nesh, make a frustrated drageal angry with me."

The friends laughed.

"What are you three laughing about?" Regnaryn asked as she joined them.

"Oh, we were just talking about Graeden setting Phrynia and Varlama on fire," Neshya answered, still laughing.

"That does not sound very funny to me." She crossed the garden to where Immic stood. He bent down, and she gently kissed his cheek. "How are you feeling, Imm?"

"Grounded and heavy."

"I am sure you will be skybound very soon."

"Oh sure, he gets a kiss and you and I are left just sitting here," Neshya began. "She's your mate, and she ignores you."

"Not always," Graeden answered slyly. They all laughed.

"I think it is time for you to get back to your training, Graeden," Regnaryn said, ignoring their comments.

Graeden shook his head. "As if it is going to change anything."

#

"How many times do we have to go through this before you two are convinced I cannot create fireballs?" Graeden asked as he once again failed to produce what his teachers demanded. He shook his head. "Seriously, I think the only way I could repeat what happened that day, and believe me, I never want to be in that situation again, is for Regnaryn to be in mortal danger."

"You are wrong," Phrynia said. "When it comes to magical abilities, you either have the talent or you do not. There is no such thing as being able to do something only once."

"Then why, after all of this training, have I been unable to conjure anything, Not even a spark."

"Because, my boy, you are using this," Varlama said, tapping the side of his head, "instead of this." She patted his chest.

Graeden shook his head. "So you keep saying."

"And you continue to not listen," Phrynia said. "Now, try again."

Try again. Try again. That is all they ever say. How can they not know I am trying? Graeden fumed in his mind.

He attempted to create a fireball. Again, he failed. And he was told to try again and again. With each failure, his frustration level grew.

Perhaps I should try doing as Neshya said, he thought. With his next attempt, he threw a fireball, a rather weak one but a fireball just the same. And before even being told, he tried again. This time, a perfect fireball exploded from his fingers and flew by Phrynia and Varlama.

"Fantastic, Graeden!" Varlama said. "We knew you could do it."

"So what made the difference today?" Phrynia asked.

"Oh, it was just something Neshya said," Graeden said and chuckled.

#

Graeden felt drained and excited as he left the training ground. He mindcalled to Regnaryn and was disappointed to realize she was already asleep. He quietly entered the house and went upstairs. For just a moment, he thought of waking her, but realized she must be exhausted if she did not wait up for him. Instead, he carefully climbed into bed and, as soon as he closed his eyes, he fell into a deep slumber.

In what seemed to be the next moment, he felt a tickling sensation on his nose. He brushed it aside with his hand as he moved from the sleeping to waking world. He opened his eyes, blinked at the brightness of the room and saw Regnaryn holding the end of her long braid over his face ready to tickle him once more. Before she had the chance, he lunged at her, rolling her onto her back and straddling her body.

"Well, good morning, sleepy head," she said.

He bent down and kissed her. She threw her arms around his neck and pulled him towards her.

"You do not think you are getting away with only a kiss this morning, do you?" she asked.

"I was not the one sound asleep so early last night."

"Excuses! You could have woken me."

He laughed. "I think not, my dear. The last time I woke you, my head was nearly bitten off."

"Well, I am awake now."

"As am I," he said.

#

"Are you meeting with Varlama and Phrynia again today?" Regnaryn asked before taking another sip of tea.

Graeden shook his head and finished chewing the mouthful of food.

"I know it is hard, love, but..."

He laughed. "No, actually it is not."

"What?" she cried. "Are you saying what I think you are?"

He nodded.

"That is wonderful. How can you be so calm about it after all the frustration you went through to get there?"

Graeden shrugged.

"Well, I am excited for you even if you do not seem to care."

"Since I have a break today, I think we should start looking for your father's journals."

"If they even exist," Regnaryn said.

CHAPTER TEN

"I STILL DO NOT understand why you think my father would keep journals," Regnaryn said after the two had walked through the house, looking for possible hiding places. "And, even if he did, why would he feel the need to hide them. Everything, everyone, here is so open and sharing."

"That is true," Graeden replied. "But old habits are not easily broken, and you must remember that your parents, especially your father, came from life at a royal court. That, my dear, is always a world fraught with intrigue and secrecy. It is just something those at court learn to live with."

Regnaryn listened, but he could see she did not understand.

"Do you feel that way? That you need to keep things secret?"

"No," he said with a hint of a smile. "Not here. Not from

you."

He saw the look of relief cross her face.

"I am glad." She squeezed his hand.

"So you see, your father may have hidden certain documents and writings from the view and knowledge of others, not due to mistrust but out of habit."

"I see, but we have not found any hiding spots, so what do we do now?"

"Well, it has been a long time and you were very young. It might not be something in the forefront of your memories."

She wrinkled her nose.

"But that does not mean it is not there. Tell me, what do you recall of your father? Of what you and he did together?"

"Not much," she replied.

"But you must have some memories of him," Graeden said as they settled onto the large couch. "Tell me anything you remember."

She thought a few moments. "He had long yellow hair. And a beard. It was soft, but it always tickled whenever he kissed me. And he always smelled good. Oh, this is silly, what good is this going to do to help us find where he hid something."

"It may. What else do you remember?"

She shook her head.

"What did you and he do together? Did he play with you? Read to you?"

After a few moments of silence, her face lit up as she remembered things, little things of what she and Grenwald had done together. How she would sit with him in the big chair, and he would wrap his arm around her as he read book after book to her. She remembered looking up into his face, watching with amusement at how the hair on his lip bounced up and down as he spoke.

"Wait. I remember something. He would go into a little room and sit at the desk. Sometimes he would let me sit in his lap as he wrote in books. Thick books. With lots of blank pages."

She turned to Graeden. "Could those have been his journals? I remember that, once he finished one book, he would begin another."

She jumped up and began to pace. "But where did he put them? Where is that room?"

"If as a child you thought it little it must be no more than a closet. But, we found no such room when we were readying the house."

"I think I remember." She grabbed Graeden's hand, almost dragging him into the library.

"No, no," she said looking around the room. "This is not right. This is not how it should be."

Her look of joyous excitement changed to disappointment.

"What is wrong?" he asked.

"Nothing looks the way it did. It is all different," she said, almost sobbing.

"How is it different?"

She turned several times to survey the room. Furniture was moved or missing. But more disturbingly, the room itself did not look right. Graeden asked her to tell him specifically what was different. As she talked, they both realized they were in the wrong room.

They went to the room at the end of the hall, Regnaryn stopped, looked around and then ran to the far wall. Almost instinctively, she ran her hand along the wall. A panel popped open, revealing a tiny room with shelves full of books lining the walls. a small desk in the corner and light coming down from a windowed shaft in the ceiling.

"This is what I remember." She entered the room and ran her

fingers along the dusty spines.

They walked around the room, perusing the many volumes. Graeden stopped at one group of books on the shelves in the corner. The books looked different than the others, smaller, not as lushly bound and unmarked. He took one from the shelf and opened it.

"You may want to look at this one," he said and held it out to her. "It is your mother's, and the date on the inside is the year she died."

She held the book to her chest, not sure if she wanted to read it.

"You do not need to read it right this moment, love," he said, sensing her hesitation. "There is time. You know they are here, and you can come to them whenever you wish."

She nodded.

"Yes, you are right," she said, still clutching the book to her chest. "Right now, we need to look for a connection between Father and the Master. But where do we begin?"

Graeden walked over to the far wall and looked at the row of larger, dated books.

"It seems these are your father's and begin when he was already an adult, probably when he left his homeland. I think we should start with those."

She agreed.

"And since it seems we have a goodly sum of reading ahead of us this day, I suggest a pot of tea is in order and, perhaps, some cakes. If you make the tea, I will carry the books to the living room," he said. "We might as well be comfortable while we read."

She nodded.

Once the tea and cakes were ready, she opened the first book and they began to read together.

CHAPTER ELEVEN

<u>*Day Three of the Second Spring Moon*</u>

It is done. Sevich's words from so many years ago have come to pass. He always told me one day I would turn tail and run, and now I have. I have abandoned my father, my countrymen and my beloved land of Aelden in their time of need. I truly am the coward my younger brother predicted I would be.

I could do no good in that place. If my words had reached a single ear, I would have stayed to fight against him. But no one would listen. It was as if no one could hear.

I hardly believe in magic, but I have no other explanation for the behavior of the court. The way everyone behaved. How even those who previously condemned Sevich's actions now obeyed his every whim, sided with his every deed. It was as if everyone was under an enchantment orchestrated by Sevich. Everyone but me.

When did this begin? Did I turn a blind eye to it at its inception? Is this somehow my fault for not insisting earlier that father do something about Sevich and his violence, his vicious behavior? Or was it already too late by the time I returned from school? I, too, let it go on. For eight years I did nothing on my own. Even when Father refused to act, should I not have done something to stop the boy?

All I can do now is mourn my homeland for I fear it will come to ruin as soon as Sevich ascends the throne. But has my abandonment taken away my right to mourn? I fear so.

<u>*Day Five of the Second Spring Moon*</u>

I wonder if Sevich is even looking for me. It has been several days since I left and I have seen neither troops nor patrols. Do I dare take the chance to stop and rest? No. The evil I saw in his eyes, especially the last few days before I left, warns me he will not let me go so easily. He will search for me.

I must find a place to stay. Somewhere with no ties to Aelden, where Sevich will have no sway. First, I need to find a village where I might get a meal, a bath and a bed.

#

Regnaryn closed the book and turned to Graeden with tears in her eyes. "My poor father."

Graeden reached over and wiped the tear from her cheek.

"His brother seems quite the villain," Graeden said.

"Yes, he does."

She reopened the book and they began to read again.

#

Day Seven of the Second Spring Moon

Now that I have passed the borders of Aelden, I can reflect on the words, unbelievable as they sound, that I heard two nights ago at that inn.

My father has been murdered, and I stand accused!

There is no doubt in my mind that this is Sevich's doing. But why? Did he hate father that much? Or was it the power of throne and crown that drove him to such an act?

In my heart, I know there will be no reasoning with him, no way I would ever be able to clear or even defend myself against him. I could not do it before on even the most trivial of matters and now he has stacked the deck against me.

So, my fate is sealed. If I choose to live, I must run. Run far away from Aelden and its allies. I must find a place that pays no heed to distant kingdoms or their renegades.

For now, I will continue south and hope to find that place.

Day Twelve of the Second Spring Moon

I have heard of a kingdom, Alexandrash, that lies a few weeks ride to the south. From what I overheard in the conversations of traveling merchants at the last few inns, it seems quite idyllic. Even if it is not all they say, it sounds like the place I need to be.

Dare I say, I have a good feeling about this?

Day Eighteen of the Second Spring Moon

I am thankful my journey continues to be uneventful save for a few spring thunderstorms. I have heard no further word of my father's murder. In fact, I have heard nothing of Aelden at all, though this kingdom does maintain ties with Aelden. Perhaps it is that the common folk, the villagers and farmers, are more concerned with getting through *their daily life than with the politics of a distant land, or even their own.*

I must laugh at myself. Even on the run from the false charges that would surely result in my execution should I be caught, I still take the time to write in these silly books. Why?

Day Twenty-Four of the Second Spring Moon

According to the merchant in the village I stopped at today, Alexandrash is only another week's ride away. I do not know why, but the closer I get to its border, the calmer I feel. I can only hope it is the sanctuary I seek.

Day Two of the Third Spring Moon

It has been three weeks to the day since I fled Aelden, and today I finally passed a wooden sign post marked ALEXANDRASH.

This sounds silly even as I write the words, but as I entered this land I felt a tranquility wash over me, as if I had been wrapped in a fine woolen blanket. For the first time in what seems an eternity, I feel safe.

As I entered the village, a few hours ride within the border, I was taken by the friendliness of the people. Almost everyone I passed greeted me with a smile and a 'Hiya'. This is not what I have experienced in the other places through which I have passed. In most, I was lucky to get a scowl, if I received any acknowledgement at all.

I am not sure if it is the mood of this place or the sense of security I feel here, but I have decided to stay a day or so at the inn. Perhaps I can gain some insight into the country and its rulers.

Not to mention, how wonderful it will feel to sleep in a bed.

Day Four of the Third Spring Moon

I am glad I decided to stay here for a few days. The people are so warm and friendly. And the love they have for their King, even so far from his capital city, makes me think I made the right decision in coming to this land. They have renewed my faith and hope in the world.

Just the way they speak of Frindlit, their king, and his court makes me realize how much I miss the comforts of that life. Perhaps if I go there, I could find a place for myself. Nothing ostentatious, nothing important. Just something comfortable.

<u>*Day Five of the Third Spring Moon*</u>

This morning I bid farewell to those at the inn. Even though it was only a stay of a few days, I will miss them. But I need to move on. Siggurna, Frindlit's city, is several weeks journey from here. I must say the vastness of this land amazes me.

It may, of course, be a fruitless trek. It would not surprise me if I never get to see the King or any of his ministers. After all, I have little to offer as proof of who I am. And the shabbiness of my appearance will lend little credence to my previous station. I am not so sure I would allow this version of myself anywhere near my father when he ruled, so why should Frindlit?

But I continue to have a good feeling for everything about this plan. I really do believe it is going to work out.

#

Regnaryn put the book on her lap.

"That is quite the tale," Graeden said. "Your father was lucky to escape his brother when he did."

"Yes, he was," she said. "Still, as evil as killing your own father and blaming your brother is, I do not think that is proof that he is the Master."

"No," Graeden said.

"Perhaps there is more in some of his other journals."

"Exactly what I was thinking," Graeden said. "I will get a few more of them. I think the most useful ones might be those he wrote before he got to Reissem Grove."

The couple spent the rest of the morning and most of the afternoon pouring over Grenwald's journals.

"Well, I must say," Graeden said as he closed the book he was reading, "your father was quite a man. Very complex."

"And verbose." Regnaryn chuckled as she pointed to the journals strewn across the room.

Graeden laughed. "Yes, that, too."

"While I loved learning so much about him and how he met and fell in love with my mother..."

"We learned nothing that could help us connect your father or your uncle to the Master," Graeden said, echoing her frustration.

Regnaryn nodded. "Are we wasting our time here?"

"No, I do not think so. Even though we have no proof, my gut tells me there is a connection between them."

"I agree. But what do we do now?"

"What about the other books, those of your mother? Maybe there is something in those," Graeden suggested.

"Good idea," Regnaryn replied.

CHAPTER TWELVE

REGNARYN AND GRAEDEN returned to the secret room to retrieve Karaleena's journals.

"Look, these are different," Regnaryn said, holding up two books.

"Is it just the covers, or are they really not the same?"

She handed him one. They began to read.

"This one seems to be a journal," Graeden said. "Is yours the same?"

"No. I do not think so, although I am not sure what it is. It contains drawings as well as entries," she replied. "Wait, I wonder if these are the books of her castings."

"Her castings?"

"Yes, her cards. Remember, one of father's entries said she was looking at cards and writing in a red book."

She showed the red cover to Graeden.

"Ah, yes. I bet that is why they are different," he said. "Do you wish to start with those or her journals?"

Regnaryn read a few random entries, skimming from page to page. She looked up at him and shook her head. "The journals, I think. The entries here seem random, to be expected, I guess, since they seem to be written to document how she cast the cards and what she saw. Unless we have specific dates for reference, I do not think these will be of much use to us."

Graeden nodded. "Shall we start with the ones around the time she and your father met? Or do you want to go back further?"

"When Father arrived. The older ones I can read when we do not have a mission to accomplish."

#

First Moon of Summer, Day One

A stranger named Grenwald was presented at Court today. Rumor has it he is a prince in exile from some distant kingdom. He is quite good looking, but seems very somber. I did not approach him, but heard he was extremely rude to anyone who did.

I hope he does not stay long. He really does not seem to be the sort of person I would like to be around.

First Moon of Summer, Day Ten

I do not know why, but this Grenwald character perturbs me far more than he should. Though we have never spoken more than a polite—well, I was polite—greeting, I feel his presence around me all the time.

First Moon of Summer, Day Eighteen

I confronted Grenwald today over the fact that he is constantly staring at me. He did not deny his actions. When I told him to stop, he actually laughed at me. The nerve!

First Moon of Summer, Day Twenty

Grenwald approached me in the garden today as I was casting cards. I felt him watching me from the shadows and when confronted, he denied it. I knew better.

He made up the pretense that he was interested in the cards, yet his demeanor and every word he uttered made it clear he is not a believer in either the art or my ability. Still, to be polite, I answered his questions only to have him laugh in my face. I stormed away.

I wish he would just stay away from me. He is truly the most boorish person I have ever met. I do not understand how the royal family tolerates him.

First Moon of Summer, Day Twenty-One

I think I have reached my limit with that lout, Grenwald. Each day his brazenness towards me increases. Today, he most definitely crossed the line.

I was hurrying along the Grand Corridor, trying not to be late for the luncheon for whatever boring dignitary was invited, when he appeared and started to walk alongside me. He asked if he could accompany me into the hall. I ignored him and walked faster to distance myself from him.

Without any warning, he grabbed my arm and dragged me into a side hall, pushed me up against the wall and had the nerve, the outright audacity, to kiss me! And it was no brotherly kiss, let me tell you. I am not, after all, a child. I know the ways of the world.

I was shocked by his actions, right there in the hallway. Naturally, I slapped his face. He stood there and smiled. The nerve!

I reminded him that I have never, not a single time since he arrived, given him the least inkling that I was now or ever would be interested in him and that his advances were not welcome. I also told him, I would rather chance the ridicule of entering the function unescorted than to be on his arm. The cad stood there, still smiling at me, so I stormed off.

After lunch, I sought out Prince Thresem. For some odd reason, he and Grenwald seem to be friends. Maybe a word from Thresem will influence that boor and make him leave me alone.

Second Moon of Summer, Day One

It has been a little over a week, and I think my talk with Thresem has done some good. Grenwald has not bothered me since then.

Still, with the new moon, I feel I need to cast his cards. I have no idea why, but he continues to occupy my thoughts. Perhaps once I do the reading I can find when we will be rid of him.

Second Moon of Summer, Day Three

I cannot believe it has taken me these last few days after Grenwald's casting to compose myself enough to sit here to put pen to paper, even about things that do not directly concern what I saw. I now understand much better why Grenwald acts so.

Even now, some of the things the cards revealed haunt me. While I did suspect a darkness in his past, this was far more than I dreamed.

At first, I could not believe my eyes. I went so far as to recast the cards. Yet, even the second time, they revealed to me the same horrors.

Grenwald's brother, Sevich, is a monster. There is no other way to state it. He has tasted power and craves more and, as he has shown by killing his father and blaming Grenwald, will stop at nothing to get it.

I saw a reign of terror brought on by Sevich that will spread much further than his little kingdom. And though I did not see it clearly at the moment, he will have a devastating effect on both Grenwald and myself. I cringe to think what.

#

"It is true, then," Regnaryn said.

"So it seems," Graeden replied. "I will tell the others what we have found."

Regnaryn was already across the room, staring out the window. "Thank you."

"I think this is something that needs to be said face-to-face, so, unless you have an objection, I will have everyone gather at Trebeh's."

She nodded, but she did not turn to him.

"They will understand if you choose not to be there," he said.

"I hope so."

Graeden crossed the room and put his arm around her shoulder. She stiffened, but he did not let go.

"What if I become the same monster he is?" she asked, looking up at him. "I already destroyed an entire colony of gawara with a mere thought. And those flying beasts, what of those? Who is to say I will not do the same to friend or family next?"

He turned her to face him. "That will never happen. There is not an evil bone in your body. Whatever you have done, you have done in the name of helping others."

"But I sent you away, and even when I knew how much pain you were in, I did not call you back. Was that not a stroke of evil?"

Graeden smiled. "No, my love. That was an act of a petulant child throwing a tantrum."

"I was a little old to be doing such things."

"In years, yes. In emotions, no."

"Still," she said, burying her face against his chest. "What if..."

He put his arms around her and held her tightly. "There is no what if. You are not your uncle. In fact, you are not even your father or your mother. You are you."

She did not look up.

"Now, I need to tell the others what we have discovered." He released his hold on her.

"You should take the journals with you," she said.

"Good idea."

CHAPTER THIRTEEN

"HOW IS SHE HANDLING this?" Trebeh asked.

"She is terrified she will turn into the same monster he is." Graeden replied.

"That is not surprising," Varlama said. "In many ways, she still fears she will lose control of her power."

"I agree," Graeden said. "But you all know her, no matter how many times we tell her she has nothing to worry about, she continues to fear the worst."

Everyone nodded.

"For now, the more pressing issue is, how do we find this Sevich?" Ayirak asked. "I, for one, have no idea where Grenwald's homeland was."

"Nor does anyone else in the Grove," Trebeh replied.

"He does not mention much about his homeland in his journals," Graeden said. "The earliest entries recount his sadness at leaving."

"Well, we need to find something," Ayirak said.

"These journals are from when he was on the road to Alexandrash, correct?" Phrynia asked.

Graeden nodded.

"Does he mention anything about direction or distance?" the drageal continued.

"Or how long it took?" Varlama added.

Graeden thought a moment. "I am not sure. We were not really looking for those kinds of details when we read them, but I can certainly reread them."

"I think we should all have a look," Trebeh said.

"Good idea," Graeden answered. "I will get the books and bring them here."

"Or we could all go there," Varlama added.

:*I was going to suggest that myself,*: Trebeh mindspoke to Varlama. :*I do not like the idea of Regnaryn being alone with this right now.*:

"I am not sure Regnaryn is up for company at the moment," Graeden said.

Ayirak slapped him on the back. "We are not company, boy. We are family."

#

"Why am I not surprised that you are all here?" Regnaryn asked with a chuckle as the group gathered in the garden.

"You did not really expect us to leave you alone too long after such a devastating discovery, did you?" Trebeh hugged the young girl.

79

Regnaryn smiled. "No. I thought you might come to have a look at the journals for yourself, so I gathered the earliest ones."

"Thank you," Trebeh said.

Graeden picked up the earliest of Grenwald's books from the table. "I think we should read the entries aloud."

"Good idea," Varlama said. "That will allow everyone to share both opinion and knowledge on any information we find in them."

"I will write down anything we discover so we do not forget it later," Regnaryn said.

"Wonderful," Trebeh said.

#

"Regnaryn and I read parts of this first journal before," Graeden said as he opened the book. "But that was before we thought it was his homeland we needed to find."

Over the next few hours, the group pored over the first journal, meticulously dissecting each entry.

"That is the last entry in this journal." Graeden closed the leather-bound book. "Should we go on to the next one or discuss what we have learned so far?"

Neshya, unusually quiet during the reading, shook his head. "There is a lot here to think about. Since the last few entries are beginning to focus more on his new life in Siggurna, I suggest we stop reading here."

"I agree," Trebeh said.

"And I could certainly go for something to eat," Neshya added. "Seriously, Regnaryn, is this how you treat guests? If I had known you planned to starve us to death, I would have stayed home."

Regnaryn playfully scowled at her brother as the others laughed.

"You of all people are not a benchmark for determining starvation. You are always hungry," Regnaryn said. "And I will have you know, I was just about to offer everyone something to eat."

#

"So, what have we learned so far?" Varlama asked as she finished the last bite of food.

"Grenwald's homeland was called Aelden, and it was some distance north of the borders of Alexandrash," Trebeh replied.

"That is not much to go on," Neshya said.

"No, but he did say the first village he came to in Alexandrash was Frelind," Graeden answered. "If we could find that on a map that would at least be one point of reference."

"Ah, but we do not have any maps of Alexandrash," Neshya said.

"But Taaryn and Ellyss do. There are dozens of maps in my father's library. Surely they could find that village on one of them."

"Well, that would be helpful, but are your father's maps detailed enough to show every small village?" Trebeh asked.

"I believe some are," Graeden replied.

"How will we get word to Ellyss and Taaryn to find that village?" Regnaryn asked.

"We could send a drageal to Hammarsh Keep," Phrynia said.

"Or," Varlama began, "Graeden could try mindspeaking to his sister."

"What? Me?" Graeden exclaimed. "I am the weakest mindspeaker here, and you want me to try and reach someone such a great distance away? Have you lost your mind, Varlama?"

The tazzamira smiled. "No, dear boy, my mind is as intact as it has ever been. And, yes, I do think you can do it. Your skills have strengthened, your mindspeaking is not what it was when you first arrived here."

"And do not forget you and Taaryn are twins," Phrynia added. "Did you not say that you two always knew what the other was doing without being together?"

"Yes, but that is different," Graeden replied.

"Is it?" Phrynia asked.

"It will do no harm to at least try," Regnaryn said.

Graeden looked around the room and found approval in everyone's eyes. *Wonderful, yet another thing I can fail at,* he thought.

"If you insist, I will try," he said.

"Good," Varlama said. "I suggest you attempt it when your body is rested and your mind relaxed."

"In the meantime," Trebeh began, "we need to pull together what we do know."

Everyone agreed. For the next hour or so, they drew up a general map of where Aelden might be in comparison to Frelind.

"That looks good, but it is pretty useless unless we discover its location." Graeden pointed to the spot marked "Frelind".

"Yeah, there is *that* tiny little detail," Neshya added with a snort.

"We must hope Ellyss and Taaryn are able to help with that," Varlama said.

"I think we have done as much as we can for now," Phrynia said. "So we should take our leave."

:And, dear boy, do not fret if your first attempt to reach your sister is not successful,: Trebeh mindspoke to him. *:If we cannot reach her this way, we do have other options. You are not under any pressure.:*

Graeden smiled at the yekcal's reassurance.

CHAPTER FOURTEEN

AFTER DINNER REGNARYN returned to the living room with several of her late mother's journals. She sat on the couch beside Graeden and placed the volumes on the cushion beside her.

"What are those?" he asked.

"Mother's journals from just before I was born," Regnaryn replied. "I want to know more of what she saw about me, about the prophecy."

"I see. Do you want to be alone?"

She shook her head. "No, please stay and read with me."

He put his arm around her shoulder as she opened the first book.

#

<u>*Day Seven of the Second Winter Moon:*</u>

Over the last few months I have felt a compulsion to cast the cards for my soon-to-be-born child and have hesitated. I feared the cards would confirm what I have seen in my dreams. And now that I have done it, I wish I had not. Never have I seen such a casting for one not yet of this world. I cannot, dare not, dismiss it. I know the power the cards hold in foretelling the future, but how do I deal with this? How will my precious daughter, yet unborn, deal with what awaits her?

I wonder whether I should tell Grenwald of this. Even now, with all that he has seen in this place, he still barely believes in the powers and abilities all around him. How can I tell him what the cards told me, what I saw? How will he believe that our daughter will change the world with her powers, if his monstrous brother does not snuff out her life force and consume her power first.

What have we done bringing a child into such a fate? How can we make it up to her? I fear for her, for I saw neither Grenwald nor I at her side. I know there will be others to guide her, but sorrow fills my heart that it will not be me.

I think I will wait to tell Grenwald. Perhaps, when I once again go over the details of the casting, I may see it differently and may change my interpretation. I hope so.

<u>*Day Fourteen of the Second Autumn Moon:*</u>

I have cast and recast the cards numerous times over the last week. There is no mistake in what I see. Each reading confirms the initial casting. Oh, if it were not so. If I were anyone else, I might hope what I saw would not come to pass, but the readings are far too strong in their confirmation of the previous foretelling.

My poor dear child.

I had so hoped these latest castings would reveal more to me about the outcome now that the child is almost here. Sadly, there remains too many things still in flux within the universe. While the cards did reveal some new information, these new revelations cause me great despair. Why will so many other beings need to unite against Sevich? Is he really that strong? That evil? Though I seek, I have yet to find any answers to those questions.

Still, I am compelled to document the prophecy that has pounded in my brain since I first realized I was with child, what I have, thus far, been too fearful to record.

Born of two kingdoms, in a place of peace and wonder, she will grow to possess great magic and power. But there will be one who will try to wrest that which is hers.

With friends and loved ones at her side, they will stand in opposition against the evil born of her bloodline. And together with another of near equal power, they will make a final stand in the battle against this evil.

I will pray every day that I have misinterpreted what I saw, but deep inside I know it will indeed, come to pass.

#

Regnaryn closed the book and stared into the distance.

"Mother knew of you and your power," she said after a few moments.

"No, I cannot be the one of near equal power," he replied. "I could never do anything even close to what you can. Surely there will be someone else. Perhaps Phrynia or Varlama will be the one of which she spoke."

"Perhaps, but she did know of you because you are indeed my

loved one."

Graeden pulled her closer. "That I am."

CHAPTER FIFTEEN

WORRELK WOKE TO THE sound of banging on his chamber door. He jumped out of bed and groped in the darkness for his dressing gown. As he grasped the fabric, he heard more rapping on the door.

"Who in the world could that be? It is the middle of the night," he muttered as he raced to the door, putting on the gown as he ran.

He opened the door just as the surly guardsman was about to bang once again.

"Why are you not ready, wizard?" He pushed past Worrelk and dropped into the large chair in the corner.

Worrelk stood motionless, wondering what the man was talking about.

"Well, get a move on, boy," the guard growled. "Or should I go tell the King you are not going on your little mission?"

"Oh, dear, I had forgotten that was today, but the sun is not yet up." Worrelk closed the door.

"Better to get an early start. Since you are far from ready, that is no longer an option," the guard said. He looked around and shook his head. "Have you any food or drink here? If you are to make me wait, the least you could do is nourish me."

Worrelk walked to the small cabinet in the corner. "I have some bread and cheese. Will that do?"

"If there is no other choice, I suppose it will have to," the guard said, taking the plate of food from Worrelk. "And to wash it down?"

"There is a jug of tea on the sideboard."

"Nothing stronger?"

The wizard shook his head.

"Well, I guess that will have to do, too."

Worrelk nodded and brought a glass and the jug to him. "I should get ready."

The guard, his mouth full of food, made a muffled sound Worrelk took as affirmation. He quickly made his way into his bed chamber.

"Is that all you are taking, boy?" the guard said when Worrelk returned with his backpack. "From what I saw of where you are wanting to go, you are likely to need something more substantial than that summer cloak."

"Ah, of course. Thank you," Worrelk said. "I have not been outside the palace walls very often so..."

"Yes, yes. Whatever. Just get what you need so we can be off, the sun has already risen."

Worrelk left the room and returned within a few moments with the cold weather clothing the guard had suggested. "Will this do, or will I need something more?"

The guard looked at the items. "Those should do fine. Now, let us be off. I would like to be to the destination you have designated before the sun is too high in the sky."

#

Once again Worrelk failed to find the plant he so desperately needed. He walked back to where the guardsman sat. The man never walked the fields to help the wizard search, rather he watched from a distance. A distance Worrelk knew was within arrow range. He stopped at his horse and saw the guardsman reach for his bow.

"Relax. I am not going anywhere. I am just retrieving the map," Worrelk said.

"That is all you better be doing," the guardsman replied, still grasping his bow.

"I do not know why you are so worried. You know I have no weapons, save this small knife that is only good for cutting herbs."

"It is not an attack I fear. I just want to ensure you do not try to run away."

"Ha! As if that was even a possibility," Worrelk said as he sat beside his companion. "Where could one go to escape the wrath of Jurcheval?"

The guardsman nodded.

Worrelk rolled out the map on the ground and marked off yet another site.

"I am not sure we will ever find that which we are searching for," Worrelk said as he scanned the map. "Who would have guessed that something so common a year or so ago, would now be impossible to find?"

The guardsman grunted.

The wizard turned his attention back to the map. After several minutes, he looked up. "I think we should try this place," he said, pointing to the map.

The guardsman looked at the map. "That is at least another day's ride. Why there?"

"It is not very close to any villages, so perhaps it has not been picked clean yet."

"It is too late to start out today," the guardsman said. "We will leave at sunrise tomorrow. If we are lucky, we might reach that place before nightfall. Then you can explore the following day."

Worrelk nodded.

"If you fail to find it there, we will go no further."

"What?" the wizard cried. "But we must. I cannot fail, I must find the plant."

"We are already beyond our own borders."

"You know what it will mean if we turn back."

The guardsman smiled. "That is your worry, wizard, not mine."

"Are you sure?"

#

"This is far more difficult a climb then I expected," Worrelk said, fighting to draw in breath. "And far colder. I am glad you made me bring warmer clothing."

"Likely the reason this place is deserted. Even the animals do not wish to traverse these rocks, especially when they are iced over," the guardsman said. "How much longer will you continue your search?"

"Until I find what I seek or die trying."

The guardsman snickered.

"Let us climb higher," Worrelk said.

"You go. I am not risking my neck any more for whatever it is you seek. My job is to ensure you do not run away, not to be a mountain goat." The guardsman sat on a boulder. "I will wait here for your return."

Worrelk nodded and started to climb further up the mountain, each step becoming more treacherous. Though numerous plants grew amongst the rocks, none were what he needed. He continued to climb.

After some time he paused, unsure he could go on, his lungs burned and his limbs cried out in pain. He looked for a place to sit, even for just a few moments to rest. Then, he saw it. There on his right grew a huge bed of the plant he sought. In his excitement, he forgot where he was and lunged toward the plant, his foot hit a patch of ice and he fell. As he slipped down the mountainside, he frantically grabbed for nearby rocks and branches, anything that could stop his descent. Each attempt only accelerated his downward momentum. He screamed as the rocky terrain tore his skin to shreds. Then, as he collided with boulders and trees, the impacts snapped his bones like twigs. Only when he crashed head first into a large boulder and his skull cracked open did his cries stop. Though silenced, his limp, lifeless body continued its descent down the rest of the mountainside.

The guardsman heard the wizard's cries and then saw what looked like a child's doll toppling down the mountain. He slowly walked to what remained of the wizard. He gathered up the battered and broken body and returned to the horses. He wrapped the wizard's broken body in a tarp, threw it over his saddle and tied it down. The guardsman then mounted his horse and began the trek home, wondering if he would be blamed for this turn of events.

CHAPTER SIXTEEN

"TAARYN, WHAT ARE YOU doing" Ellyss asked as he grabbed for her.

"What?" she replied.

"You nearly walked in front of that horse."

"Oh, I am sorry. I guess my mind was elsewhere."

"Apparently so. Had I not been with you, you might have been seriously hurt."

She smiled weakly. She could not tell him, had he not been with her she would not have been distracted. How could she explain how much he confused her? On one hand, he seemed interested in her. On more than one occasion, she had caught him watching her from across the room. And, whenever they were out in the cold, he would wrap his cloak and his arm around her. Yet, whenever she attempted to sit by him, he would make up an excuse and depart. Could she be wrong? Was he only being nice to her as a courtesy to the sister of a friend? She was not sure she wanted to know.

"I know the weather is bitter cold," Ellyss said as the pair reached the bottom of the stairs, "but could we go to the garden, to that bench by the stream? There is something I need to speak with you about. Alone."

Taaryn's heart leapt and plummeted simultaneously. His tone sounded serious, though not somber. Her mind raced. What did he want to discuss? Would he tell her he had feelings for her? That he was leaving? Or, something worse?

She nodded, afraid if she spoke her voice would reveal the fear and excitement his request had spawned within her.

"Good. I do not believe it is snowing at the moment," he said as they reached the cloak rack. "Still, you should bring an additional cloak, just in case."

He smiled as he wrapped the cloak around her shoulders and reached for a second one.

"What about you?" she asked, measuring each word so as not to betray the emotions ebbing and flowing inside her. "You should also take a second cloak. You are no more impervious to the cold than I."

"Yes, yes, my dear lady," he said with a laugh, "those were my intentions."

He haphazardly donned a few cloaks. Taaryn tsked at him as she fixed the garments around him.

"Really, you are not a child," she said.

"Far from it, to be sure."

"Exactly my point. Yet, like a child you cannot even dress yourself for the cold."

He smiled, allowing her to finish fussing over him.

"Shall we go?" she asked when she was satisfied.

He nodded, and they walked toward the door. Both shivered as the first rush of frigid air hit them. Ellyss thought of postponing this meeting, at least not having it in the garden, but Taaryn was already across the courtyard. He hurried to catch up to her.

#

"Do you see that?" Emmaus said, pointing to the courtyard outside.

"Taaryn and Ellyss?" Prescia asked.

"Yes, of course, Taaryn and Ellyss. Look how they are walking. He has his arm around her."

"Emmaus, it is cold out; he is trying to keep her warm. That is all."

"Hrmph. That girl has never needed anyone to shelter her from the cold before. She has her own cloak, and a far warmer one than his. I do not like those two always being together," Emmaus snarled. "What is going on there?"

"Whatever it is, it is no concern of yours. She is a grown woman," Prescia responded.

"She is not."

Prescia laughed. "She is the same age as Graeden and you have no problem with him having a mate."

"That is different."

"Why? Because he is a male?"

Emmaus glared at her. "No, of course not. It is just that I am not sure I trust Ellyss. He has an oddness about him. Surely you, of all people, have noticed."

"He is different. But he is from another land. Perhaps, if we were in his home, we would be looked upon as the odd ones."

"Still..."

"You realize you have the same reaction every time one of your daughters takes more than a passing glance at any young man," she said with a laugh. "You see every male as a threat to your child's safety, even if you have known the boy from when he himself was a babe."

"I do not!"

Her husband's protest just made Prescia laugh harder. "Then I suppose the incident with Kyra and Jereth never happened," she began. "If I recall, you swore he was after her fortune even though you knew his family was quite wealthy in their own right and he alone stood to inherit."

Emmaus just glared at her. "All right, maybe I overreacted just that once."

Prescia smiled coyly at him. "Just once, eh? I could give you more examples if you would like."

"No, no, my love," he said, shaking his head. "You have made your point, as always."

"As for Ellyss and Taaryn, what if there is more to it than his just keeping her warm. What if she likes having his arms around her? If she likes being around him?"

Emmaus was taken aback. He had not expected such a response.

"What do you think you can do about it if that is, indeed, the case?" Prescia asked, not giving him time to reply. "Well?"

"I am not sure...exactly. I would talk to her, make her see the folly in it. That is what I would do."

"And if she did not agree with your opinion?"

"I would forbid her to continue seeing him."

"Ha!" Prescia snorted. She walked away, shaking her head and laughing. "As if that would make a difference."

Emmaus followed. "What do you mean by that?"

"You will forbid her, eh? And you think she, the most stubborn of all of your children, will just obey your wishes and give up the one she loves?" Prescia worked hard not to laugh again. "You would have a better chance of sprouting wings than changing that girl's mind once it is set."

"Not Taaryn. She would never defy me...some of the others perhaps, but not Taaryn."

"And what makes you think that?"

"She has never defied me in the past. She would not defy me now."

Prescia shook her head. "You are so naive, my love. Have you ever told her to do anything she truly did not want to do? Something important. Not chores or schoolwork or watching the little ones. I am talking about challenging her when she believes in it with her entire being. Think about it."

He stared at her for a moment. "We forbade her to follow Graeden and she did not."

Prescia nodded. "True. That was only because she could barely move after the incident. As for this relationship with Ellyss, we might be jumping to conclusions. This may be nothing more than friendship."

Emmaus sighed. "Fine, Prescia. I will let this thing between them run its course without interference. But I am telling you, I do not like it."

#

"Well, then," Taaryn said, wrapping her cloaks tightly around her as she sat on the bench by the now frozen stream, "what did you need to say?"

She patted the bench beside her. Ellyss dutifully sat down.

"This is difficult for me to tell you, Taaryn," he began.

"It is not Graeden, is it?" she interrupted.

"No, as far as I know Graeden and the others are fine. I have had no word from anyone in Reissem Grove."

"Thank goodness. I am sorry I interrupted you. Do go on."

"What I wanted to speak to you about is..." He hesitated, as if trying to find just the right words. "I mean..." He laughed. "You know I have gone over this conversation a million times in my head. Yet, when I come face to face with you, the words escape me."

She smiled.

"What I am trying to say is...Oh, damn. I am just going to say it outright. I, we, must discuss your feelings for me."

Her mind raced, torn between the hope he shared her feelings and the fear he did not. She swallowed hard, trying unsuccessfully to dislodge the lump in her throat.

"You have seen into my soul. You know my history, at least some of it, and still you wish to pursue what, and correct me if I am wrong, seems to be more than just a friendship. I do not understand how or why you would want such a thing."

She looked into his face and saw the turmoil in his eyes.

"I do not understand, either. I just know I want you, need you." She struggled to keep her voice calm. "Ellyss, I love you. I have loved you since I first set eyes upon you at the wood's edge that night. I desire you. No, I crave you. Just being close to you....well...I fear you do not share the same desire for me."

"If it were but that simple," he said, holding her hands to his lips and kissing them.

Even through the heavy gloves, she felt his kiss and her heart leapt.

"The sentence I serve for my past wrongdoings does not include love or happiness," he continued. "And now I fear I have dragged you into my misfortune."

"What you were then is not who you are now. I do not care what you did eons before I, or any of my kinsmen, walked upon this world. You have not answered me. Do you share the same feelings for me..." She hesitated, then continued, "Even just a little?"

She watched him struggle to come up with an answer.

"Yes. I do. More than you know. More than I have a right to. From the first moment I laid eyes upon you before you even came down to meet us, I felt something I had never felt before. And when you stood next to me, I cannot even describe the joy I felt. As the days passed, being with you, my joy increased as did my desire. But..." He turned, gazed off into the distance, and let his words trail off.

Taaryn wanted to throw her arms around his neck and smother him in kisses. She did not. Though his words spoke of joy, his voice revealed turmoil and pain within.

"I do not understand."

"It is not an easy thing for me to say," he answered. "I am afraid."

"Afraid?" she asked. "Afraid of what? Of me?"

He smiled, reached for her face and brushed a strand of long black hair back behind her ear. She reached up and pressed his hand to her face.

"No, it is not you I fear, although, it would be more appropriate if you were afraid of me."

He saw the confusion in her eyes.

"You are the only one who knows anything of my past. In all these countless lives I have lived in atonement, no one has ever seen into me as you have. I can only wonder what this means. Am I finally at the end of my punishment? Has my debt to the gods finally been paid, and can I now live the life of a normal man? Is that what you represent? Are you my salvation?"

She listened and squeezed his hand.

"Or are you just another deception? Are you here to torment me? To give me hope of salvation only to pull it away." He saw the look in her eyes. "No, my dearest Taaryn, I do not say you are at the helm of this ploy. If it is a deception contrived yet again by the gods, then you are a mere pawn, a puppet in their hands."

He was relieved to see she believed him. "My fear is for you. If this is a deception, then what will become of you when it is complete?"

"Do not fear for me," she answered. "Never having known the plans or ploys of the gods, I can only do what I think is right for me and those around me. And what is right for me, for us, at this moment in time, is to enjoy each other in every way possible. If it is meant to be, if I am your salvation, then so be it. And if not, I for one would rather have a short time of love and joy with the hope that it will last forever than to deny myself your company for fear of what might be."

She smiled and led him back toward the Keep.

CHAPTER SEVENTEEN

TAARYN CLOSED AND locked the door to her room behind them.

"I have been wanting to do this since the night we met." She threw her arms around his neck and kissed him.

Ellyss was momentarily taken aback. It had been quite some time since a woman had reacted to him in this manner. He held her tightly, returning the kiss with equal passion. It did not take long before they discarded cloaks and clothes and shared a heart-stopping passion neither had ever known before.

#

They awoke, still wrapped in each other's arms, to the sound of knocking.

"What is it?"

"Mistress Taaryn," a young girl replied. "Her Ladyship sent me to tell you everyone is waiting for you to come to dinner."

Taaryn sat up and looked around the nearly dark room. She smiled, remembering the afternoon's activities. She reached across the bedside table and lit the lamp.

"Please assure my mother, Ellyss and I shall be down shortly," Taaryn answered.

"Yes, Mistress."

Ellyss squirmed slightly at Taaryn's response to the servant. Taaryn saw his reaction and smiled broadly. She rolled back toward him and kissed him again. He gently pushed her away.

"You told your mother we would be down shortly. If I allow that to go on, I fear we will not make an appearance until after breakfast."

"Ah, true," she answered and rose from the bed. She flipped back her hair and looked over her shoulder at him. "There is always tonight."

The last rays of sunlight streamed through the window, glittering across her naked body as she crossed the room to the pile of discarded clothes on the floor. He felt his body respond to the sight of her.

She tossed his clothes to him and then began to dress. He sat on the side of the bed, watching her before he donned his own clothes.

They left the bedroom and proceeded to the dining room.

"Since you will be coming back to my, or should I say our room tonight, we will need to have one of the servants bring your things from your room."

She smiled at his reaction. "You did not think I was going to let you leave me, did you? My bed is far more comfortable than the one in the room you were in and, since I plan on spending a lot of time in bed with you, my love, well..."

Before he had a chance to reply, they reached the dining hall door. They entered together, Taaryn tightly clasping his hand in hers.

Ellyss surveyed the room for reaction. He thought he saw a passing shadow of concern on Emmaus' face, but it was gone before he was sure he had even seen it. He was both surprised and relieved to see no reaction from any of the others, save for their tardiness. It was as if was perfectly natural for them to be entering together in such a manner.

#

"So that is it? Your family continues on as if nothing between us has changed?" Ellyss asked as they returned to their room.

Taaryn looked at him, unsure of where his questions would lead.

"I do not understand what you are getting at. Nothing has changed between you and my family," she said. "No one treated you any different this night than before, did they?"

"No. But I do not think Emmaus is happy with this."

She laughed. "My father is never happy when he must face the fact one of his daughters is no longer a child. But my family, my father, is not what is troubling you, is it?"

"Already you know me almost as well as I know myself. No, it is not them, it is me. Who I am, what I was."

"I thought we settled that question in the garden," she said.

He shook his head. "You settled it, but I am still afraid for you. For what you represent. This is the first time in all of my existence that someone has made everything else in life insignificant.

That terrifies me."

He saw the puzzlement in her eyes and gently squeezed her hands before he continued.

"I fear you will be used as another payment toward my atonement by making me sacrifice one thing for another. Perhaps your life for something else—which would I choose to sacrifice?"

"But surely, your judges cannot still be that vengeful against you after all this time, all these lifetimes you have endured."

He shook his head. "All the lifetimes I have spent represent less than a single grain of sand in a vast desert to one who knows eternity."

"But they, the gods, would not hurt me just to get to you." She sounded as innocent as a newborn babe.

He stood and crossed the room. "That, my love, is the basest of misconceptions held by mortals. True, there are a handful of benevolent gods, but most are, at best, indifferent to all creatures in this place and all others. You see, my dearest Taaryn, mortal beings are looked upon as objects, pieces on a game board to be manipulated and discarded as the gods' whims dictate. So, to answer your question, yes. Yes, I do believe if it would suit their fancy, the gods would sacrifice you."

She shook her head and drew in a breath. "So you are saying these gods will do as they please to us with no regard for what we want or do."

Ellyss nodded.

"Then, I say again, let them. If we cannot alter or influence their actions, we must do what we feel best for us."

"How can you say that?"

Taaryn laughed. "Because I am mortal. And as such, I am not promised next year, next week or even tomorrow. Be it the gods or fate or just chance that decides when my life starts and ends is immaterial to me. The only thing I can do is live each moment of my life the best way I can. And right now, the best way is with you."

CHAPTER EIGHTEEN

TAARYN SHOT STRAIGHT up in bed, her sudden movement waking Ellyss.

"What is the matter?" he asked. "You are shaking."

She turned to him, her face ashen. He reached for her, and she fell into his arms.

"I heard him. I heard his voice calling to me," she said, hesitating between words.

"Who, my love? Whose voice was called to you?" Ellyss asked, fearing the Master, or something far worse, had located her and the family.

"Graeden. It was Graeden. But his voice was so soft."

Ellyss breathed a sigh of relief. "There, there, love," he said, stroking her hair. "What did Graeden say?"

She pulled back and looked at him.

"He called my name and asked if I could hear him," she answered. "Do you think it could really be him?"

"It is possible." Ellyss noted the hope in her eyes at his response. "Did you answer him?"

She thought for a moment. "No. I do not think I did."

Ellyss stroked her hair again. "Well, perhaps you should."

"How?"

"Speak to him in your mind, as I have taught you to speak to me."

"But he is so far away."

"You heard him, so you may be able to reach him, as well."

She nodded and he could tell how hard she was trying to mindspeak to her distant brother. A few moments later she turned to Ellyss, looking disappointed.

"Nothing," she said. "Oh damn, it was probably just a silly dream."

Ellyss kissed her on the forehead. "Maybe and maybe not. Let me try to help you."

Her face brightened. "Could you?" she asked excitedly. "What do I need to do?"

He smiled at her enthusiasm.

:*Just concentrate,*: he mindspoke to her. :*Think of Graeden and talk to him with your mind just as if he were sitting next to you. Just like you do to me:*

:*Yes. I can do that.*:

Ellyss joined with her mind ready to add his power to her thoughts. Stunned by the strength he found there, he quickly realized his job would be to help her focus. He tightened her thoughts of Graeden until they were like an arrow on its way to a target.

When they received no immediate response, he continued to keep her focus on Graeden. Soon, they both heard Graeden's voice.

:Taaryn, is it really you?: he mindspoke joyfully to his twin. *:I was not sure I would be able to reach you nor you able to respond to me. This is wonderful.:*

:Graeden! Graeden!: she thought excitedly, blind to the fact that tears of joy streamed down her cheeks. *:It is you. Ellyss said it was. He said I, we, could reach you.:*

Then the conscious words ceased, leaving only the twins' emotions and thoughts rapidly flowing between them. Their excitement resembled a raging flood of thoughts.

:Graeden. Slow down, please: Ellyss broke into their minds. *:This pace is too much for her.:*

All three minds fell silent.

:Is she all right?: Graeden asked with concern. He felt Taaryn sigh within his mind.

:Yes, I am fine.:

:Thank the heavens.:

The twins' mindspeak continued on for a bit longer at a much slower pace. A few minutes later, Ellyss again interrupted. He feared Taaryn was fatiguing from the strain. Though she protested, Graeden agreed. He told her what he needed her to do for him and then said farewell.

Taaryn collapsed into Ellyss's arms.

"Thank you," she said softly.

"Shh," he replied, cradling her in his arms. "Sleep now. We will talk of this in the morning."

The words had barely left his lips and she was asleep. He gently laid her back down on her pillow, pulled the covers up over her and lay beside her, his head propped up on his arm as he watched her for a few moments. He closed his eyes, going over what had just transpired. He was amazed and excited that they were able to mindspeak over that great distance, but his concern lingered over how much it had physically taken out of Taaryn. Hopefully, her exhaustion was merely due to excitement and inexperience.

#

Graeden bounded down the stairs. Regnaryn looked up from her book.

"I did it! I spoke with her! With them! I did not think it possible, but it was."

"That is wonderful," she replied. "How is everything in Hammarsh Keep?"

"Everything is fine. No sign of trouble of any sort. But, I did find it odd that Ellyss was with Taaryn. You do not think..."

"Think, what?"

"That there is something going on between them."

"And if there is?"

"No, that is impossible. He is... well, he is just not right for her. I am sure it is no more than him keeping an eye on her, as he did for me."

Regnaryn smiled. "Perhaps. You said you spoke to both of them?"

Graeden nodded.

"Do you think it is possible for me to speak to them also? I so want to meet your sister."

"With your power, I am certain you could reach them on your own," he said with a chuckle. "But I will be more than willing to act as the intermediary."

"Yes, I would like that. When can we contact them?"

"Not too soon. I fear our first encounter seemed to take a lot out of Taaryn."

"I am certain Ellyss will keep her safe," Regnaryn answered. "As you said, he looked after you, so I am sure he will do the same for her."

#

"Just what do you think you are doing?" Taaryn asked angrily as Ellyss blocked her exit from their room.

"Look at yourself. You are exhausted."

"I am fine."

"No, you are not. You tossed and turned all night. You need to rest."

She tried to push by him. He would not move. She raised her hands and pounded on his chest. He stood silently, but still did not move. She stopped hitting him and fell against him.

"Let me by," she sobbed unable to fight him any longer.

He wrapped his arms around her and touched his lips to her forehead. "No," he said quietly. "I cannot do that. You must rest."

He picked her up, carried her to the bed, and gently laid her down.

She looked up into his face. "I need to, we need to find the information for Graeden."

He wiped the tears from her cheeks. "Shh, my love. Sleep now. When you are rested, we will search for the information. I promise. But now, you need to sleep...Sleep...Sleep..."

His words flowed over her like the gentle waves of a brook on a warm summer day. His words, his glance engulfed her in comfort. She did not resist. Could not resist. She welcomed it. It was so peaceful, so warm. She barely noticed her eyes closing as she fell asleep.

"That is good, my beautiful Taaryn. Sleep."

\#

He kissed her softly on the lips, gently covered her with the blanket from the foot of the bed, and stood watching her restful breathing as she slumbered. Once certain she was deep in sleep, he wrote a quick note to Prescia saying the couple would not be coming down to breakfast as Taaryn was not feeling well. He summoned a servant to take the note and to bring him food.

The servant quickly returned with his food and a reply from Prescia. He read the note and sat down to his meal.

Once he had satisfied his hunger, he perused the books on the shelf and chose one. He sat on the bench by the window and began to read. On more than one occasion, he looked over at Taaryn's sleeping body and found his interest in the book was replaced by his desire to just watch the beautiful young woman sleep.

After several hours, Taaryn began to stir. Ellyss went to her side and sat on the edge of the bed. He watched her as her eyes began to flutter and then open. She smiled up at him.

He nodded. She drew him close and kissed him.

"I saved some food for you. I doubt if it is still warm, but if you want something fresher, I will get you something else," he said as she released him and got up from the bed.

"I am sure this will be fine." She filled her plate, then sat down by the small table. "Please come sit by me."

He sat across from her. "I have a message from your mother." He handed her the note. "She wishes to see you when you are feeling better."

Taaryn nodded.

"Should I tell her about talking to Graeden?"

Ellyss thought a moment. "Perhaps not just yet."

"I agree."

"After you visit with your mother," Ellyss said, "I think we should begin to look for that information. Any ideas on where we should begin on our quest?"

"The library," she said.

"I surmised that. I meant any ideas to narrow the search within the library?"

"A few."

CHAPTER NINETEEN

:I AM DONE SPEAKING with Mother,: Taaryn mindspoke to Ellyss. *:I think you should meet me in the library to begin our search.:*

Ellyss chuckled. *:We really are of one mind. I am already there.:*

:Fine, then I shall meet you shortly,: she replied and hastened her step.

She entered the large library and closed the door behind her. When she turned, Ellyss was by her side.

"I have found the maps." He took her hand and led her to bank of shelves in the far right corner of the room.

"Good. Are there a lot of them?" she asked.

Ellyss looked at her sideways, and she laughed at her own question.

"Oh, I do not question out of laziness but rather out of anticipation of how many volumes we will need to peruse before we are through."

She looked at him again and realized he was only teasing her. "Oh, you!" she exclaimed.

He smiled. "There are a few, but I do not think it will take us too long to get through them."

He abruptly stopped in front of a huge bookcase, and she nearly ran into him. "You really cannot believe this is just a *few*. Can you?"

Before he had a chance to answer, she continued. "Surely there is a way you can just lay your hand on the books and find out which, if any, are the ones we need to read more carefully."

He laughed. "No, I am afraid that is not how it works. There is no easy way out. We will need to at least glance through the volumes to find what we seek."

She smiled. "Well, it was worth a try. Where do you think we should begin?"

He walked over to a table that held a stack of about twenty books. "I thought we might begin with these. They are dated a few years after Grenwald arrived in Alexandrash."

"You do realize," Taaryn said, "this may come to nothing. If that village is as small as Grenwald said it was, it might not be shown on any of these maps."

Ellyss nodded. "I know. Perhaps, if we are lucky, these were meticulous mapmakers who captured every village."

"And if not?"

"Well, we will have to hope that, in later volumes, the village grew enough to be noted."

The pair opened the large book of beautifully drawn maps

and began to search for the small village of Frelind.

They perused volume after volume, finishing not only the stack of books Ellyss had originally brought out, but numerous others with no success. It was not until a young servant boy came with a note from Prescia, asking if Taaryn was well enough to come to dinner, that Taaryn and Ellyss realized all the lamps had been silently lit around them.

Taaryn dismissed the servant, instructing him to tell her parents they would arrive shortly.

Ellyss began putting the books back on their shelves but was interrupted by an older gentleman.

"Lady Taaryn. Sir. I will replace those for you," the elderly man said as he looked at the stack of books. "Planning a trip?"

Taaryn shook her head. "No, Olferd, just looking for a place, a tiny village. Well, it was tiny thirty odd years ago."

"Hmm," the old man said. "And I am guessing from the look on your face you were not successful."

"No."

He looked again at the books. "These might not be your best source to find it from that time. If you tell me what you are looking for, I would be more than willing to research it for you. That is, after all, one of my duties."

"Thank you, but I think we would rather find it ourselves," Taaryn said.

"As you wish, my lady," the librarian said. "Then I will bring some other books that may hold the information you desire."

"We have looked at all the map books," Taaryn said.

He ran his fingers along the spines of the books and smiled. "Not quite all of them. This is not the only library within the Keep."

Taaryn looked a bit surprised.

"Perhaps you can tell me the region you are exploring?" the man asked, ignoring her reaction.

Ellyss nodded. "We only know that it is somewhere on the northern border."

"Good. That will narrow the search and perhaps allow you to find more detail for those regions. Now you two should be on your way. You do not wish to keep Lady Prescia waiting. I will put whatever books I find here for you."

#

After dinner, Taaryn and Ellyss rose from the table and started for the door.

"Taaryn, please stay," Prescia said. "Your father and I wish to speak to you and Ellyss."

They joined Prescia and Emmaus where the two sat.

"We want to know what you two are up to," Emmaus said. "The servant we sent to fetch you said you were in the library. I must say, at first I did not believe him. I was not aware you even knew we had a library, never mind visited it."

Taaryn's face reddened.

"Now, Emmaus, stop teasing her," Prescia said. "Are you going to tell us what you are looking for?"

"Or should I summon the librarian?" Emmaus asked.

Taaryn looked at Ellyss. *:Shall we tell them?:*

:It is not a secret:

"We are looking for the location of a small village in the north. A village called Frelind," she said.

"Why?"

"Because Graeden thinks it is important in the search to find the Master."

"Graeden? How would you know what Graeden thinks?" Emmaus asked.

"He told me," she replied.

"And how would he do that?"

"We mindspoke to each other last night," she replied, not at all surprised by her father's disbelief.

"What? That is nonsense," Emmaus said. "You cannot do such a thing, and even if you could, the distance is too great."

Prescia softly touched Taaryn's cheek and then turned toward her husband. "No, my love, it is not nonsense. She has done what she says. I can see it in her eyes."

Taaryn grasped her mother's hand. "Thank you."

Emmaus slumped into his chair, mumbling and shaking his head. "I dare not ask, even in my own mind, what else can or will happen around here for fear of what the answer might be."

Taaryn moved toward her father and knelt in front of him. She took his hands in hers. "I know, Father. I feel the same. So many changes, so many things we never thought possible. Magic and monsters, creatures we thought myth, we now know to be real."

"Real and apparently knocking on our front gate," Emmaus replied.

"And you will face them as you have faced every other terror that has confronted you and your kind," Ellyss said.

"What do you mean, 'our kind'?" Prescia asked. "You say that as if you are not one of us."

Ellyss coughed nervously. "I mean your family. While in the library waiting for Taaryn, I did a bit of reading on this family's history. While your lives have been calm for the last few generations, there was a time when your ancestors faced and overcame great ordeals."

"Ah, yes. Of course," Prescia said and then turned to Taaryn. "So, child, tell us more of your talk with your brother." She motioned the couple to sit in nearby chairs.

"Is this the first time you and Graeden have done such a thing?" Prescia asked.

"I guess we never thought to try it when he was here. It never crossed our minds that such a thing might be possible."

"Why does Graeden think this village is important?" Emmaus asked.

"It was the first village in Alexandrash that Grenwald stayed in," Ellyss replied.

"Wait! Did you say Grenwald?" Prescia asked.

"Yes. He was Regnaryn's father," Taaryn answered. "Why do you ask?"

Prescia shook her head and began to mumble. "Surely it cannot be the same Grenwald. Yet, that is far from a common name..."

"The same Grenwald? Mother, are you saying you knew Grenwald? How can that be?"

Prescia chuckled. "I have not spent my entire life as someone's mother nor here in Hammarsh Keep, child. I did have a life before I met your father."

Taaryn blushed.

"How do you know Grenwald?" Ellyss asked.

"Until I wed Emmaus, I lived in Siggurna at the Royal Court."

Taaryn looked shocked. "You? You were at the Royal Court?"

Prescia nodded. "As a matter of fact, Queen Jansen was one of my best friends. Of course that was before she became Queen. Oh, the times she, Karaleena and I had back in those days."

"You knew Karaleena, as well?" Ellyss interrupted.

"Yes. Oh, I see, if Grenwald is Regnaryn's father, then Karaleena is her mother. My, my, how things happen."

"Do you recall anything about Grenwald? Where he came from?" Ellyss asked.

Prescia shook her head. "No. As a matter of fact, when he first arrived he was quite the disagreeable fellow. Prince or not, there is no excuse for rudeness! Of course, we did not know he was a prince at first, just a very obnoxious young noble from a distant land." She chuckled. "We all thought it quite odd that Karaleena was interested in him, but after they fell in love, he changed. He remained quite secretive, but at least he was civil."

"Is there anything else?" Ellyss asked.

"Not really. Shortly after those two became a couple, I came here to marry Emmaus. I heard the two of them wed and then left Siggurna, but that was all I knew."

"Grenwald is dead, is he not?" Emmaus asked.

Ellyss nodded.

"Then why the interest in him now?"

Taaryn turned away from her parents.

"This is not easy to say, or to believe, but it seems Grenwald's brother, Sevich, is the Master," Ellyss said.

Prescia and Emmaus looked shocked.

"We are trying to find their homeland, in hopes of finding and confronting him."

"I see," Emmaus said. "From the looks on your faces, I do not think you were successful in your search."

Taaryn shook her head. "No, but Olferd said he would try to find other books for us to look at."

"Good."

"What will you do if you still cannot locate what you seek here?" Prescia asked.

"I suppose we will need to travel to Siggurna," Taaryn said.

"You do not seem to relish that prospect, Ellyss," Emmaus said.

"No, I do not. The more people who know of our quest, the more likely the Master, Sevich, might hear about it."

"That is a good point," Emmaus replied.

"When will you be speaking to Graeden again?" Prescia asked.

Taaryn shrugged and looked to Ellyss.

"Mindspeaking over such a long distance takes a great deal out of Taaryn, both physically and mentally," he began.

Prescia smiled. "Hence your being ill this morning."

Taaryn nodded.

"And is there nothing you can do to make this task take less out of her?" Emmaus asked.

"There is. It will still be an ordeal, not as easy as you and Prescia mindspeaking across the Keep..."

"How did you know?" Prescia asked.

Ellyss momentarily toyed with the idea of allowing Emmaus and Prescia to think that he had some mysterious ability to know, but thought better of it. "Graeden told me."

He smiled at the sense of relief that passed over her face.

"What makes it even more taxing is we need to be shielding the conversation. After all, we do not want the Master or his people finding us."

Taaryn looked at him, slightly shocked. She had not even considered that.

:I was not shielding my thoughts,: she mindspoke to him in a near panic.

:Actually you were, my love,: Ellyss answered. *:And Graeden and I were helping. I will tell you more about it later.:*

She sighed with relief into his mind, and he smiled.

"And?" Emmaus asked impatiently.

"I can work with Taaryn to help her build up the strength of the ability to the point where it will not be so exhausting. It will still be hard work, not unlike physical labor, but just as with physical labor with practice and strengthening it will become less of a strain."

"Good," Emmaus replied. "When will you begin?"

"In the morning," Ellyss said,

"Is there anything we can do to help you, both of you?" Prescia added.

"Not at this time."

#

"I think we should go back to the library to see what Olferd has discovered, if anything," Taaryn said.

"It has only been a few hours, and evening hours at that. Do you really think he already started looking?"

Taaryn laughed. "Well, since the shock of seeing me in the library reading did not cause him to faint dead away, yes, I am sure he did."

"If you say so."

#

"Ah, see I told you," Taaryn said, pointing to a new stack of books on the table. "Shall we have a look at what he found?"

The couple sat and opened the first book.

"These books are amazing," Ellyss said.

"What do you mean?"

"Not only are they magnificently crafted, but just look at the detail on the maps," he replied.

"Be that as it may," Taaryn said, stifling a yawn, "if they do not contain the information we need, then they are useless."

"That is true, but let us not give up hope just yet."

She nodded.

"This is odd." Ellyss pointed to a map in the third book he looked at.

Taaryn glanced up from the book she was perusing. "What?"

"Did they not say Frelind was a small village?"

"Yes, that is what they said."

"Well, this map shows it as a good-sized town."

"And the date on the book?" Taaryn asked.

"About a year before Grenwald would have been there."

"Could we have gotten the name wrong?"

Ellyss shook his head. "I do not think so. This town is very near the northern border. See."

She looked and nodded. "Perhaps, his perception of small was different than ours."

"You are probably right."

"So, do you think this is truly the place where Grenwald entered the country?"

"I do."

He hurriedly began to make notes on the paper the librarian had conveniently left for them. When he finished, he looked up at Taaryn and smiled.

"The others will be glad to hear what we have found."

"Should we contact them now? Here?" she asked unable to hide her excitement.

Ellyss put his arm around her shoulder. "Not yet. Let us go back to our rooms where you can be comfortable."

CHAPTER TWENTY

"THE GOOD NEWS IS Taaryn and Ellyss were able to find the village we sought. It seems what Grenwald considered a tiny village was not so small, after all. Now we have a way to find his homeland, Aelden," Graeden said.

"Do you really think we can do that? If father's perception of what the size of the village was, perhaps his sense of direction was not that spot on, either," Regnaryn remarked.

Ayirak shook his head. "No. While his assessment of the size of towns may have been off, he was after all comparing them to the capital city of his land, his sense of direction was impeccable. Have you never seen any of his maps?"

"He drew maps?" Graeden asked.

"Oh, yes, I remember now," Phrynia said. "When Reissem

Grove was just getting settled, he drew up the maps to ensure each group received ample land. So, I agree with Ayirak, his directional accounts of his journey from Aelden to Alexandrash are surely accurate."

"We will need to reread the journals dealing with his trip and find Aelden," Graeden said.

"And then what?" Regnaryn asked.

"Once we determine the general area of Grenwald's former kingdom," Phrynia replied, "we will send a scouting party of drageals to give us more accurate information."

#

"I had hoped to determine a more accurate location for not only Aelden, but its capital." Graeden pointed at the map they had drawn after pouring over Grenwald's journal entries.

"Yes, that would have been nice. We have narrowed it down to this area," Phrynia said, circling an area on the map with her talon.

Neshya drew in a whistle. "That still seems like a lot of land to cover."

"It would be if we were scouting it by foot. Remember, we will be in the air," Phrynia replied.

"How will they contact us with what they find?" Neshya asked. "That is quite a distance, and none of us share the same long range mindspeaking abilities as Graeden and his sister."

"We will create a relay system to keep in contact. That will lengthen the journey a bit, but in this situation communication outweighs the need for speed."

"Agreed. Have you decided who will be in the party?" Varlama asked.

"I volunteer, Mother," Immic said.

"No, son, you are not ready to fly that distance. You are not yet fully healed."

"I can do it. At least, the first leg of the journey," Immic said.

"No."

Immic glared at his mother and stormed out.

:You could have been easier on the boy,: Varlama mindspoke to Phrynia.

:I only spoke the truth. If it was any other time, even a month or so from now, he would have been my first choice to go all the way to Aelden. He knows that. But I will not risk permanently injuring him, when there are others who can handle the mission.:

#

The scouting party, led by Curme, set out to find Aelden on a crisp, bright morning. As they took off, those on the ground shouted well wishes and waved. Many of the other drageals, old and young, flew some distance with them.

"What do you think they will find?" Neshya asked Graeden as the scouting party soared high above them.

"I am not sure," Graeden replied. "And to be perfectly honest, I do not really know what I want them to find."

"I feel the same way."

The two friends stood in silence as Curme and the others flew out of sight.

#

:I think we have gone as far as we can to still be able to contact the Grove, so it is time to find a place to camp for the night,: Curme mindspoke to the others.

:In this flatland? Will we not be seen?: Qhiak, the smallest of

the drageals, asked.

:I sense nothing more than the local wildlife in this area,: Curme replied.

:Do not tell me you are afraid, little one,: Helam snorted.

:Of course not, and do not call me little one. We are the same age,: Qhiak responded.

:Yes, but I am not small and weak.:

:Enough!: Curme shouted. *:We have more important things to discuss than your childish prattling.:*

Neither replied.

:I have found a suitable spot,: Curme said. *:Follow me.:*

In the next moment, the three drageals landed with only the slightest disturbance to the surroundings. Helam set up a makeshift camp, more of a rearrangement of leaves and such to soften the ground, while the others went in search of food.

"So, what is the plan?" Helam asked after they finished eating.

"Qhiak will stay here," Curme began.

"What? Why?" Qhiak sputtered. "I can fly as well as Helam, maybe even better."

"That may be true, Qhiak, but you are a stronger mindspeaker than he. This position is likely the most important of all. The one that will ensure our messages reach Reissem Grove."

Qhiak nodded. She had not thought of it in that way.

"Now, it is time to let those at home know we have reached our first destination," Curme said.

"Ah, yes, of course," Qhiak replied, trying to hide the fear within her that she might not be able to do as asked.

After Qhiak completed the communication with those at home, the three drageals discussed the strategy for the rest of their journey.

"Do you think we will encounter any of those beasts that attacked Reissem Grove?" Helam asked.

"I am not sure what we will find. But if all goes as we hope, we will be able to locate the Master's lair without being detected."

"And if we are seen? There will be only two of us...if they attack in force..." Helam said.

"Well, Helam, you and I will just have to make sure we can fly higher and faster than anything we encounter."

#

:Something is not right,: Curme said.

:What do you mean?: asked Helam. *:I sense nothing.:*

:That is just it. This is where Aelden should be, but there is nothing here. Nothing at all. I do not even detect a single animal.:

:How can that be?:

:I do not know. I have never felt such an emptiness. It is as if everything has been wiped away.:

:Could it be a powerful shield blocking our senses?: asked Helam.

Curme shook his head. *:I do not think so,:* he replied to the younger drageal.

If it is, Regnaryn and the others are in for what may prove to be an insurmountable enemy, he thought.

:What is it then?: Helam asked

:There is only one way to find out. I am going lower to get a better look. You wait here. Contact Qhiak. We need to let those at home know what is going on here now, just in case...:

Helam mindcalled to Qhiak.

:Have you found it already?: the other drageal cheerfully asked.

:We are not sure.:

:What is wrong?:

:I do not know. Not yet, anyway. Curme went to investigate.:

:Investigate what?:

:The nothingness below,: Curme answered as he rejoined Helam. *:There is nothing there but a large blackened crater. No vegetation. No animals. Nothing save a massively burnt out landscape as far as the eye can see.:*

:Could it be we are in the wrong place?: Helam asked again.

:No, this is where it should be. There are the peaks we were told to look for.:

Helam nodded.

:Contact those at home, Qhiak. We are heading back to meet you now,: Curme said. *:I wish to leave here quickly. There is something about this place I do not like.:*

CHAPTER TWENTY-ONE

A STENCH UNLIKE anything she had ever encountered wakened Taaryn. She opened her eyes to find herself enshrouded in a black and red mist.

Taaryn had all she could do to suppress the panic she felt swelling within. She immediately feared Sevich had found her, but tried to convince herself this was nothing more than a dream.

"What is going on here?" she called to the blackness. "What do you want from me?"

Her question was met with vicious laughter.

"Want? From you? You are barely significant enough to warrant my attention," a voice that permeated her very being replied.

"Then, why am I here?"

"How dare you address me directly?" the voice asked.

Taaryn did not answer.

The voice laughed, amused at her lack of response.

Taaryn felt something brush against her shoulder. She had all she could do to keep from jumping.

"You amuse me, mortal," the voice said as wisps of black smoke circled around her and a large column of red smoke formed directly in front of her.

"He truly has found a worthwhile comrade this time. Or are you more than just comrades?" the red smoke asked, sniffing the air. "Hmm, this could be very interesting."

The black smoke wisps snickered as they continued to slither around Taaryn.

"What do you mean?" Taaryn asked, trying her best to sound unconcerned. "Just who is this he you speak of?"

The wisps of black smoke moved to form a semicircle behind her.

She watched as the red smoke formed into a shape that resembled Ellyss. Taaryn could not help but gasp at the sight.

"Ah, so I am correct. You do know this creature in his current form."

"I do not know what you mean," she answered, trying to cover her reaction.

The voice laughed. "You cannot fool me. We can feel it in your essence, you not only know him, you are intimate with him, with Ellyss. That is the name he is using now, is it not?"

"I do not know what you are talking about," Taaryn answered.

The voice laughed heartily, and the black smoke wisps tittered at her words.

"Is she really that stupid?" one of the black smoke wisps asked.

"Or is she trying to fool us?" a second one continued.

"As if she could," the third one replied.

"Enough," the red smoke thundered, making the black smoke wisps waver.

The red smoke figure approached her and caressed her face in its hand. Taaryn shuddered at its touch.

"You are truly unaware of what you are. How delightful, yet so typical of your kind," the voice said as it moved around her. "But you see, that will not do. You must be fully aware of everything. What you are. What he was and is. And, most importantly, what is truly at stake here."

Once again, the wisps of black smoke snickered.

Taaryn did her best to quiet the growing fear within herself. "I do not understand," she said with all the calm and decorum she could muster

"Exactly," the voice replied, once again caressing her face. "So it is not yet time. I will wait until you do. Then, well, let me just say, we will meet again."

#

Taaryn opened her eyes to Ellyss' gentle shake. She gasped and then choked on what felt like a puff of smoke as she became aware she was again in her room.

"What is wrong, my love?" he asked when she was finally aware of his presence. "You were thrashing about in your sleep."

Taaryn coughed a few more times then reached for Ellyss.

He saw the terror in her eyes and felt her tremble in his arms.

"Was it Sevich?" he asked. "Tell me."

She shook her head as if its mere mention would bring it back. He held onto her, stroked her head and whispered words of comfort.

After a few moments, she relaxed enough to speak.

Taaryn told him what she had seen and heard. Ellyss sat in silence, continuing to stroke her hair. When she finished, he rose from the bed and began to pace. He shook his head as if that action would change what he knew. She saw the torment in his eyes and did not interrupt.

"This is not good," he said after several moments.

"Are you saying it was more than a dream?" she asked.

"It is as I feared." He cursed. "I knew it. I knew they would not allow me to have even a moment's happiness."

He ran his hands through his hair, pulling on it as if that might help. He walked back to where Taaryn sat upon the bed, and he knelt in front of her. He took her hands in his own.

"I am so sorry, my love. The being you describe sounds like Xanchad, one of the ancients who condemned me to my fate."

He stopped her before she could speak. "Do you remember when we first met, when you saw into my soul? I told you my greatest fear was that those from my past would use you to torment me."

Taaryn nodded.

"I believe that is what this is."

He stood and again paced, muttering and cursing. "Damn, what am I to do? I cannot leave this place. Not yet. I have vowed to help these good people in the fight against the evil that might threaten them. Yet, if I stay, I put you in danger from the eternal ones. If I go, I put everyone else in danger from the Master. This is playing right into their hands."

"Stay or leave, I will remain at your side, regardless of what this Xanchad creature has in store for us," Taaryn insisted.

He stopped pacing and looked at her. "I am sorry. As much as I love you, I should never have gotten involved with you. I, of all people, should have known better."

"Tish, tosh. Are we going to do this again? How many times do I need to remind you that neither of us had much choice. Call it fate, or whatever you like. As soon as we met, we were involved and there was, is, nothing either of us can do to change it. Am I wrong?" she asked, motioning him to her side.

He did not reply.

"Also, there is little we can do about what these gods of yours have planned for us."

He nodded again.

"Well, then," she said, trying just a bit too hard to sound cheerful, "let us not worry about them. We can just as easily get killed being thrown from a horse or by Sevich or in a thousand other ways, right?"

Ellyss nodded and refrained from reminding her that death was not always the worst outcome of a situation.

"Good, then we are in agreement. Now, let us dress, surely it must be time for breakfast. I am starving!"

Ellyss could not help but smile.

CHAPTER TWENTY-TWO

"IS SOMETHING WRONG?" Taaryn lifted herself up on one elbow, after waking to find Ellyss standing by the window and staring into the distance.

Ellyss turned to her. "I am sorry. Did my rising wake you?"

"No."

"I was just thinking about your encounter with Xanchad."

"What about it?" She sat up. "Please tell me you are not still brooding over our relationship."

He smiled. "No, not this time."

"Good, then what is it?"

"It is what he said to you. That you did not know what you were." He sat beside her. "You are sure he said what and not who?"

She nodded. "But what importance does that one word

have?"

"That is just it," he replied, "the ancient ones, and most especially Xanchad, choose their words with the utmost care. So, there is something else he wishes to convey to us. What are you that you do not know you are?"

Taaryn shook her head.

"He cannot possibly mean human, you obviously know that. And, unlike me, you do not have a dark past, do you?"

"Not one I am aware of," she replied.

They looked at each other, chuckling at her response.

"No, I am sure I would have sensed such a thing. So, what is it?"

She shrugged and watched as he walked back to the window, mumbling "what you are" over and over.

"Of course!" Ellyss shouted after a few moments.

"Of course what?" Taaryn asked.

"What you are. You, too, are a magicker."

Taaryn looked at him with disbelief and then laughed. "That is ridiculous. We do not have magic in this land."

"Ah, that is where you are wrong. Magic is everywhere. It is as natural a talent as a beautiful singing voice. But as I said before, in this land, for some reason, the recognition and nurturing of it no longer happens."

"Even if it is true, you cannot be serious that I possess such a talent."

"Why not? Graeden does. And you picked up mindspeaking as easily as breathing."

"That is different."

"Really? How?"

"Graeden is in Reissem Grove, and that is more likely the

reason for what he can do. As for the mindspeaking, that is not really magic."

Ellyss smiled, remembering the story that Regnaryn had made a similar argument to Varlama.

"Even if I agree with you that mindspeaking is not magic, which I do not, tell me how you can do so across such great distances?"

"It is Graeden. Even you said we have a special bond being twins."

"Is that all there is to it?"

She thought a moment. "That, and his being in Reissem Grove. You know what that place is. I am sure that is contributing to our being able to speak together. That is all, it is nothing special."

"You are wrong," he said. "Even if it is just between you and Graeden, you accomplished it naturally. No one taught you how to do it." He sensed she was readying a rebuttal, but he continued before she could interrupt him. "Yes, I know what you are going to say. I taught you, but that is not true. I just helped you refine the skills that were already there."

She still appeared skeptical. "Still, it is only with Graeden."

"But you have not tried contacting anyone else in Reissem Grove, have you?"

"No, but I am sure it will not work with anyone else."

"Perhaps, but I think we should try. Tonight. Before we retire. And as for other magic," he quickly added before she had a chance to argue with him about the mindspeaking, "we can discuss that later."

#

After dinner, Ellyss watched Taaryn bound up the stairs and race down the hall to their room. He was not surprised at her burst of energy. She had been trying to quell her excitement all day.

"So, what do we do now?" she asked the instant he closed the door. "Should I try to reach Regnaryn and have her tell Graeden to answer if she hears."

"I think Regnaryn and Graeden, well..."

"Of course, because they are soulbound there may be a kind of spillover from one to the other. That is possible."

He thought a moment. "Try to reach Neshya or Immic. I do not believe either of them have extraordinary mindspeaking ability."

"But what if it does not work? If I cannot do it."

"Then you will know that at least part of your ability comes from the bond you and Graeden have."

Ellyss knew this experiment had the potential of backfiring. If she truly was only able to reach Graeden, she might resist any attempt to find magic in herself. But between what Xanchad had said and his own gut feeling, he sensed there was more to this than just the bond between twins.

"Right," she said with a matter of fact tone. "At least we will know one way or the other, and we can go on from there. I will try to reach Neshya."

She sat down and cleared her thoughts. She no longer had to do that when she mindspoke with Graeden, but that was Graeden. She took a deep breath and mindcalled to Neshya. She told him what she wanted him to do and ended by saying how much she hoped this message would find him.

She finished and looked at Ellyss. "It is done," she said. "Now what do we do?"

"We wait," he replied. "As much as I know you want an immediate response, you must remember that we have no idea what either Neshya or Graeden are doing at this moment."

He was about to continue when he noticed her face light up with elation and excitement. He knew Graeden was mindspeaking to her in response to her mindcall to Neshya. He waited. He would not interrupt. She would tell him all when she was done with Graeden.

A moment later, she leapt from her chair and jumped at him, throwing her arms around his neck and kissing him madly all over his face.

"You were right. Neshya heard me! He told Graeden that, if he did not know better, he would swear I was right there within the Grove it was so strong."

She thought for a moment. "You do not think he meant that I was loud as if I were shouting, do you? I think I was, just a little. I was so afraid it would not get through."

Ellyss laughed. "From what I know of that young yekcal, he probably thoroughly enjoyed it, loud or not."

She nodded, released her grip on him and began to giggle and dance around the room. Ellyss watched her with amusement. She acted as giddy as a child. After several moments, she threw herself backwards onto the bed, breathless.

"So what do we do now?" she asked after a few moments.

"Now, we need to see if we can uncover any other abilities."

"Bah, I told you before, I do not possess any magic."

"Then, explain to me how you saw into my soul? How you were able to easily breach barriers the likes of which have stopped even the best magickers through the ages?"

She shook her head. "I do not know."

"Well, even if you have no other talents, we will work on you honing your shielding abilities. You have already displayed an innate talent for shielding your mindspeaking conversations."

"I have?"

Ellyss laughed and pulled her close to him in a hug. "See, it comes so naturally, you are not aware you are doing it. That, my dear, is an extraordinary gift. Most novice mind speakers are like a person standing in a room and shouting so that everyone within earshot can hear them. You were not only able to immediately pinpoint your thoughts to Graeden, you were shielding them from anyone besides him and me."

"Wait," she said, pulling back from him. "I thought you told me that first night, you and Graeden were shielding those thoughts from outside minds."

"We were prepared to do so, but found you were doing the same, not fully, but to a remarkable degree. We merely fine-tuned your shielding."

"And that is unusual?"

He laughed. "Oh, yes, most unusual. Just ask Graeden sometime how much difficulty he had doing that."

She grinned broadly. "You mean I did something Graeden could not?"

He nodded. "Is that a bit of sibling rivalry I sense?"

"Perhaps just a little." And then, as if to curtail any further discussion of that subject, she continued. "When will you do this?"

"Tomorrow. But we need to be somewhere safe."

"Safe?" she asked. "Is the Keep not safe?"

He smiled. "The Keep is quite safe against non-magical attacks and accidents."

"Accidents?"

He took her hand. "Such things are rare, but there is always a chance that as we work on one skill another untrained power can manifest in an uncontrolled manner. So, it is best we are prepared. And it is better to be away from all other distractions."

She nodded. "Is there such a place nearby?"

He nodded. "Yes, it is near the black rock face not far from the Keep."

"But that is a sheer cliff with a dense forest on one side and a river on the other. There is no way to access the cliff nor swim the river. There is nothing else there."

He smiled. "It is not the rock face itself that I speak of, but just past it in the woods where the river forks into a small stream. That is the place."

"By the stream? There is nothing but impassable woods there."

"Ah, you would be surprised at what you can find if you know where and what to look for."

He smiled at her skeptical look.

CHAPTER TWENTY-THREE

THE NEXT MORNING, the couple headed out toward the woods that bordered the looming black rock face.

"So, where is this magical place that has eluded everyone in the Keep for ages?" she asked as they exited the Keep's gate.

The sarcasm in her voice did not escape Ellyss. He stopped abruptly and Taaryn almost ran into him. He turned and glared at her.

"It is called a troilhan. If you are unable to open your mind, cannot at least consider other possibilities than what you are accustomed to, go back to the Keep, for you will never achieve anything."

He turned and walked on, shaking his head and muttering. "After all she has heard and seen, all that has happened..."

She stood in silence, stunned by his reaction. She wondered if it was because he was afraid of what he might find in her mind. Or was it something else?

She watched him for a moment, and then she followed.

"Troilhan, you say. I have never heard such a word."

"It is of an ancient tongue."

No more was said until they reached the stream. He waded into the cold water that just barely came up to his ankles. He motioned Taaryn to follow, and she did without comment. They followed the stream as it snaked its way through the dense foliage.

"By your reaction to this place," he said, "I am guessing you have never come this way before."

"No, I have not," she replied in a voice just above a whisper. "This is the first time I have traced the path of the stream. This is absolutely beautiful. I had no idea."

After a little way, the stream widened, though the water level neither rose nor subsided, then seemed to end as the forest crossed its path.

"Now where do we go?" Taaryn asked.

"We continue to follow the stream."

"But it ends, there is nowhere to go. Nothing to follow."

"Look more closely. Look for more than what you expect to see." He pointed toward two large trees directly in front of them.

At first she could see nothing but the trees, so close together she was sure not even a piece of paper could pass between them. But, as she concentrated, she saw an opening large enough for even a horse to pass through.

"Ah, yes, now I see it," she said excitedly.

He nodded, walked forward to the opening, and stepped through it. Taaryn followed. They continued along the stream through the trees until it emptied into a modest sized lake encircled by trees so densely packed, they seemed more a wall than foliage. The shore of the lake was covered with what looked like shimmering black silk. In reality, it was an exceptionally fine sand that reflected the sunlight.

"So, it is as I surmised," Ellyss said.

Taaryn did not respond, too busy staring in awe at her surroundings.

"This place and the rock face," he went on as much to himself as to her, "are connected."

Taaryn shook her head. "I am sorry, I was not listening. It is hard to believe this place is here. I have hunted and played in these woods since I was a child and never..."

Ellyss put his arm around her shoulder. She touched his hand.

"What do you mean, these two things are connected?"

"They resonate with the same tone. Like two musical instruments playing the same note exactly the same as if they were one. I have been to many of these hidden places..."

"Wait," she interrupted him. "You mean there are other places like this?"

He smiled at the look of amazement on her face. "Yes, they are scattered throughout the world but known by only a select few."

She drew in a breath.

"Each resonates slightly differently than their surroundings. This is the first time that I can feel the connection between the two. Look at the sand. See how the sunlight catches it? Does that not remind you of the rock face?"

"Now that you mention it, yes. Are you saying they are the same? But how?" She bent down, picked up a handful of the black sand, and let it run through her fingers. "How could the cliff have been pulverized into this?"

He shook his head. "I do not know…" His voice drifted off as he stared into the distance, as if looking somewhere well beyond the boundaries of this place. "All I can tell you is what I feel. The sand and the rock are the same."

He turned back towards her, looking almost apologetic for his lack of an answer to her questions.

She smiled. "So, what do we do now?"

"For the moment, let us sit by the water's edge and enjoy the beauty of this place."

#

"I thought you said I had a talent for this," she remarked after Ellyss broke through her latest shielding attempt.

"You do."

"If that is so, I am glad we are not trying something I have no affinity for. Shall we try again?"

He shook his head. "No, it is time for a rest, you are fatigued."

She wanted to argue with him, but knew he was right.

Ellyss sat in the black sand and motioned her to join him. She snuggled up against him and he put his arm around her shoulder. Within a few moments, she slept. He sat quietly, content to be beside her.

She slept for almost an hour.

"Oh, my," she said, rubbing her eyes. "I guess I really was spent."

He smiled and drew her close.

"Do you think we can try again?" she asked.

"I am not sure that is wise. You do not want to tire yourself to the point you cannot train again tomorrow, or worse, make yourself ill," he replied. "It might be better to just go back to the Keep for the night and try again tomorrow."

"I know. But just one more attempt and then I promise we will leave." She looked at him in a way both knew he could not resist.

"All right, but just one attempt, and it will need to be a short one. Remember, you are not expected to master this technique in one day."

"I know." She stood up. "But I think I can do just a little better than I did before."

He watched her, and though he could not see what she was drawing up around herself, he sensed a convergence of her energy to a focused point. He waited until he felt no more changes in her energy, then he called her name. Which, in previous attempts, had been enough to break her concentration, she looked at him in response to his call. This time her energy did not falter. He then tried to pierce her shielding with a mental push.

He felt the shield waver ever so slightly, but she recovered. She smiled in victory and that lapse in concentration caused the shielding to falter and drop away.

"That was wonderful, Taaryn," he exclaimed. "You were able to maintain your shield against an attack."

"I hardly call that an attack," she replied.

"I am serious, my love. That was extraordinary."

"Now you are just patronizing me."

"You know me better than that," he replied. "And before you ask, no, you cannot try it again. You promised, remember?"

She nodded. Even though she really did want to try again, she knew he was right.

CHAPTER TWENTY-FOUR

THE COUPLE GATHERED up their things and prepared to return to the Keep.

"Remember what I told you earlier. Before we leave, we must give a bit of magic back to the land to keep it strong."

She watched Ellyss walk down to the water's edge and kneel in the black sand. He sat there motionless for several moments, then returned to her side.

"Shall we?" He motioned to the opening in the trees where they had entered.

"What?" she asked in disbelief. "You are done? But..."

"What were you expecting?"

She blushed. "Umm, I am not sure, but certainly more than you just sitting there."

He laughed. "Magic is not all thunder and lightning, you know."

"Yes, but...Oh, come on, let us head back."

She grabbed his hand and pulled him toward the path leading back to the Keep. He said nothing. They were almost to the edge of the forest when she stopped so suddenly, Ellyss nearly knocked her over.

"Wait," she said. "What about the others?"

"What do you mean?"

"Should we tell them about what we are doing?" she asked. "This place? All of it?"

"No, I think we should wait."

"Hmm, perhaps you are right. But if we go off each day for hours at a time, we may just have to offer some reason to them."

"I am sure you can come up with a feasible explanation," he said with a twinkle in his eye.

She nodded.

"And I am not so sure they are ready for any more magic being sprung on them. I think some of them are still having a hard time with the idea of Graeden's actions in Reissem Grove."

"True, true. And if they doubt my explanation that we simply wish to be alone," she looked at him with just the slightest hint of mischief in her eyes, "you could make them forget...like you did with Graeden at that inn."

He shifted his glance away from her. Even at the time it was done, he was not comfortable with erasing Graeden's memory.

"It was just a joke," she quickly added when she saw his reaction to her words.

He smiled weakly but still looked uncomfortable.

"I am sure it must be dinner time," she said changing the

subject, "I am famished."

She did not wait for a response.

#

It did not take long for Taaryn to master maintaining her shielding against both mental and physical attacks. Ellyss had gone far beyond the casual play. He now bombarded her with attacks that if she lost her shield, could injure her. He would not attempt a lethal attack, but he veered close to it.

He also noticed she could alter her shieldings. Although not something he could put his finger on, he sensed that even during an attack the shielding would change. He had planned to tell her about doing such things but, just like shielding, it came naturally to her.

He wondered what other surprises she would present to him as he attacked her with a burst of mental energy. It had no sooner left his mind than he found himself on the ground, knocked down by his own attack.

"Wait...What did you just do?" he asked rubbing his head. "How did you do that?"

She looked at him unsure, of how he had fallen and what he was asking her. "What do you mean?"

"Do you not know what you just did?"

"I deflected your attack, just like I have been doing all along."

"No. This was different. This time you reflected my attack."

She looked confused.

"You just turned my own attack back upon me and, in the process, increased its strength."

She still did not understand.

"Do you know how amazing this is?" He did not give her time to reply. "I have heard of it, but have never actually seen anyone use it. Even more amazing, I do not think there have been more than just a handful of people through the ages who perfected that technique. You have just managed to make your shielding an offensive as well as defensive weapon!"

She just stared at him.

"How did you do it?" he asked.

She shrugged.

"Think. What was different about what you did to fend off that attack?"

She stared at him for several moments. "I was annoyed that you were still attacking me. And, with that last attack, which by the way was a bit harsh, I got angry."

"I see."

She waited for him to elaborate, but he did not. He just turned and stared off across the water.

"Is that good or bad?" she asked when she could no longer wait for his response.

He turned back to her and smiled. "I am not sure. It is good that you can do it and know to a degree what caused you to do it. But bad if we, you, cannot determine how to do it at will without the necessity of outside stimuli."

"You mean like Graeden and his fireballs?"

"Hmm, I had not thought of that, but yes, very similar to that." He smiled. "I guess you two are alike in more ways than anyone ever imagined."

"So, how do we proceed?" she asked.

He shook his head and pondered her question. "I am not sure. I think this is beyond my abilities."

"You are not saying we are going to quit, are you?" she asked in dismay.

"No, no. That is not what I am saying. What I mean is, we need another opinion...some outside input on how to proceed."

"And where do we get that?"

"Varlama," he replied. "After all, she was the one who trained Regnaryn, and it is she and Phrynia who are helping Graeden."

"Of course. Shall we try to contact her now?" Taaryn asked excitedly.

"Not just yet."

"Why not? Why do we need to wait? The faster we get her opinion, the faster we can get on with this. I just do not understand your..."

"Hold on a moment. You seem to forget, my love. This place is shielded, remember?" he said. "Not even your formidable mindspeaking talent could get through this barrier."

"Yes, I had forgotten that," she said sheepishly.

CHAPTER TWENTY-FIVE

"WHAT ARE WE TO DO now?" Regnaryn asked.

The others shook their heads.

"Could we have misinterpreted what we found and sent them to the wrong location?" Graeden asked.

"No, you sent them to Aelden," an unfamiliar voice replied from the shadows. "At least, what is left of it. I apologize for not getting here sooner so your drageals could have avoided that unnecessary trip."

The presence of the grizzled old man emerging from the darkened corner of the room startled everyone.

"Who are you?" Ayirak growled, his hackles rising.

"And how did you get in here?" Phrynia asked.

The old man smiled. "Do you mean through Reissem Grove's

barriers or into this particular room?"

"Both," Regnaryn replied.

"Ah, Regnaryn. You have your grandmother's eyes." He nodded at the chair. "May I sit? My old bones do not fare as well crouching in the shadows as they once did."

"You have yet to answer our questions," Ayirak boomed as he blocked the man's path.

"I am the wizard Romeiko, a name which has no meaning to any of you. Long have I desired to come to this place, a place I have watched from afar. It was only after I parted ways with Sevich, that I realized this is where I truly belong. Oh, how I yearned to come here, but I knew I needed to wait until the time was right. When all of you, especially you, Regnaryn, kin of my childhood friend, needed me most." The old man paused and looked around the room. "I can help you find the one you seek, the one that goes by many names...Sevich. The Master. Jurcheval."

The others looked confused.

"Yes, of course, you do not recognize his latest name, the one he resurrected himself as. That makes it even more important that I am here now."

"And why should we believe you?" Ayirak growled. "How do we know you are not one of his agents?"

"Because, my fierce friend, had I meant you harm, or intended to take Regnaryn, I could have easily done so at any time and accomplished the task completely undetected."

He paused, allowing his words to take hold. He chuckled at the tickle in his mind. "Your talent at exploring minds far surpasses my expectations, Phrynia. Still, you will see nothing more than I wish."

The drageal did not respond.

Again, he nodded at the chair. "If you will be so kind as to allow me to sit, I will answer your questions."

Ayirak reluctantly stepped out of his path.

"Tell us who you are," Neshya demanded. "And not just your meaningless name."

"How do you know not only of us, but of this place?" Graeden asked. "And what did you mean by you were once in his service?"

"How much do you know of your father and his family, Regnaryn?" the old man asked, ignoring the others' questions.

"Little of him, and less of his family, only what I recently read in his journals from the times after he had escaped his brother," Regnaryn said, not sure why she felt comfortable answering this strange old man.

"I never had the privilege of meeting Grenwald, but from the contempt and hatred Sevich had for him, I imagine he was a good man. I did know your father's mother and her family. We grew up together, her brother, Yarrow, and I were the best of friends. Friends until he, like Sevich, turned into a monster. It runs in the family, you know," he said.

Regnaryn grabbed Graeden's arm. "What do you mean? Am I to become like him?"

The old wizard smiled. "No, child, you will not, not ever."

"Then what did you mean by those words?" Graeden asked.

"Generations ago, a curse was set upon Regnaryn's family."

"Surely you cannot be serious. A curse?" Graeden said.

Romeiko's face became very stern. "There was a time you did not believe in drageals either and now, well, here you are. You should have learned by now not to so quickly discount that which you do not know." He shook his head. "I really thought you had become more open over the last bit of time, young Graeden of Hammarsh Keep. Perhaps you, too, should look into your family history."

Graeden looked at the old wizard, confused by his words.

The old man chuckled. "But that is a tale for another time. Perhaps when we have dispatched Jurcheval, you and I, and perhaps some others, will talk of those days. It is indeed a fine tale."

"What of this curse upon my family? Do I bear it?" Regnaryn asked, remembering the destruction she had bore down upon the gawara.

Romeiko smiled. "No, child, you are the antithesis of evil. And, it seems, the curse only manifests itself upon the second son of the accursed or his sister. You are neither of those. And since neither Yarrow nor Jurcheval begat children, this will end here, either with his demise or the end of the world as we know it."

"Why would anyone curse my family?" she asked.

"That I do not know. Its origin is ancient, and has been a bane on your family for uncountable generations, perhaps from as far back as when gods and demons walked amongst men." He looked at her and saw the fear in her eyes. "But that is just conjecture on my part."

"So, you are saying Sevich, er, Jurcheval's children will also carry the curse and the next generation may face one even worse than him?" Phrynia asked.

"Yes. Unless he has changed since I knew him, Jurcheval has no desires except to gain power and inflict pain. Carnal pleasure holds no place in his life."

Everyone in the room fell silent for a moment.

"And just how do you know all of this?" Neshya asked.

"As I said, I knew his uncle. We were friends in our youth."

"That does not explain how you know Sevich," Ayirak said.

"I served Sevich when he was a youth," Romeiko said.

"No! That is not all," Phrynia snapped. "It was much more than that. You sought him out. You were his teacher. You taught him how to hone his heinous skills."

"Are you saying you did such a thing knowing what he was? What he would become?" Graeden asked.

The old man nodded and looked away. "Yes."

"But why?" Regnaryn asked. "If you knew what he would become, why did you aid him?"

"I was young and full of myself. I thought I could control his darkness, keep it at bay. Help him overcome that which plagued him."

"Liar!" Phrynia shouted. "You had no desire for such altruism. Yes, you wanted to control him, but not to help him. No, you wanted his power for yourself."

Romeiko turned to the drageal and smiled. "Ah, yes, I had forgotten the power of drageals to see the truth, even if one tries to hide it in the depths of their soul."

"You tried to take his power from him?" Regnaryn asked. "Like he is trying to do to me."

The old wizard turned to her. "Not to actually take it. I think I wanted more to manipulate it. To have him do my bidding. He was after all just a child, barely thirteen, when I first sought him out. I should have realized at our first meeting that he would not bend to my will. But, I was arrogant and I did not accept that fact until it was almost too late."

"Then it is you we should blame for all of the pain and suffering that was wrought down upon us," Trebeh said.

"Sevich already had the power, the evil, within him. Even at that young age, he was already far stronger than his uncle, Yarrow, was at the time of his death."

"But you stayed, anyway," Regnaryn said. "You continued to

help him."

The old man turned to face her. "Yes, sadly I did. Evil, true evil, is quite the seductress, my dear. She tempts and teases, cajoles you into thinking that doing this one thing will not be so bad. 'Just show him how to do this, or that. It is nothing major, nothing that will cause harm,' she purrs into your mind. And, before you know it, you have embroiled yourself into a situation you never thought you could be in."

"Pretty words but nothing more than excuses," Phrynia said. "We are all faced with choices, large and small. All tempted by that siren's voice, but not all of us choose to succumb to her wiles."

"You are right, and I will not attempt to condone my actions. Truth be told, there are no words, no true words to do so. That is something I have had to live with since the day I escaped his grasp. It was only when I saw you, my dear," he said and turned again to Regnaryn, "that I felt I might have a chance to atone for my sins by helping you defeat him."

"Why should we believe you? Believe that you are actually here to help us and not merely to try to manipulate Regnaryn as you tried to do with Sevich?" Graeden asked.

"You are right to be cautious about one such as myself, suddenly showing up at your doorstep," Romeiko replied.

"Yet," Phrynia interrupted. "You were able to enter the Grove. And for as long as we have lived here, the defenses of this place have never let anything in that could harm us, be it beast or enemy."

Everyone in the room agreed.

"Tell us what you know of Sevich and how you plan to help us defeat him?" Regnaryn asked.

The old wizard turned and looked at her for several moments before speaking. "I am sorry, child, I do not mean to stare but you so resemble your grandmother. I was taken back to the happy times of my youth, before the curse showed itself in her brother."

"You said that before, now stop stalling and answer her question," Neshya said.

"Of course, forgive me," Romeiko replied. "Your mother saw the power you would achieve and the fact that you would need to face an evil force."

Regnaryn nodded.

"What she did not see, or perhaps did not want to acknowledge, was that the confrontation with the evil one would decide the fate of the world. If you, alone or with your comrades, are unable to defeat Jurcheval, if he is able to attain your power, all will be lost. He is quite powerful on his own. If the unthinkable happens, and if he is able to obtain your power, there will be no stopping him. I fear it would not be long until the entire world would lay in ashen ruins, as does Aelden, even these many years after he destroyed it."

"Yes, yes," Neshya said. "We know all of that. Well, all except the setting the world aflame."

"Really? She saw all of that?" Romeiko shook his head. "Forgive me, I did not realize the full extent of her abilities."

"Yes, she did. It is all written in her journals from just before I was born."

"Amazing," the old man said. "Perhaps one day you will let me read them."

"Enough stalling," Ayirak snapped. "How do you plan on helping us find and defeat him?"

"Finding him is simple. As I said before, I already know where he is," Romeiko said.

"Wonderful, then let us go face him," Neshya said and turned to the door.

"Knowing where he is and knowing how to defeat him are two very different things," Romeiko said.

"As much as I hate to agree with him," Ayirak said, "Romeiko is right. We have already seen what that monster is capable of, so just running blindly to confront him would result in certain failure."

The old man nodded. "And I fear you have not seen the true extent of his power. Up until now, your encounters have been through his agents, those he controls. You have yet to come face to face with him," Romeiko said. "His power and cunning, especially his mind control, is formidable when one stands before him."

Graeden squirmed, remembering his encounter at the inn.

"So, what do you suggest we do?" Regnaryn asked.

Romeiko shook his head. "I do not have an exact answer..."

"Then why are you here? Why are you wasting our time?" Neshya snarled.

Romeiko ignored the interruption. "I do not have an exact answer, no plan carved in stone. Not yet."

"It sounds to me as if you are stalling, old man," Graeden said.

"Yes, I am sure it does, but there is another aspect of this quest that has yet to come to fruition. And until it does, until the rest of your forces are ready, the future is obscured as is the plan of attack." He turned to Trebeh and Phrynia. "I am sure you understand."

They nodded.

"We must wait to see how certain events, events away from Reissem Grove, unfold before we can move forward."

"Bah!" Ayirak snorted. "Yet another example of seer prattle, meaning you have no idea."

"What do you mean by the rest of our forces?" Graeden asked. "We have no other forces within or outside of Reissem Grove."

"Ah, but you do," Romeiko said and turned to Phrynia and

Varlama. "I am surprised you two have not sensed them. Have you been so focused on what is here before you that you have been blind to what lies beyond these borders?"

"Tell us more. Enlighten us to our blindness," Varlama said.

"All in good time. All in good time."

CHAPTER TWENTY-SIX

"WHAT ARE YOU doing?" Ellyss asked when Taaryn plopped herself down on the grass almost as soon as they had broken through the trees.

"This is as good a place as any to try to reach Varlama, is it not?"

"I thought we would do it in our room," he said. "You will be more comfortable there."

"Really? More comfortable? Is that the true reason?"

He smiled. "You know me too well, my love. I had hoped to use the time walking back to the Keep to decide what to tell them."

"I would think that is pretty straight forward. We are trying to discover if I possess any magical abilities."

"Ah, but why were we doing such a thing?"

"Because of what Xanchad said," she began and then stopped. "Of course. We cannot tell them of Xanchad, because none of them know your true past."

He nodded.

"Still, it is such a lovely day and this place is so serene, we can just as easily think of a reason here as on the walk back. And now, both of us are thinking about it."

"True." He sat beside her.

They sat for almost an hour, discussing and discarding ideas of the reason why they chose to look for magic in her. For every idea they came up with, they found a reason to discount it.

"This is harder than I thought it would be," Taaryn said.

"Fabrications usually are," he replied. "I think our best path is staying as close to the truth as possible."

"But leaving out one little detail, eh?" she said with a smirk.

Ellyss nodded. He rose and extended his hand to help her up.

They looked around, realizing it was nearly sunset.

"Where did the day go?" Taaryn mused as they began the trek back to the Keep.

#

As the couple entered the Keep, Ellyss took Taaryn's arm. "You do realize we cannot do this just now."

"What? Why?"

"Because, we have been away all day and it is nearly dinner time. Do you not think your parents will expect us at the table?"

"Maybe they will not realize we have returned," Taaryn said. "Or we could say we were tired or something and beg off. I really want to contact Varlama as soon as possible."

Ellyss raised an eyebrow and laughed. "Seriously? Your

mother knows everything that goes on in this place. As for the evening meal, well…"

Taaryn sighed. "Of course. So, I guess it will be dinner first. Still, we must clean up. Neither Mother nor Father would appreciate us at the table looking like this."

Ellyss followed her up the stairs, wondering what she was up to. She was not one to give in so easily, and she always endeavored to honor her obligations.

#

"Shall we contact Graeden now?" he asked as they entered their room. "I do not think we should keep Varlama waiting too long."

Taaryn turned toward him. "What do you mean?"

He smiled. "I know you already contacted her."

"Why would you say that?"

"Because you were far too calm during dinner for it to be any other way. I surmise you mindcalled to Varlama earlier, probably while we were dressing and told her to go to Graeden."

He knew from her reaction he was right.

"I am not foolish enough, nor are you, to think that you still require certain trappings to mindspeak, even across long distances."

"As you said earlier, we know each other too well," she replied.

"Actually," Ellyss continued, "I am surprised you did not just talk to her through Graeden earlier."

She blushed. "I had thought of that, but…"

"But?"

"Well, I thought it would be better with both of us here. I need you to explain what exactly I did and…"

"And you are unsure how Graeden will react to this turn of

events."

She nodded. "Even when he was home, when he spoke of his magic, at that time merely mindspeaking in Reissem Grove, I sensed a level of uncomfortableness, almost a fear, in him. I think on some level he doubts the existence of his own magic. And when we tell him you suspect I have more magic than just being able to mindspeak, I think he may be a bit more than unhappy."

"That is a possibility, but we will never know until we talk to him. Shall we begin?"

The two joined their minds, and Taaryn called out to her brother.

CHAPTER TWENTY-SEVEN

:*IT IS ABOUT TIME you contacted us,*: Graeden said, not trying to hide his frustration.

Varlama laughed. :*I told him you said it would be some time, because you had things to do.*:

:*He does not like being in the dark about what is going on,*: Taaryn said. :*Though he feels no remorse for putting others in the same position.*:

:*Hrrmph,*: Graeden replied. :*What is going on there? Why did you contact Varlama directly?*:

:*It was my idea,*: Ellyss said. :*I have found a rather unique ability within Taaryn, and I need guidance as to how to proceed.*:

:*What do you mean by ability? You are not saying that you went seeking out magic in her, are you? I gave no permission for such a thing.*:

Graeden snapped. *:Surely you, of all people, are aware of the consequences.:*

:Since when do I need to ask your permission? Just who do you think you are?: Taaryn shouted. *:You have no say in anything I do.:*

:Stop it both of you,: Varlama said. *:This is neither the time nor the place for such silly squabbling. Whether you approve or whether it is your place to approve is not the issue at hand.:*

Even with no further response from the twins, it was clear neither was happy with the other.

:Ellyss, please continue,: Varlama said. *:Just how did you find this ability and, as I am sure Graeden would like to know, why did you even look?:*

:You are already aware of Taaryn's ability to mindspeak across amazing distances, but I am not sure if Graeden has told you that she naturally shielded her mindspeaking during her first conversation,: Ellyss replied.

:I was not aware of that.:

:Obviously it was not perfect the first time, but with each passing conversation, her shielding has progressed to the point that I no longer need to augment it. That got me thinking she could enhance her shielding abilities even further, perhaps to the point of creating a barrier against physical attacks.:

:A fair assumption,: Varlama said. *:And? Can she?:*

:Yes, she can deflect anything I throw at her, mentally or physically.:

:Wait!: Graeden interrupted. *:Are you saying you have been putting my sister in danger?:*

:Only if she is not paying attention,: Ellyss answered, understanding Graeden's concern. *:I am not putting her in any more peril than Phrynia and Varlama have put you in during your training.:*

:That is exactly what I am afraid of,: Graeden replied with a bit more levity.

:So, you found what you expected. Is there more? I somehow think if that was all you found, you would not be contacting me.:

Ellyss chuckled. *:Always the perceptive one, eh, Varlama. As I was saying, the intensity of the attacks have been increasing and today, well, I guess I went a bit over the top and...:*

:And he made me angry,: Taaryn interrupted.

:Yes, I made her angry because she asked me to stop and I did not. At least, not until she reflected one of my attacks back at me with almost double the force as I had generated!:

:Wait. Did you say she reflected the attack? Are you sure?: Varlama asked.

:Oh, yes, I am sure. I had all I could do to protect myself.:

Taaryn looked at him with shock. She had no idea that she had put him in danger. His glance assured her it was all right.

:The problem is that, similar to both Regnaryn and Graeden when their magic first manifested, she is not sure how she did it, other than she was angry at me,: he continued. *:That is my predicament. I do not know exactly how to proceed. In fact, I am not even sure I have the skill to train her in this ability.:*

There was several moments of silence. Taaryn felt nervous at the lack of response, but Ellyss told her that he surmised Varlama might be contacting Phrynia.

:Now I understand both your excitement and your distress,: Varlama said, breaking the silence. *:Reflective shielding is a rare ability in itself, but enhanced reflective shielding, which is what you are telling me Taaryn is exhibiting, is almost unheard of. So, it seems these twins both appear to be far more extraordinary than we were led to believe.:*

:What do you mean?: the twins asked simultaneously.

Varlama ignored the question and continued. *:The nature of her ability presents us with the dilemma of how to progress. We, obviously, cannot leave her talent untrained and uncontrolled. Yet, who will be able to train our young protégée? You were right in contacting us, Ellyss. This is indeed beyond your capability.:*

:Yes,: Ellyss replied, *:that is what I thought. So, who can teach her to control this if I cannot?:*

:There are only a handful of beings qualified to do so. The problem is that most of them cannot be contacted without running the risk of alerting Jurcheval to not only what is going on but also to your whereabouts.:

:Jurcheval?: Ellyss asked.

:Oh, I am sorry. I thought Graeden would have told you, that is the name Sevich reinvented himself as. Have you heard of him in your travels?:

:No. How would I? : Ellyss replied.

:I suppose you would not. His new name apparently means follower of Jurcena, or something like that.:

Ellyss snorted. *:Why am I not surprised?:*

The sharpness of Ellyss' response took both Varlama and Taaryn by surprise.

:Who is Jurcena?: Taaryn asked.

:From what I understand, he was an ancient demon. But that is of little consequence. As for your training, I think I am the only person who can train Taaryn,: Varlama said. *:The question is, should it be here in Reissem Grove or there in Hammarsh Keep?:*

Ellyss felt the excitement grow within Taaryn at the thought of going to Reissem Grove.

:Both options have their drawbacks and dangers,: Varlama continued. *:But, the first thing I must know is, just where are you*

conducting this training? Is there a secure area close to Hammarsh Keep?:

:Yes,: Ellyss said. *:And it is within walking distance. It is a goodly size and its barriers are some of the strongest I have ever encountered.:*

:What?: Graeden interrupted. *:Where? I do not know of any such place.:*

:Nor did I, until Ellyss showed me,: Taaryn said to her brother.

:Splendid! Then I will come there,: Varlama said.

:So, Graeden's training is going well enough that you can leave him?: Ellyss asked.

:Oh, yes. He has made great strides since last you saw him. I will let Romeiko continue his training while I am gone.:

:Romeiko?:

:I will tell you about him when I get there.:

:How will you get here?: Taaryn asked.

Varlama laughed, *:The same way Ellyss did.:*

:Of course, how silly of me,: Taaryn said sheepishly.

:When will you arrive?: Ellyss asked.

:Well, that will depend on you,: Varlama replied. *:I will need you to do a few things in preparation for my arrival. And it takes three days to get there.:*

:Anything. What do you need?:

:I will need some sort of shelter within the secure area in which to reside during my stay.:

:There is plenty of room here at the Keep,: Taaryn said.

Varlama chuckled. *:No, child, I do not think that would do. I am not sure that, even as extraordinary as your family is, they are ready for that yet.:*

:Oh, of course, how silly of me,: Taaryn said. *:And even if the*

family would understand, there are too many others in residence there who would not.:

:*True,*: Ellyss said. : *As for the shelter, since I will have to work alone...*"

:*What do you mean, alone?:* Taaryn interrupted. :*I can help you.:*

:*Of course, I am sorry,:* he continued. :*I think we can have something serviceable ready within about five days. It may not be fancy...:*

:*I am a tazzamira,:* Varlama responded, :*we do not require fancy...serviceable will be fine. Then, it is settled. I will depart in six days, that should give you sufficient time to do whatever you need.:*

#

"Is this not wonderful?" Taaryn asked, barely able to contain her excitement. "I will admit, the thought of going to Reissem Grove was amazing, but getting to meet Varlama here will be almost as good, right?"

"Yes, my love, it will. Varlama is a very interesting being."

Taaryn thought for a moment. "I do not think Graeden ever mentioned a tazza...Oh, what was it she called herself?"

"A tazzamira. When last you saw Graeden, he had not yet met Varlama."

"I see. So, tell me about her."

"All right, but only if you sit beside me," he said. "I am getting dizzy watching you twirl around the room."

She laughed and bounced onto the bed beside him.

Ellyss told her all he was supposed to know, leaving out anything he knew of the tazzamira from previous lives. He did not wish her to divulge something neither of them should be aware of.

"Oh, she sounds amazing," Taaryn said. "And, I daresay, a bit intimidating."

"Yes, that she is. Now, my love, we need to figure out what we are going to do since we do not have a great deal of time to build the shelter. The first thing is to get the tools and materials we need out to the troilhan without anyone finding out what we are up to," he said. "Any ideas?"

"If I remember correctly, there is a small hunting cabin with tools. No, wait, that is at least a day's ride from here. It would take too long to get there and get back." She thought a bit more. "Of course, how stupid of me. There is a shed behind the stables that is rarely used, and I am pretty sure there are tools in there. As for supplies, how good a thief are you?"

He smiled. "Oh, you would be surprised."

"Good. Then we can get the tools we need from the shed and nails and such you can acquire from the carpenter's shop. What about wood?"

"I believe we can get all we need and then some in the forest."

"This is going to be so exciting." She jumped up and began to twirl around the room again.

"Slow down," Ellyss said with a smile. "You know you are going to have to curb your excitement a bit. Remember, you cannot tell anyone else what we are up to or of her presence."

Taaryn stopped. "Oh my, you are right. I had almost forgotten."

Ellyss nodded. "Well, we had better get a good night's sleep. We are in for an exhausting day tomorrow."

CHAPTER TWENTY-EIGHT

"WELL, THAT WAS unexpected, eh, Graeden?" Varlama asked.

Graeden glared at her. "I am not happy that both you and Ellyss are so eager to put my sister in danger."

"She has always been in danger, as have we all. The difference is now she will be more able to protect herself."

"She has no idea what could happen."

"I am sure Ellyss has told her. And, young man, you should be glad Ellyss was there when these powers awoke, so she knows what they are and how to use them."

Graeden shook his head. "Are you sure he is not the reason they awoke? His probing and prodding."

"You do realize, it might have been you who awakened her powers."

"Me? How? When?"

"The first night you mindspoke to her and she answered."

"No. That cannot be."

Varlama nodded. "I believe it is. Think about it, had she ever shown any such talent before? Even when you went home after learning how to mindspeak, did she ever do it?"

"No. But I did not try then. I thought that was just something to be done here, amid this magic."

"It is probably just as well you did not. After all, would you have known how to help her understand it?" Varlama asked.

"No. Even now, I barely understand it myself," Graeden said. "But what of this reflection. You say it is rare, then how is my sister able to do it? We are not of magic. So why, how could she possess such an ability?"

Varlama shrugged. "Who is to say why such things occur."

Graeden clearly did not like her reply. Before he could respond, Varlama pushed up from her chair and headed for the door.

"I must speak with Phrynia. She and I have some planning to do," she said as she departed.

#

"Do you really think the girl is as powerful as Ellyss purports?" Phrynia asked.

Varlama nodded. "I actually think she may be more so."

"Really?"

"Have you ever known Ellyss to exaggerate?"

The drageal thought a moment, then shook her head.

"Neither have I," Varlama replied. "And it is a very rare occasion, indeed, when he asks for help."

"I had not thought of that. How powerful do you think she

is?"

"We will not know until we meet her."

Phrynia cocked her head to the side. "We?"

"Of course, we. You do not think I would fly with anyone else, do you?"

"I suppose. After all, you are far from fond of not having your feet firmly planted on the ground," Phrynia interrupted.

"Exactly. And I have no intention of risking life and limb, my life and limb, to another drageal."

"Nor would I burden any another drageal with your antics once aloft."

The two friends laughed.

"I think you should stay there as well and help me with the girl," Varlama said. "If she is as powerful as Ellyss thinks..."

"Or as stubborn as her brother," Phrynia added with a snicker.

"Exactly. If she is either of those things, I would really like you there with me."

"Of course. When do you wish to leave? There are a few things that need to be dealt with before we depart. Specifically, Graeden and his training."

"Ah, yes, Graeden. He has made remarkable strides in perfecting his abilities."

"I am not sure what Neshya said to him, but whatever it was it worked. He is now at a point where he just needs to fine-tune a few things," Phrynia said.

"Yes, but I do not want him to stop training just because we were not here to insist."

"My thoughts exactly. What do you think of letting Romeiko take over? The man seems to be quite talented."

Varlama walked to the doorway and looked out at the moon. "Are you sure we can trust him?"

"I sense no more deception in him than I do in anyone else."

Varlama raised an eyebrow but let the comment pass. "And what of his past penchant for darkness?"

Phrynia shook her head. "I do not sense that in him. We really have no other choice. No one else here, not even Trebeh, is sufficiently adept at physical magic to do it. Had Aloysius remained…"

The tazzamira softly growled under her breath at the chetoga's leaving. "I guess you are right. But I would still like to have both Regnaryn and Trebeh around during the sessions, just to ensure he does not return to his former ways."

"I was thinking the same thing," Phrynia said. "So, when do we leave?"

"Ellyss said it would take about five days for the two of them to erect a shelter of sorts for me," Varlama said. "Oh my, I did not tell them to do anything for you."

"I will be fine," the drageal said.

The tazzamira breathed a sigh of relief.

"The flight will take about three days, right?" Varlama asked.

"At a normal speed, yes," Phrynia replied.

Varlama winced.

"We could always speed up or slow down the pace to make the trip shorter or longer."

"What a decision," Varlama said. "None are truly to my liking, but I guess it is better to go at a normal pace."

From their initial meeting, it always amazed Phrynia that the tazzamira could be so ferocious and fearless in battle and so terrified of flight.

"Good, then we will leave in six days," Phrynia said. "Shall we go and talk to the others?"

#

"What is the matter, Graeden?" Regnaryn asked.

"Why are they both going?"

"Varlama needs transport and from what I hear, she is not the easiest passenger."

"Are you sure that is the only reason two of the most powerful teachers are going off together to assess someone's talents. What are they keeping from us?"

Regnaryn started to laugh, but she stopped when she saw the scowl on his face. "Are you just now realizing those two have secrets built on secrets. If they are keeping something from you, from us, I am sure they have good reason."

Graeden grumbled under his breath. "What about my training? Are they just going to abandon me half-trained and run off to another challenge?"

"You are being childish. We both know your training is complete."

Graeden glared at her, but she chose to ignore it.

"Tell me what is really bothering you about this," she said as she slid her arm around his shoulder.

He patted her hand and grinned. "I never can fool you, can I?"

She smiled.

"It is just, well, you do not know my sister. She is not one to be content to sit idly by while others act."

Regnaryn did not speak

"What worries me about this offensive skill she has..."

Graeden rose and began to pace. "I do not think she will be content to attack only those assailing her. She is more likely to try to defend everyone else."

Not very different from you, my love, Regnaryn thought but did not say aloud.

"She has always been like that, even when we were children. She could never tolerate the sight of anyone else getting hurt. She would rather it be her. I mean there was one time when this little was standing in the path of a runaway cart. Taaryn pushed the child out of the way, only to have her leg run over by the cart. She was lucky her leg was not completely crushed or worse. And then there was the time..."

Regnaryn did not interrupt Graeden's reminiscences of his twin's reckless behaviors through the years. She sat quietly and listened.

"Do you now understand just why I am so concerned about Taaryn?" Graeden asked after completing his tirade.

"Somewhat, but you know," she said as she smiled, "she sounds very much like someone else I know. So, while it is true that I do not know Taaryn, from all I have heard about her, you and she truly are the epitome of twins, one mindset, one way of reacting. I do not know your past well enough to cite specific instances, but I am sure that, if asked, your sister could regale me with your escapades."

He was not sure how to react to her answer. She laughed at the look of shock on his face at her words. She stood and approached him. She put her arms around his waist and looked up into his face.

"I do understand your concern for Taaryn's safety, but you have to look at it from her point of view," Regnaryn said. "No, actually, what you need to do is think back a bit. Remember when everyone around you was battling the Master's beasts, and all you could do was throw rocks. How did you feel?"

She watched his face, the memories were painful to both of them and rarely discussed, but this time she felt it necessary to make him recall. He did not answer. He did not need to. They both knew.

"Would you really want Taaryn to feel that way?" she continued. "From all that you have just told me about her, you must know that even if she did not have any magical abilities, she would 'throw herself under the cart' to try to be helpful."

The expression on his face showed her that, as she suspected, he had not thought of the situation in those terms.

"You should be thankful she has manifested those abilities," Regnaryn said. "Now she will be better equipped to face the battle she would have thrown herself into, anyway."

"Yes, you are right." He hugged her tightly.

"So are you all right with this now?" she asked.

"Well, I will still worry about her."

Regnaryn laughed. "I am sure we will all be worried about each other. I know I will. I will be worried for you as well as all the others. But my worry will be tempered by the knowledge that we will face this enemy as well-trained as we can be."

Graeden nodded, but a new look of concern crossed his face.

"What is it?" Regnaryn asked.

Graeden smiled. "Oh, I was just thinking of what hell my poor sister is going to be put through with those two as her teachers."

Regnaryn laughed. "True, so true."

CHAPTER TWENTY-NINE

"I NEVER REALIZED you were such a skillful thief," Ellyss said as they carried the purloined tools and supplies through the woods. "Are there any other nefarious talents I should know about?"

Taaryn smiled.

"Do you really think we will be able to build a suitable shelter in only five days?" she asked, avoiding his question.

"I do. It will be a far cry from luxurious, but it will suffice. Fortunately, Varlama was telling the truth when she said she was not fancy."

"Still…" Taaryn pondered. "How long do you think she will be here?"

"That will depend on you."

"On me?"

"Well, dearest, you are the reason she is coming. So the length of her stay will be determined by what she finds."

"If you are wrong in your assessment of my talents, she may leave the day after she arrives."

"Quite possibly." Ellyss saw the crestfallen look on her face. "But I doubt that will be the case."

She shook her head. "Perhaps."

#

"Varlama's shelter is coming along far better, and faster, than I expected," Ellyss said.

"Faster maybe, but I would not go so far as to call it better," Taaryn said, eyeing their handiwork.

Ellyss hit the wall with the side of his fist. "It is sturdy, and will certainly keep out the weather," he said. "I do not think anyone could ask for more within such a short time. Just a few finishing touches tomorrow, and it will be in fine fettle for Varlama's arrival."

"And since she is not due until the day after, perhaps we can add a few niceties."

"Like what?" he asked.

"I am not sure, just something to make it look less shabby. Something nicer than a tarp for the doorway. And something for the floor, whether she likes fancy or not, I am sure she would prefer not to sleep on the dirt."

He put his arm around her and smiled. "Let us see what we can do."

"I just want her to like this place... and me," Taaryn said. "Even if my abilities turn out to be less than what you expected, I do not want to be a disappointment."

She slipped out of his embrace and walked to the water's edge.

He followed her and again took her in his arms.

"Regardless of the level of your talent or the accommodations, Varlama will not be disappointed with you. You are remarkable, and she will see that as soon as she lays eyes on you. Just as I did."

She looked up at him, surprised by his last comment.

Ellyss chuckled. "Did you not know how smitten I was with you that first night?"

Taaryn shook her head.

He laughed. "So, I was able to keep something from you. That is good to know."

"Are you saying there are things you wish to keep from me?" she asked, trying to mask her fear and sound lighthearted.

"Never." He took her chin is his hand and gently kissed her lips.

She responded by pulling him closer, pushing her hips against him. His body responded to hers. He removed her shirt and ran his thumb across her hard nipple before pinching it between his fingers. She moaned into his mouth.

He removed the remainder of her clothes, tossing them up and away from the water's edge. He reveled in her beauty as she sprawled on the soft sand, her body beckoning him. He stripped off his clothes and accepted her invitation.

#

The sensation of lightly falling raindrops on their naked bodies woke the sleeping couple. It took a moment to remember where they were and another to realize that the sun was already setting.

"Oh, my," Taaryn said, scrambling to her feet and looking for her clothes. "Mother is going to be furious at our tardiness. And I doubt we will have time to wash up before dinner, which definitely will not sit well with her."

"I am afraid so." He looked around and shook his head. "I had hoped to return the tools we borrowed tonight."

Taaryn shook her head. "No. There is no time for that. We will need to do that tomorrow or some other time." She looked at him just standing there. "For goodness sake, stop dillydallying and get dressed. We must hurry."

He did as told and in a matter of minutes the couple were beyond the woods on the way to the Keep.

"We must decide what will we say if asked why we are so late," Taaryn said as they hurried down the path.

"And why we look so," Ellyss added.

She frowned and nodded. "Damn, I wish we had not..."

He grabbed her arm and pulled her toward him. "Not made love?"

Taaryn smiled. "No, not that. That was, as always, wonderful. I wish we had not fallen asleep."

"I agree, but with as hard as we have been working, I am not overly surprised. At least the rains came and woke us, else we might have slept through morning. And that would have taken a great deal more explaining."

Taaryn nodded, and they hurried to the Keep.

#

The sidelong glances of the gate guards did not escape the couple as they entered. Both knew the family's reaction, especially Prescia and Emmaus, would be far more than just a look.

Taaryn and Ellyss entered the dining hall, looking flushed and disheveled. Their appearance did not go unnoticed but the only overt response was Prescia shaking her head.

"I believe an apology is in order from the both of you for making everyone else wait upon you," Prescia said, her voice calm but clearly unhappy.

"After dinner, you can explain both your tardiness and appearance," Emmaus added and rang the bell for the meal to be served.

Taaryn and Ellyss remained in their seats until everyone else had left the dining hall, then rose and approached Prescia and Emmaus.

"I apologize for our rude behavior," Ellyss said. "We had been out walking and lost track of the time."

"And then we got caught in the rain," Taaryn added.

Emmaus grumbled under his breath, but did not respond.

"You need to be more considerate of others," Prescia said. "We were beginning to worry and were getting ready to send a party out to look for you."

"I am sorry, Mother," Taaryn replied.

"You two have been leaving the Keep a great deal lately," Emmaus said. "What are you up to?"

Ellyss squirmed a bit, even though he had been expecting the question. He knew all along it would only be a matter of time before they would have to explain their absences. He had still not come up with a good reason. And he was not ready to tell anyone the truth. Not yet.

"Oh, Emmaus," Prescia said nudging him. "Have you really forgotten what it is like to be young and in love and living in the hustle and bustle of the Keep?"

Emmaus stared at her.

"They need some time alone."

"They can be alone here," he replied. "There is no reason to go wandering off to who knows where."

Prescia laughed. "That was not what you thought when we were their age."

"That was different," he replied.

She laughed again and turned toward Taaryn and Ellyss. "Please, just try to be more aware of the time so I, we, do not worry about you."

Taaryn took her mother's hand and squeezed it. "We will. I promise."

As they left, Ellyss wondered how long Emmaus would accept these flimsy excuses for their absences. If they could just hold out until Varlama finished training Taaryn, then most could be revealed.

#

"If I have not lost a day due to exhaustion," Taaryn said with a smile as she climbed into bed, "Varlama should be arriving the day after tomorrow."

"Yes," Ellyss replied.

"When will they get here?"

"I would think after nightfall. I do not think any of us want to try to explain the presence of two so-called mythical beings arriving midday. They should be within a reasonable distance to communicate with us by tomorrow, so we will have more information then."

Taaryn nodded and looked at him. "So, if all is going according to plan, what is troubling you?"

"What makes you think something is troubling me?"

She laughed but did not answer.

"All right, you are correct. I am concerned about what we will do while she is here."

"What do you mean? Can we not carry on doing what we

have been doing?"

Ellyss got out of bed and began pacing. "We could indeed leave every morning and return for dinner but, as your training intensifies, you run the risk of being injured."

"Injured? How?"

"Nothing serious. More than likely just a few bumps and bruises. The problem will be explaining them to the others. I, for one, do not wish your parents, nor any of your family, to think I am brutalizing you."

Taaryn got out of bed and walked to him. She put her arms around his waist and pulled him toward her. "I know you would never do such a thing."

"Yes, but do they? I still sense your father does not fully trust me and would be more than happy to see me gone."

She looked up into his face. "If you go, so do I. If he or any of the others do not already know that, I will be more than happy to explain it to them in no uncertain terms."

Ellyss smiled. "I am sure you would, but that still leaves us with the dilemma."

Taaryn walked to the sideboard and poured two glasses of wine. She sat on the bed, held out one of the glasses, and motioned him to join her. He did and the two sat, sipping their wine in silence for a few moments.

"What we need is a logical excuse to be gone for an extended period of time."

"Yes," Ellyss said, "and one that will not raise questions or alarm at my absence in regard to Jurcheval's threat."

"Yes, of course. Funny, I had almost forgotten about him." Taaryn took another sip of wine. "Do you have to be physically present for your shielding of the Keep to remain intact?"

"Not really, it only needs to be reinforced periodically. I am sure once Varlama arrives, she can make it even stronger than I have. Why do you ask?"

"If you do not need to be here, we could say we wish to go off, away for a bit. A sort of hunting trip."

Ellyss rubbed his chin. "That might work."

"With everyone already thinking we have been slipping away to be alone, no one will question us any further."

"And we could get whatever supplies we need without any more subterfuge."

"Good, then it is settled." Taaryn stroked his shoulder. "I am looking forward to seeing Curme again."

Ellyss decided he would not tell her that it would not be Curme bringing Varlama.

CHAPTER THIRTY

"AFTER ALL THIS TIME, this is all you have to give me? I told you I wanted twenty people and you bring me a list of five." Jurcheval threw the list of names across the table. "Why do I even bother with you? I will just send those in my private guard out to complete this mission."

The council members looked at each other, none wanting to be the first to speak. All knew someone needed to.

"Sire, I do not wish to disagree with you," Undell said.

Jurcheval arched an eyebrow. "Then, perhaps you should not."

The man took a deep breath and ran his hand through his gray hair, as if that might help to bolster his courage. "From what you have told us of the one you seek, the members of your private guard would more than likely have a difficult time infiltrating the places the boy and his family might be known. And, in this situation, intimidation may not be the best way to get information."

The other two men at the table cautiously nodded in agreement.

"So, you think my men are brutes?" Jurcheval asked.

"Well, they are far from genteel. Our list of names, though short, contains those we think would be most able to gain the trust of villagers and find the information you seek, Sire," Undell said.

"Even then, there are still several problems," Ilyan began.

"Do tell," Jurcheval said, not trying to mask his sarcasm.

"The first," the man continued, "is, as we stated previously, the area you wish to search is quite expansive."

"If you find enough people, it will not be," Jurcheval said and watched the three men squirm.

"I am not sure, even if we find a hundred people, we will be able to adequately search that large an area," Ilyan said.

Jurcheval glared at them. "First, I suggest you find the twenty. Once that is done, I will find a way for them to accomplish their task."

"Even if we find that number of people, how will we communicate with them? If they find something, how long will it take for them to let us know?" Orem asked.

Undell turned to him, whispering, "The listening stones."

Orem gulped as he realized his lapse of memory. "When do you wish to have them set out," he asked, trying to change the subject.

"I will summon you when the time is closer at hand. Now, go. Find more people."

#

"What is this?" Jurcheval frowned at the tarp covered lump the guardsman had just dropped on the floor in front of him.

The guardsman gulped. Even as large and fierce as he was, he, like everyone else in the kingdom, cowered in the presence of Jurcheval.

"It is Worrelk's body, Sire."

It took a moment for the full extent of the man's words to become clear to Jurcheval. As they did, his rage welled inside, his face contorted and he let our an ear shattering roar.

The guardsman became physically afraid as the flames in the fireplaces around the room suddenly tried to escape their confinement and the temperature in the room rose. He wondered if he should, or even could, run. Before he came to a decision, the flames subsided and the room returned to normal. The guardsman looked at the king and saw, while he remained visibly angry, his face no longer resembled that of a demon.

"How did this happen?" Jurcheval asked.

The guardsman explained, watching the king's expression, half-expecting to be struck down at any moment.

"Take that thing and get rid of it," Jurcheval ordered once the guardsman had completed his explanation.

The guardsman gathered up the body and nearly ran out of the room, thankful to have escaped the king's wrath.

#

"This is your doing, niece. I do not know how," Jurcheval ranted to the empty room, "but I am certain you are the reason my wizard failed and my council cannot find the people I need."

He drew in a breath, and his face contorted into a maniacal grin. "No matter, this little setback will not stop me. I am still stronger than you. Oh, how I will savor the moment when, at last, I defeat you.”

He pulled the rope cord and a young servant immediately appeared.

“Summon the Council members.”

The young boy bowed and backed out of the room.

#

“There has been a change in plans,” Jurcheval said to his Council. “That inept wizard went and got himself killed, so there is no need for further delay. Unless, of course, you have found no one else.”

“Sire, it has only been two days since last we met,” Ilyan said, “that has not been sufficient time to complete the task you set for us.”

Jurcheval glared at the man.

“We have found a few more people, but not the desired twenty you requested,” Undell quickly added.

“Show me the list of names,” Jurcheval said.

Undell gave the paper to the young servant boy, who silently appeared from the shadows.

Jurcheval scanned the list and growled. “Only five more. Do you seriously think the plan will succeed with only ten people? And what is this? Why are there females on this list? What good will they be on this mission.?”

“Sire,” Ilyan said, “the women are likely the key.”

“It is true, Majesty, oft times people, especially the sort likely to know of this boy you seek, are more willing to talk to a woman, alone or with a male companion, asking questions than to a lone man,” Undell added. “That is why we are sending out couples.”

“Couples!” Jurcheval shouted and pounded his fist on the table. “Instead of exploring the twenty areas I requested, or the ten you have found people for, the search will now only cover five areas.”

"Unless you can give us more time," Undell said, "that is what we feel is the best plan."

"There is no more time. You had all best hope you are correct in your assessment of the situation."

The three men nervously looked at each other and then back at Jurcheval.

"Bring them to me in the morning, and I will tell you and them the plan," Jurcheval replied.

"Should we not hear of it before then, Sire?" Orem asked. "After all, we are your Council, and we are here to advise you in such matters."

"Do you doubt my ability to devise such a plan?" Jurcheval demanded as he slowly walked behind the questioning man.

Before Orem could reply, Jurcheval snapped his neck.

"Any other questions?" he asked.

Undell and Ilyan silently shook their heads.

"Good. Then I shall see you and your spies in the morning."

"They," Jurcheval said, pointing to the two remaining Council members, "tell me you are the ones to successfully complete the mission I have in store for you. By the looks of you, I am not so sure. Sadly, I have no choice but to make due with what I am given."

The ten soon-to-be spies and the Council members squirmed nervously, but all remained silent. Jurcheval nodded and a servant set a large map on the table. The twelve moved closer for a better look.

"This is where, in just a few days time, you will carry out your mission," Jurcheval said, running his finger over a large area of the map.

One of the men drew in a deep breath, summoned his inner

courage and spoke. "That is quite the distance away. I see no way we can be there in that short amount of time, Sire. Surely it will take over a month to get there on horseback."

"Ah, perhaps you are not as dimwitted as you look. Yes, it would take over a month to travel there by horse, but I have something else in mind. Come. Follow me," Jurcheval said.

He smiled to himself at the confused looks on their faces as he strode past them and through the open door.

#

Jurcheval strode down one passageway and then another, with the others hurrying behind him to keep up. They were more than a little concerned when he turned down a hall that ended in a wall. Jurcheval slowed his pace, savoring the fear emanating from them.

He stopped just short of the end of the hall. Without any visible action on his part, the solid wall evaporated into thin air, eliciting gasps of astonishment and panic from those gathered around him. Jurcheval reached into the opening, seized an already lighted torch from the wall and stepped through the doorway onto the narrow staircase.

The others cautiously followed.

"Do you know where we are going?" Ilyan whispered to Undell as they entered the stairwell after the others.

Undell shook his head. "I have been down this corridor more times than I can count, and I have never been aware of this passageway. I have no idea where it leads."

The men looked at each other, neither wanting to voice the dread they felt.

At the bottom of the stairs, Jurcheval turned down a narrow passageway on the right. After a short time it opened to what appeared to be a massive stable. Fear once again gripped those following him as their minds raced to fathom what could be kept there. It did not take long for their question to be answered.

After just a moment, there was movement in the darkness and first one and then more immense creatures lumbered into view. Several in the group turned to run away, only to find the doorway they entered through was gone, replaced by a solid wall.

Jurcheval approached the beasts. "These are my sevi."

The others turned away in fear.

"Yes, they are quite the sight, are they not? They will be your transport."

"I am sorry to question you, Sire," the spy who had questioned the mode of travel said.

Jurcheval turned and scowled at him.

The spy swallowed hard. "I do not see how these beasts can be any faster than horses. In fact, they seem to be rather slow."

The king let out a hearty laugh, taking everyone by surprise. "That is true. On land they are indeed far slower than a horse, but, these beasts are the result of crossbreeding swamp lizards and dragons. So you see, you will not be traveling by land, you will be flying on their backs."

A collective gasp went up from the would-be spies and the Council members.

"We cannot do that," one of the spies blurted, then quickly covered his mouth.

Jurcheval turned and glared. The spy cowered.

"I think what he means, Sire, is we do not know how to travel upon such beasts," the woman next to him said.

Jurcheval turned his attention to the speaker, then looked around to the other frightened faces and laughed. "If that is your only concern, that should be no problem. They can be quite docile and easier to ride than many a horse I have encountered. "

"Perhaps, Majesty, it would be a good idea for them to have a chance to practice riding on them, even just a short run, before they head out for their destination," Undell suggested.

Jurcheval waved his hand in the air. "Fine. After we finish with the rest of the details of the mission, they can do so this afternoon."

The spies, still stunned not only by the sevi themselves, but by the fact they would be flying on their backs, fell silent.

The king turned and headed toward the exit which, like the doorway upstairs, suddenly reappeared. "Come along now. Do not dawdle. It is almost their feeding time, and I would not want you to be mistaken for dinner."

The spies quickened their step, maintaining their distance behind the king, but wanting to be as far away from the beasts as they could manage.

Once out of the underground stable, the group let out a collective sigh of relief. Upon reaching the throne room, Jurcheval laid out his plan.

"I do not wish to question you, Sire, but do you really think it feasible for us to get from here to there," one of the men asked, pointing to the map, "in only seven days, even if we fly?"

Jurcheval did not reply. The expression on his face told the man his answer.

"Sire, how will we communicate across such a distance?" asked one of the women.

Jurcheval nodded to the young servant boy standing against the wall. The boy brought an ornately decorated cask to the table. The king opened it, revealing ten black stones that reflected the room's light like a crystal prism but one made of obsidian, yet on closer inspection, were neither. Jurcheval reached in and took one of the stones, which fit almost perfectly into the palm of his hand. He showed it to the spies. "With these."

"Are those the famed listening stones?" someone asked.

"Yes," Jurcheval said. "With these I will be able to hear and speak to you and you to me."

The spies and the Council members looked at each other, then at Jurcheval in amazement.

"I have heard of them, but I was not sure they were real," one man whispered.

"Even though you will be traveling in pairs," Jurcheval said, putting the stone back in the cask, "you will each have your own stone."

The king nodded to the servant. He presented the cask to each spy, nodding for them to take a stone from the box. Each gingerly reached into the box and removed a stone, surprised at how they felt.

When the last stone was taken and the servant retreated back into the shadows, Jurcheval looked around the room. "You will keep these stones with you at all times. As of this moment, they are bound to you and you to them," he lied, relishing the distress he knew such a thought would cause them. "I will not elaborate on what will happen if you try to dispose of them. Be warned, it will not be pretty."

The spies said nothing.

"Now, be off to your practice flight. You will leave at dawn tomorrow."

"Sire," Ilyan said. "How do they get back to beasts'..."

Jurcheval scowled.

"I mean, sevi's ," Ilyan quickly corrected himself, "stable so they can ride them?"

Jurcheval smirked and pointed out the window to the grounds behind the palace. "They are already waiting for you."

CHAPTER THIRTY-ONE

"WILL THE WEATHER affect their flight?" Taaryn asked, looking out the window at the gray skies threatening rain.

"I doubt it. After all, drageals are a hearty bunch and a little rain will not stop them. As for Varlama, well, she will not be overjoyed, but she will make do."

"Good."

The couple finished dressing and went downstairs to share the morning meal with the family as they did every day.

"Mother, may I speak to you?" Taaryn asked as the dining hall cleared out.

Prescia stopped and turned to her daughter. "Of course, child, what is it?"

"Ellyss and I would, with your permission, of course, like to go away alone together for a bit."

Prescia eyed the young couple. "I am not surprised, but please do not tell me you plan to leave today in this dreary, wet weather."

The couple nodded. Prescia sighed.

"Fine, fine. I assume there is no point in asking you to wait" Prescia said, not really expecting a response. "How long will you be gone?"

"A few weeks, I think," Ellyss said.

"That is a long time. Just what are you two up to?" she asked, then shook her head. "No, no. I am not sure I really want to know. Just be sure you take enough supplies and such."

Taaryn kissed her mother on the cheek. She and Ellyss quickly left the room to prepare for their departure.

They gathered the supplies they needed and headed down the hall to leave, unsurprised to find Prescia waiting for them at the door. She shook her head at their approach. The two cringed, knowing how difficult it would be to lie to her.

"It is as I thought," she said.

They looked at each other in panic. Prescia smiled.

"I knew you two would forget your rain gear." Prescia laughed at the expression of relief that crossed their faces. "Are you sure you have enough food and supplies for however long you will be gone?"

"I think so," Ellyss said. "And we can hunt for whatever other food we might need."

Prescia handed them the gear and walked away,

"Take care and please be careful," she said without turning back to look at them.

Taaryn and Ellyss stared at each other.

"Oh, I am sure of it. Mother suspects something," Taaryn said as they left.

\#

The rain showed no sign of stopping, so Taaryn and Ellyss decided to spend the night in the shelter they had built for Varlama. They would set up their own camp the next day when the weather improved.

Just after sunset, the couple left the troilhan and called to Varlama.

:*Good evening, you two,*: she said.

:*Hello,*: Taaryn replied. :*How is the trip going?*:

:*A bit on the bumpy side,*: Varlama sighed. :*Thankfully it should only be one more day's flight.*:

:*That is what I thought. You have indeed made good time,*: Ellyss said.

:*So I am told,*: Varlama said.

:*Everything is ready here,*: Taaryn said. :*And I do hope you will like it.*:

:*I am sure it is just fine, my dear. In fact, after being on a drageal's back for three days, even sleeping on a pile of sharp rocks would be comfortable.*:

:*If that is what you want,*: Ellyss laughed, :*we have just enough time to go find them before you arrive.*:

:*That will not be necessary.*:

All three laughed.

:*When do you expect to arrive?*: Ellyss asked.

:*We could be there about this time tomorrow. Dusk should give us enough cover. I am told there is a rock face we could land on in order to stay hidden if we arrive during daylight.*:

:*Yes, there is a rock face, though I know of no one who has ever scaled it,*: Taaryn said.

:*I am sure it will do for the short time we might need it,*:

Varlama replied. *:So, we will see you tomorrow evening then.:*

:Safe flight, my friend,: Ellyss said.

He turned to Taaryn and was not surprised at the large grin on her face.

"Well, my love," he said, "it is a good thing we do not have to return to the Keep tonight. I do not think you would be able to contain yourself."

She nodded. "I know. I am not sure I will even be able to sleep tonight,"

"You had better try."

Taaryn looked at him, as if asking why.

"Knowing Varlama as I do, I would not be in the least bit surprised if she began testing you almost immediately after you two meet."

"No. You cannot be serious. Really?" Taaryn asked.

"It is possible, so I suggest you be prepared."

#

Taaryn woke from a restless night's sleep to another rainy morning.

"Oh, I was hoping the rain would have gone by now. I did not want the weather to be an issue for Varlama," she said as she and Ellyss sat inside the shelter, eating their morning meal of meat pies.

"Other than being wet and probably grumpy, it should be of no concern," he replied. "There is still time for the skies to clear."

"I hope so. What shall we do until then?" she asked.

"I can think of a few things to pass the time." He took her into his arms and kissed her.

She did not object.

#

As hoped, by late afternoon the sky cleared and the rain stopped. With dusk's approach, Taaryn's excitement mounted.

Then, with just the slightest wisp of wind, a drageal appeared. As it came to rest, a figure slid off its back and landed gracefully on the ground beside it.

Taaryn was somewhat surprised. She had assumed Curme would be the drageal who brought Varlama. This was definitely not him. The golden drageal was larger and carried itself with a distinct air of confidence and nobility. As Taaryn watched, she felt an immediate recognition.

She turned her attention to Varlama. Even from this distance, she could tell the tazzamira was somewhat taller than Ellyss and covered with silky white hair that extended from head to foot. The only place not concealed was her face, which radiated an indescribable beauty and purity.

"Ellyss," the white-haired figure said as she waved and loosened the harness-like contraption from the drageals neck. "So good to see you again."

"Taaryn, wonderful to finally meet you," the drageal said.

"Taaryn, may I present Varlama and Phrynia," Ellyss said.

Taaryn stood speechless, staring at the two women.

"I am sure we are quite the sight, child," Varlama said with a smile, "but surely it is not so bad that it frightens you into silence."

Taaryn's face reddened.

"Yes, I must apologize for my appearance. A long flight, bad weather and a less than cooperative passenger," Phrynia said, casting a sidelong glance at the tazzamira, "does little for how one looks."

"It was not that I was uncooperative," Varlama replied, "it was that your flying was reckless at best."

"Reckless? Ha! If I wanted to be reckless, we would have been here two days ago."

:Do not fret, my love,: Ellyss said into Taaryn's mind in response to the concerned look on her face. *:These two always bicker, but they are the best of friends.:*

Taaryn turned to Phrynia.

"I am sorry, I did not mean to be rude," Taaryn said to the drageal. "It is just that you look remarkably like the drageal in the window in the Great Hall of the Keep. Did Graeden not mention that to you?"

Phrynia nodded, acknowledging Taaryn's comment. She did not elaborate.

:Are you ever going to tell those two the truth?: Varlama asked the drageal.

:Perhaps...in time.:

"Where are my manners? Allow me to welcome you to our troilhan," Taaryn said.

"Troilhan? Where did you hear that word?" Varlama asked.

"That is what Ellyss told me these places are called. Is that not right?"

"That is one of its names, one from a time long gone by and a name I have not heard for many years." Varlama turned toward Ellyss. "Where did you learn it?"

"I must have heard it from you. How else would I know it?" Ellyss replied and then cursed himself for making such a blunder.

:What is it?: Phrynia asked the tazzamira.

:I am not sure. I sense there is something different about Ellyss.:

Phrynia chuckled in her friend's mind. *:I think Taaryn may be at the root of that.:*

:No, there is something else, something I cannot quite put my finger on.:

:*Because he used an ancient word? With all his travels, I do not find it odd he knows such a thing. What else has happened that has made your mind uneasy?:*

:*When we first mentioned Jurcheval's name and its meaning, Ellyss definitely overreacted. It was as if the name or its derivation had some meaning to him. Now, his use of a word he should not know, one I am sure I never mentioned to him. You are much older than he is, and you did not know it, did you?:*

Phrynia shook her head. :*I think you may be overreacting.:*

:*Maybe, but in these times, we dare not ignore anything suspicious or out of the ordinary.:*

The drageal agreed.

"Now, let me get a closer look at this shelter you two have built for us," Varlama said. "From here, it looks quite remarkable."

Ellyss laughed. "Well, I would not go that far, but it is adequate."

"I am sorry," Taaryn began, "but I do not believe it is large enough to accommodate both of you."

"I think she was expecting Curme to merely drop Varlama off and then be on his way," Ellyss said.

"Yes, I guess I was, when he brought Ellyss he left the same night. So..." Taaryn was visibly embarrassed at her oversight. "Oh, I am sorry. I was just not expecting you to stay."

:*Did you know Phrynia was coming and staying?:* Taaryn asked Ellyss.

:*I had a feeling that would be the case,:* he replied. :*But I did not tell you because you were already so excited and...:*

She glared at him.

"Do not fear, child. To be honest, I had thought of sending Curme," Phrynia said, lying to try to ease Taaryn's stress. "No one else could handle her." She motioned to Varlama. "She is afraid of flying, or heights, or both. Though, knowing the mountain top she lives on, it makes no sense to me. I swear, if I could not fly, I would not go near it for fear of falling to my death."

"I am not afraid," Varlama said. "I just like to have my feet planted firmly on the ground no matter how high up it is."

"Ha," the drageal snorted. "Be that as it may, you are not a good passenger."

"Honestly, even if we had told you I was staying, there is no way I would have expected a drageal-sized shelter in so short a time," Phrynia said.

"But where will you sleep?" Taaryn asked. "I could go back to the Keep to see if I could get some sort of tarp to make a tent. But...."

"Relax, child," Phrynia said. "If the weather turns nasty, there is shelter to be had nearby. Otherwise, sleeping in this beautiful, soft black sand will do just fine."

"I wanted to talk to you about this sand," Ellyss said. "It is fascinating, almost as if it is alive."

"I agree," Varlama said. "This sand is from the nearby black cliffs."

"I thought so," Ellyss replied.

"It is said, black mountains such as these began their lives as black ice glaciers that were magically solidified. That is why this place is so powerful," Phrynia said.

"Yes," Varlama agreed. "I surmise this is an ancient place, forged near the beginning of time."

"Ah, I see," he replied.

"Will you two be staying here or returning to the Keep?" Phrynia asked.

"We decided it would be best to remain here." Ellyss pointed to the tent off to the side of the shelter.

"And your mother, Taaryn? How did she react to that?" Phrynia asked. "From what Graeden has told us about her, she is quite intuitive. I would not be surprised if she too possessed formidable talents that have just never fully awakened. Perhaps, that is the bloodline from which you both receive your powers."

The drageal chuckled at the surprised look on Taaryn's face.

"Umm, she seemed fine with it, I guess. Though, as you already seem to know, I am sure she suspects something more than us wanting time alone."

"I must say, I am quite impressed with both the shelter and the food stores," Varlama said emerging from the shelter. "Now, let us sit and enjoy a meal and a glass or two of wine while we get to know each other. We will also tell you what we are planning over the next few days."

CHAPTER THIRTY-TWO

"I THINK THAT IS enough for today," Varlama said.

"What? It is barely mid-day," Taaryn replied.

"I know and you are very close to a complete physical collapse, child," Phrynia replied. "Look at yourself, you can barely stand."

"I am fine. Maybe just a short break. To catch my breath and then..."

"No," Ellyss interrupted. "They are right. You are on the brink of damaging both your mind and your body. You need rest."

"I know it has only been a few days, but I have so much to learn," she replied.

"It will do none of us any good, least of all you, if you kill yourself in training," Varlama said. "If that happens, we will not only lose you, but think what that would do to your family."

"And Ellyss," Phrynia added.

"It is about time you stopped being so stubborn and listened. Is all of your family so damned headstrong, or is it just you and Graeden?" Varlama asked.

"I fear it is all of us. Would you not agree, Ellyss?"

He nodded.

"But," Taaryn said, "there is no time to rest. I have accomplished so little."

"I hope it is just your state of fatigue that is clouding your judgment, child," Varlama responded. "You have accomplished far more than any of us had expected in such a short time."

Taaryn looked surprised at her teacher's praise.

"Look at what you can do, not what you have not yet mastered."

Varlama could see the young girl still did not understand.

"When we first arrived, you could neither reflect an attack on command, nor did you know how you had previously done it. Now, you can easily make your shielding reflective at will."

"Yes," Taaryn replied, "but I have yet to gain control over how I reflect the attack."

Phrynia threw up her hands in disbelief. "This is maddening. First Regnaryn, then Graeden, and now you. You all act the same."

Taaryn looked confused.

"The three of you have no concept of your own powers and how amazing you are."

Taaryn's face reddened.

"How long have you been training? In fact, how long have you even been aware you possessed such an ability?" Phrynia asked.

"Umm," Taaryn began, "not very long. Less than a month."

"And you think in less than a month you should be further

along?"

Taaryn opened her mouth to answer, but Varlama cut her off.

"Have you any idea just how long most people train in order to simply recognize the mechanism necessary to use even the most commonplace of abilities?"

Taaryn shook her head.

"Well, I do. It can sometimes be a lifetime."

"A lifetime? We do not have that kind of time. If that is the case, I wish I had never found out about them. Partially trained will be worse than not being trained at all."

Varlama laughed. "Oh, the drama of youth." She turned to Phrynia. "How many times have we seen such emotions in the last few years?"

"From all three of them. Were we that overly dramatic to our teachers?"

"Probably, but enough reminiscing." Varlama smiled and turned back to the girl. "Taaryn, we all know it will take you far less than a lifetime to master your abilities, but it will still take time. During that time, you must be at your best, lest you get hurt or hurt someone else."

"We are not trying to impede your training by making you rest, we are trying to keep you safe," Phrynia said. "You must remember that reflective shielding is an extremely rare ability. The main reason an ability is rarely seen is that it is extremely difficult to unveil, not to mention master. You have not only unveiled it, you are well on your way to mastering it."

Ellyss added, "When you add the fact that you also mastered another ability shortly before that, your abilities are unbelievable."

"That is right. In a matter of a few months, you have exhibited two very rare and powerful abilities and a third more common but nonetheless powerful one," Varlama said.

"Two rare abilities?" Taaryn asked.

Phrynia again threw up her hands and walked away muttering to herself.

"Yes, two. Do you not consider your ability to mindspeak to anyone over the distances you do rare? I certainly do. None of us can do it. Even Graeden can only speak to you."

Taaryn's face reddened slightly. "Oh, I had forgotten about that."

"Exactly. That is because you have made it and your shielding abilities a part of you, and in a very brief amount of time."

"But," Taaryn replied, "it is imperative that I master this ability as quickly as possible."

"That is true," Varlama said. "We do not have years for you to accomplish this. Had Phrynia and I suspected it would take that long, we would not have even begun your training. In all of my years, I have only had one student who was a faster learner than you, and she, well, she too is extraordinary. While our time may be at a premium, I do not believe taking a day or two off will upset the balance of the universe."

"As we said earlier," Phrynia added, "what good will it be if you injure, or worst yet, kill yourself in the process of learning."

Taaryn wanted to argue, but her mind and body told her they were right. She reluctantly conceded.

"All right," she said, mustering a half-hearted smile. "I see that I am outnumbered. I guess I am a little tired, a bit of a rest might be good."

She leaned against Ellyss, yawned, closed her eyes and allowed her exhaustion to take over. Ellyss picked her up and carried her to their tent. He laid her down, covered her and kissed her forehead.

#

Ellyss returned to the two women. "I am glad we finally got her to rest. How long do you think she will sleep?"

"At her level of exhaustion," Varlama replied, "she probably needs at least three days to fully recover. Even with the shield I set in place to block all outside intrusions, I would not be surprised if she awakens well before then. If her rest is peaceful, that might be enough."

Ellyss drew in a breath. "Do you really think she is that fatigued. How did I not notice it before now?"

"It seems my friend that she has also learned how to shield her physical state. Neither of us were aware of the extent of it until just a little while ago," Varlama replied.

"Yes," Phrynia added, "it was only when her mental state reached a point where she could no longer maintain the shield that we detected the truth. It is amazing she kept her strength up as long as she did. She will be a formidable force to reckon with. I am glad she is an ally."

Ellyss said, "She has been training at less than maximum or even near maximum strength?"

"Yes, that is what I believe. So, when she resumes training, her ability to fully control the reflective shield should happen in a very short time," Varlama replied. "I would not be surprised to see the level of intensity of her reflective attacks increase, too."

"In that case, we will need to ensure we, too, are well rested," Phrynia said.

The others agreed.

"I am going to sit with her," Ellyss said. "Shall we meet for dinner or is there something else we need to discuss?"

Varlama patted his shoulder. "No, dinner will be fine."

#

"I have been thinking," Varlama said when she and Phrynia were alone.

"About what?"

"Karaleena's prophecy and Romeiko's chiding of us. Could Taaryn be the one Karaleena spoke of standing beside Regnaryn and not Graeden?"

"That thought crossed my mind, as well. If Romeiko was correct about outside forces coming to our aid, she would fit that, as well."

"When do you think we should tell her of this?"

The drageal looked off into the distance. "After she has completed her training. I think then she will be better able and willing to accept this additional responsibility."

"And what of her relationship with Ellyss? It seems quite serious."

The tazzamira snorted. "That is an understatement. In all the years I have known Ellyss, this is the first time I have ever seen him involved with anyone. There seems to be something unique in what they have, something beyond even a soulbond."

"Ah, good, you sense that, too. I wondered if it was just my imagination. So, should we tell him now or when we tell her?"

"I think they should be told at the same time," Varlama replied.

Phrynia nodded. "And once told of the prophecy and what we think it means, we can contact the others in Reissem Grove and make final plans to stop Jurcheval."

CHAPTER THIRTY-THREE

AT DAWN THE SPIES gathered, each carrying their gear and the listening stones. Though it was not spoken, each harbored fears of flying on the backs of the beasts. Fears the few trial runs they had the day before did nothing to remove.

"Lord Undell," one of the women said, "I understand how we will speak with the King, but how will we communicate with the beasts?"

Undell shook his head. "You will not. They have been instructed by the King, in whatever way he speaks with them, where they are to take you."

The spies all looked at each other in horror.

"Surely, you do not mean we will fly the entire time without landing?" one of the others asked.

"No. From what I have been told, and mind you, it is very little, you will fly from dawn until just after sunset each day until you reach your destination."

Undell's reply only sparked more questions. Before they could be asked, the King arrived.

Jurcheval strode past the spies and went to each of the sevi and stroked their necks. Then he turned and faced Undell and the others.

"It is time. Do not fail me," Jurcheval said and walked away.

The spies approached the waiting sevi. As they had done the day before, they climbed into the two-person harnesses attached to the beast's back and, with no prodding from the riders, the sevi took flight.

#

It was almost dark when the sevi landed. As soon as their passengers were off their backs, the beasts were quickly aloft again.

"That had to be one of the worst days of my life," one of the men said as he dropped on all fours and kissed the earth beneath him. "It is unnatural for man to not have his feet firmly on solid ground."

"I think one of the worst things is not having any control," another said. "Being at their mercy."

"Or any way to communicate with them," a third spy said.

Everyone agreed.

"Well, we had better get used to it, since we have to do this again for the next several days," one of the others said.

The first man shook his head. "Please do not remind me. Perhaps the beasts will not return."

"Somehow, I doubt that will happen."

"I know, but one can always hope," the first man said with a smile.

"That may be, but for now we need to eat and then rest," someone said.

The others agreed. A short while later the group sat around the fire, eating and chatting.

"You know, I bet if we wanted to, we could slip away and not have to go through with this mission at all," one of the men said.

The others quickly shushed him.

He laughed. "Ha! What can happen?"

"Do you not recall we each carry one of the King's listening stones?"

"You do not really think these silly things work, do you?" He removed the stone from his pocket. "It is merely a rock, grant you a pretty one, but a rock just the same, with no more power than any strewn around this campsite."

In the next moment, the man gasped for air. He dropped the listening stone, and he clawed at his throat as if trying to remove some unseen thing from around his neck.

"Do you really want to know the pretty rock's true power? To find out what can happen if you try to disobey me?" Jurcheval's voice boomed seemingly from everywhere.

The man struggled against the unseen force until it finally released him. He fell to his knees, coughing as the air once again filled his lungs.

"Be thankful I am in a generous mood today," Jurcheval said, his voice calm but nonetheless menacing. "Should I hear such talk again, from any of you..."

He did not finish, he did not need to. The threat was clear and all knew it.

The spies sputtered words of loyalty, all the while glaring at the man who had incited the anger of the king. They cowered, fearful he might change his mind and strike out at them. After several moments of silence, they looked at each other, shaking their heads, still afraid to utter a single word.

"It is late," one of them whispered after a few more minutes. "We should retire. There is yet another long day ahead of us tomorrow."

#

The spies awoke to find the sevi had returned. The beasts sat motionless a fair distance from the camp.

"They are quite disarming, sitting there glaring at us," one woman said.

"I think we should make haste to eat and prepare to leave," another said. "My gut tells me they are not a patient breed."

When the last of the campfire's embers were extinguished, one of the sevi reared its head and let out an ear splitting, dissonant bellow. The noise took the spies by surprise: up until that moment, the beasts had never made any noise, not even the slightest grunt. Now, they felt as if their heads would explode from it.

It took a few moments for the spies to recover and feel it safe to remove their hands from their ears.

"I do believe it thinks it is time for us to be on our way," one of the spies said.

"But how does it know that?" asked another.

"I am not sure I really want to know," a third said. "But I suggest we hurry up and be on our way lest they all decide to speak."

The others agreed. Within a few moments, all sat atop their rides after bidding farewell and good luck to each other.

Almost as soon as the humans settled on their backs, the five sevi took flight on their appointed paths.

#

Another four days of the same routine ensued—flying from dawn until almost dark, then being left by the sevi only to have them reappear the next morning. The only difference now was that each team was alone.

On the sixth morning, Pavela and Castell, the only married couple, awoke to find the sevi had not returned.

"Does this mean we have reached our destination?" Pavela asked.

"It would appear so," Castell replied.

"I wonder how the others are doing," she said.

"I am sure they are all fine," he replied, "though, I do believe we are the first to be done with the flying beasts. Can you hand me the map from my pack?"

She reached into the bag lying on the ground next to her and handed him the map.

"If all went according to plan, we should be here." He pointed to a spot marked on the map

She nodded. "After we eat, we should head toward this village."

"Yes, it looks like it should take a full day's walk, maybe two, from here. Then we will see if we can discern any information about the boy."

"In the meantime, we need to come up with a more solid plan, a reason why we are asking about him."

Castell nodded. "I am sure your devious little mind can come up with something before we get there."

She smiled. "If we are lucky, they will know of whom we

speak. Otherwise, we will need to continue our travels to the next village and the next. Do we have enough money to buy a horse? That would make the travel so much easier and faster."

"I believe we do."

"Good. The sooner we can finish this mission, the sooner we can get home."

"Shh," he said. "Do not forget, he is listening."

CHAPTER THIRTY-FOUR

TAARYN OPENED HER eyes and immediately recognized her location.

"Why have you brought me here again?" she asked into the darkness.

Her question resulted in muffled snickers.

"Why am I here?" she shouted. "If you will not speak to me, send me back."

Her words had barely left her lips when the red column of smoke appeared before her.

"Your bravado tells me you have discovered what you are."

"If you mean my abilities, yes, I now know that."

"And what do you mean to do with these abilities? Take over the world?"

"Of course, not. We are trying to defend against another who has that intent."

"And once you defeat that one, what then?" He swirled around her until he formed a blur of red before her eyes. "Will he charm you into then taking over the world as he once attempted? Is that why he is having you trained by those two? So he can make another play for power? Did he tell you of his past? When he was Jurcena, a minor demon with delusions of grandeur and power? Has he mentioned any of the monstrous things he did?"

Taaryn stood her ground. "I know of his past and yours, Xanchad."

The smoke re-formed into a column before her. "Ah, so he has not forgotten me. That is good. What did he tell you of me?"

"I know what you have condemned him to. Has he not yet paid for his crimes? How many lifetimes have you made him endure? How many times have you given him a glimmer of hope or happiness only to snatch it away? Who is the real monster here?"

In the next moment the cave was filled with black smoke figures. "Kill her. Kill her now," they hissed. They swirled around her until they engulfed her body and filled her lungs.

Taaryn choked and clawed at the air to free herself. And then, they disappeared. She opened her eyes to see Xanchad, in the shape of Ellyss, standing before her.

"I am impressed, human. You have come a long way in a short time. You are no longer the same frightened child as the last time we met."

She did not respond. He moved closer, touching her face and making it burn. She tried to recoil, but she could not move. He walked around her and leaned in until his lips brushed against her ear, his breath making her skin feel as if it would burst into flame.

"Let me show you what the future holds for you and him."

In the next moment, Taaryn was swept into a vision. Similar to the one she experienced the first time she looked into Ellyss' eyes, now the visions were controlled. She clearly saw each thing Xanchad wanted her to view. She tried to look away, but she could not.

"What is your purpose?" she asked.

"So you know the truth. All of it, even that which he does not yet know."

#

"Good morning, sleepy head," Ellyss said as Taaryn emerged from the tent. He walked to her. "I assume you had a good rest."

She nodded as he gently kissed her. "I guess I really did need a good night's sleep, after all."

"Closer to two days of sleep," Phrynia replied.

Taaryn looked confused. "Why did someone not wake me?"

"With how far you allowed your strength to be depleted, we knew it would be best to let your body decide when to wake," Varlama said.

"And now that you are fully rested, we can continue with your training," Phrynia said and attacked her from the rear with a large rock.

Taaryn easily deflected it.

"Please, come sit and eat," Varlama said. "There will be no more attacks until you have finished your meal. I promise."

"Thank you," the young girl said as she took the chunk of bread the tazzamira held out. She took a small bite and then quickly devoured the rest of it.

"I think I will be able to better control the reflective attacks today," she said when she finished both the hunk of bread and several pieces of meat.

Varlama was glad to hear the girl's assertion, but coyly asked, "And why is that, child?"

"Because I saw myself doing it," Taaryn answered. "I had a dream where I was able to do it with complete control."

Taaryn was careful not to reveal anything else she had seen in her dream.

"It is good that you feel that way," Varlama said. "But dreams and reality are not the same thing. I am not saying you cannot do this today. I just do not want you to lose confidence if your dreams and reality do not match immediately."

:I was just going to say the same thing,: Ellyss mindspoke to Varlama.

:I thought as much. But those words will hold less of a sting coming from me than from you. A teacher's words do not stab one's heart as deeply as those of a lover.:

"Yes, I know that," Taaryn replied after swallowing the mouthful of tea. "In my dreams, not only did I see myself controlling the attacks but for the first time I clearly saw how to control them. Now, I understand, and I will be able to do it. I am certain of it."

"All right then," Varlama said, "as soon as you are done with your meal, we will start."

#

"Today did not go nearly as well as I had hoped it would," Taaryn said as the group prepared for dinner. "My aim is still off, and I am not yet able to control the intensity of the reflection. I expected to be much better."

Ellyss almost spit out the tea he was drinking.

"My goodness, woman," he said. "Just a short time ago, you

were barely able to keep your reflective power intact. Now, in just one day, you can call it up on demand, and you are complaining about not being able to control it completely. Not only that, but look at yourself. You do not seem to be fatigued at all and today's session was not an easy one, not by any stretch of the imagination."

Taaryn laughed. "I guess you are right. It is just that I had such high hopes of mastering it all today."

"You accomplished a great deal, child," Varlama said. "Far more than we expected, even with your dream claim."

Phrynia and Ellyss nodded in agreement.

"Still, I expected to do better," Taaryn said. "Oh well, there is always tomorrow."

#

Ellyss and Taaryn bid the others good night and headed off to their tent.

"What do you think of our charge's change in attitude?" Phrynia asked.

"I am not sure. I think there is more to this dream than she is telling us," Varlama replied.

"Do you think we should try to find out what else there was to it?"

"No, if it was something she wanted us to know, she would tell us. It will be interesting to see if she shares the rest of it with Ellyss."

"Even if she does, would he tell us?" Phrynia asked.

"If it were important to the fight against Jurcheval, he would."

"I hope so. And if she says nothing to him?"

"Hmm, I am not sure," Varlama said. "You know, old friend, we could just be creating imaginary monsters in the shadows. "

"Or the dream could have more serious ramifications."

"You are not thinking Jurcheval might have somehow found her in her dreams, are you?"

"I certainly hope not," Phrynia said. "But we both know dreams are one of the methods he employs to control people. I remember what he did to Regnaryn."

"Still, I doubt he could have found Taaryn in this place, even on the dream plane. I doubt the shieldings of this place could be breached by anyone, but her attitude changed far more than one would think even a good rest would cause. We will just have to be watchful and wait to see what happens."

Phrynia nodded. "Speaking of a good rest, I think it is time we afford ourselves the same luxury."

CHAPTER THIRTY-FIVE

"TAARYN, WE HAVE taught you as much as we can," Varlama said. "It is now up to you to maintain and possibly enhance your skills through practice."

"I am not sure what to say," Taaryn replied.

Her two teachers smiled.

"There is something we need to tell you. Something we learned from Karaleena's journals that we believe affects you," Phrynia said.

"Me?" Taaryn asked. "How could Karaleena know of me? I know she knew my mother, but that was years before I was born and long after the two had parted company."

"Your mother knew Karaleena? That is, indeed, a coincidence," Varlama said.

:More like the fates closing the circle,: Phrynia mindspoke to Varlama.

"Are Graeden and Regnaryn aware of this?" Phrynia asked.

Taaryn looked to Ellyss, and he shrugged. "I am not sure if we told him. We found out when we were first looking for the village."

"Ah, I see," Varlama said. "I am sure your mother is thrilled to have her son mated to the daughter of her old friend."

"As would Karaleena herself," Phrynia added.

Taaryn nodded. "But you said there was a prophecy that mentioned me?"

Varlama recited the prophecy and then looked to Taaryn. "At first, we thought Graeden would be the one of near equal power. Now, we feel it is you."

"No, that cannot be right," Taaryn said, shaking her head. She walked away from the others, pacing and muttering to herself.

After several moments, she turned back toward the others. "Surely, you are mistaken. From what I have heard of Regnaryn's powers, what she can do, I am nowhere near her equal. Not now, not ever."

"We disagree," Phrynia said. "It is true that right now, Regnaryn has more power than you, but that is because she has had more time and training. And who knows what other abilities might awaken within you in time. "

"Do not forget," Ellyss added, "she has been subjected to several ordeals that forced her magic and powers to come forth faster and in a far more explosive fashion."

As the others tried to convince her, Taaryn realized this was what Xanchad had been alluding to in their last meeting, what she had not understood at the time. Now, his words and those of Karaleena's prophecy made so much of what was happening make sense.

"It still seems pretty far-fetched to me, but if all of you are convinced, I will accept it."

The others were relieved.

"I think we have found the outside forces Romeiko told us about," Varlama said.

"Should we contact those in Reissem Grove and tell them we are ready?" Ellyss asked.

"Ready? I think not," Varlama said.

"I do not understand," Ellyss replied.

"We should have some semblance of a plan together before we contact them. I am sure they will devise one, as well," Varlama said.

"I agree," Phrynia said. "Our first decision is do we go to him or let him come to us."

For the next few hours, they discussed and argued both scenarios until they reached a consensus.

"Now, it is time to contact those in Reissem Grove," Varlama said, "and learn of their plan."

"But we need to leave this place in order to do that," Taaryn said. "Where will we go?"

"It must be somewhere where you two will not be seen, in case someone happens by," Ellyss added.

"And where we can stay a few days," Varlama said.

"I have the perfect spot," Phrynia said. The lilt in her voice made Varlama cringe.

"You do not mean?" the tazzamira asked. "Surely, there is somewhere else we could go."

The drageal laughed. "There is no better place. It has the height you so love, it will afford us great visibility in all directions and no one will be able to see us so we can easily stay there as long as we need to."

Varlama groaned. "I was afraid that was where you were thinking."

"Where?" Taaryn asked, no longer able to contain her curiosity.

"Up there." Phrynia pointed to the nearby black cliff.

"There is no way to get there," Taaryn replied.

The drageal chuckled.

"That old lizard means to fly us up there," Varlama snapped.

"Of course, how silly of me to forget." Taaryn flushed a deep red. "But is there really a place for us to even stand? We have always thought the summit was sharp, jutting rock points."

"Yes, you would," Phrynia said. "That is indeed how it appears from the ground. From the air, the jagged rocks are only on the edges of the cliff, almost like a wall, and the interior is quite flat."

"How will you get us up there?" Taaryn asked. "Surely, you cannot carry us all at once."

"No, I will make three trips, one with each of you. We will leave tomorrow, just after sunset. Who wants to go first?"

Taaryn could barely contain her excitement. "Me. Please, take me first. I have never flown and it seems so exciting an adventure."

Varlama harrumphed and turned away, grumbling to herself.

The drageal smiled and nodded.

#

Taaryn was up before sunrise. She walked down to the water's edge and sat staring at the cliff.

"Why am I not surprised you were unable to sleep," Phrynia said as she approached.

"I am sorry. Did I disturb you?"

"No. I have actually been expecting you. Would you like to go to the cliff top now, before the day breaks?"

"Could I? That would be wonderful."

"Good, then let us go."

"Do I need to take anything?" Taaryn asked.

"Some food and something to keep yourself warm. It tends to be a bit brisk atop cliffs."

The girl nodded and ran off to get what the two would need. She returned in a matter of minutes.

"What should I do?" Taaryn asked as the drageal crouched low to the ground.

"Just climb up on my back and find a comfortable spot close to my neck, then wrap the straps around your waist and hold on to my feathers."

Taaryn nodded and quickly did as instructed.

"You can hold on my feathers a bit tighter, child. You will not hurt me."

As soon as Phrynia felt Taaryn had a good grip, she took off.

Taaryn gasped as the tops of the trees were in her sightline. "This is amazing," she shouted. "Such a beautiful sight."

"We have a bit of time," Phrynia said, "would you like to stay aloft a little longer before we land?"

"Oh, yes. Yes."

The drageal soared higher into the still star-filled sky. She felt Taaryn's excitement as the girl clung to her neck.

Too soon, the sky began to lighten with the hint of the dawn and the soaring pair headed to the cliff top.

Once they landed, Taaryn slid off Phrynia's back. Phrynia turned to see the young girl grinning from ear to ear.

"Words cannot describe the joy I am feeling right now.

Thank you so much."

"It was my pleasure, child. I must say, you are a far better passenger on your first flight than Varlama is even after all these years."

Taaryn shook her head. "I do not understand how she cannot appreciate the beauty of what one can see from the sky and the feel of the wind across your face. Even in darkness, it was amazing. I can only dare to imagine what it is like in daylight."

"Yes, the sights are magnificent. The beauty of the land and the sky still astound me. Now that the sun is up, you and I can decide where to set up camp for our stay here."

"But how can we let Ellyss and Varlama know where we are?" Taaryn asked.

Phrynia laughed. "I am sure they will figure it out."

#

"I think those two left early so they would not have to help gather supplies," Varlama said.

"It is probably just as well they did. I am not sure Taaryn could have contained her excitement all day," Ellyss said.

"You may be right. So, tell me about you two."

He stiffened at the request. "There is nothing to tell."

"Oh, come now, old friend. In all the years I have known you, you have never been with a woman for more than a night or two of lust and frolic. You have not been quite yourself lately, and I am curious to know if it is her, or something else."

Ellyss gulped. He had feared Varlama suspected something. He cursed himself for the blunders he had made and wondered what Varlama was thinking.

"Believe me, I was as surprised as you, maybe even more so,

when this turned into what it is. But that is the way these things happen, right? There is never a rhyme or reason, it just happens."

"Yes, that is true."

He hoped she meant her words, and there would be no more questions. He also knew he needed to be far more careful about what he said about things he should have no knowledge of.

They gathered the supplies for the stay on the cliff with no further discussion of anything but what they should take.

Once gathered, it became apparent that even the bare necessities were more than Ellyss could carry alone. Varlama reluctantly agreed and grumbled that at least it was only a short trip.

"Well, now that is done, what is your plan for your day?" Varlama asked.

"I am going to lie down and get a good sleep. Taaryn has been so stressed and excited since this all began, she has not slept well, which means I have not slept well."

"I am sure you two found something to do with those wakeful hours."

For the first time since she had met him, Ellyss blushed. "Well, yes, but even as enjoyable as that might be, one still requires sleep. So, if there is nothing more you need of me, I shall get some rest. Please wake me a bit before Phrynia is due back."

#

Just after dusk, Phrynia arrived. "Well, I see you two have been busy," she said, pointing to the supplies.

"Yes, and with no help from you. Is that why you brought Taaryn up there this morning? To get out of helping?" Varlama asked with a sly grin.

"You found me out, old friend. That was exactly my plan."

All three laughed.

"I think you should take Varlama first," Ellyss said. "I think she will be more at ease with some visibility of her surroundings."

"Ha! As if it matters, broad daylight, dusk, dark of night, it is all the same to her. She just hates to fly. Taaryn, on the other hand, took to it like a one of my own babes. If she had not been in such awe of the experience, I would have thought she had been flying her entire life."

"Wonderful, she loves to fly, and I do not," Varlama grumbled. "Shall we get this over with. At least this time, it will be over quickly."

Ellyss chuckled as the two friends continued to bicker. Once out of earshot, he gathered the things he would take.

In a short time, Phrynia returned. He climbed onto her back, and they were off.

#

When they landed, Ellyss and Phrynia were a little surprised to see Varlama and Taaryn had set up the tent and were now chatting away. The pair immediately stopped and came over to help get the new supplies sorted out.

"You do know we will not be able to have a fire after dark," Ellyss said. "The sight of light or smoke up here might cause alarm below."

"Ah, of course," Taaryn replied. "I had not really thought of that. So, that is why you brought only those things we could eat as is."

Ellyss nodded.

"We have picked a good few days to stay up here, the moon is almost full, so we shall not be stumbling around in complete blackness and possibly fall off the edge," Varlama said.

"Yes, the timing was indeed fortuitous. Now, I suggest we gather our dinner and contact Reissem Grove," Phrynia said.

"I already spoke with Graeden and told him to gather the others together," Taaryn said. "I am sure they are waiting for us."

"Good thinking, child," Phrynia replied.

CHAPTER THIRTY-SIX

:WHERE ARE YOU? Surely you are not strong enough to break through one of those places' barriers. Are you?: Graeden's last question was asked almost as an aside, as if he really did not want to know.

:No. We are atop the black cliff.:

:What! How can that be? They are merely sharp-edged rocks.:

Taaryn chuckled. *:That is what I said, but it turns out they are very flat and full of lovely vegetation.:*

:But, how? How did you get up there?:

:The same way the others got here. On the back of a drageal. And, if you have never done so, I will tell you, flying is an amazing adventure.:

Graeden was taken aback by his sister on several levels. Her confidence far exceeded the way she had acted the last time they had spoken. And now, flying on a drageal's back. If he were honest with himself, he was not sure he would be so thrilled to do such a thing.

:*I understand you two have a lot to say to each other, but right now we have more pressing matters to attend to than where we are and how we got here,*: Phrynia interrupted.

:*I am sorry,*: the twins said in unison and then laughed.

:*Where are our manners?*: Regnaryn said. :*Taaryn, you have yet to meet all that are here. Allow me to introduce everyone.*:

#

After the introductions concluded, Varlama spoke. :*We have news that will interest all of you. First, Taaryn's powers are, indeed, real and far more impressive than Ellyss led us to believe. With time and the right training, she will be quite formidable, almost as powerful as Regnaryn.*:

:*You cannot be serious,*: Graeden said.

:*I am very serious. In fact, I believe she is the one mentioned in Karaleena's prophecy and the outside force Romeiko spoke of.*:

Even without him saying anything, Taaryn sensed Graeden's disbelief and distress over that statement.

:*I did not believe it either, Graeden, when they first told me, but...*:

:*But, what? What nonsense have you been filling my sister's head with? Tales of fame and glory? Well, there is no such thing in battle. There is only terror and pain and loss.*:

:*Graeden,*: Taaryn snapped. :*You know better. These are our allies. No, they are more than that. They are our friends, our family, and they would never do such a thing. I know you worry about me, you always have, but I will be fine. I understand what we are facing, and I would rather meet it head on than to quiver in hiding like a feckless coward.*:

Graeden was shocked not only at his sister's words, but at her tone. Though never meek, she now spoke with the voice of a warrior.

He apologized. Varlama continued. *:Have we had any news of what Jurcheval is up to?:* She waited a few moments and then continued. *:Your silence leads me to believe we have not, and that concerns me. He does not strike me as one who would simply give up. Yet, that seems to be the case.:*

Everyone agreed.

:So, why have we heard nothing? Has he found a new, even more surreptitious means to exact his evil? Is he even still within his castle?: Phrynia asked.

:Romeiko, you are the one who gave us not only his name but his location. Are you still able to see him? See what he is doing?: Varlama continued the questions.

:My vision is limited from within the confines of the Grove, and I dare not leave just yet. But from what I can glean, he is still in his castle and still trying to find a way to get to Regnaryn. I must tell you, if the curse manifests the same in him as it did in his uncle, each defeat he has suffered at Regnaryn's hands has eaten away at any semblance of sanity within him, thus making him even more dangerous and unpredictable when he does decide to strike.:

:And you just thought to tell us that little tidbit now?: Graeden asked.

Romeiko did not respond.

:Then, we must strike first,: Phrynia said, ignoring Graeden's question.

:Do you have a plan?: Ayirak asked.

:We do.:

:As do we,: Ayirak added.

Both groups revealed their plans and surprisingly, or possibly not, both proved to be very similar. Both still needed some fine-tuning, but all agreed they had a good start. The meeting ended with each group having some things to consider. They decided to speak again in two days.

#

"What is it, Taaryn?" Phrynia asked. "Did the meeting fatigue you?"

Taaryn shook her head. "No, that is not it. I am unsure how I should feel right now. I am both excited and afraid."

"If you were not afraid of the coming battle, I would fear for your sanity," Varlama said.

The girl smiled.

"I have been thinking that, once you and Ellyss join the others, Phrynia and I should make our camp here."

"You will not be coming with us?" Taaryn asked.

"No, we will need to remain here so Jurcheval will not be able to detect Hammarsh Keep and possibly launch an attack to distract you should he hear of our plans."

"Of course," Taaryn said. "But why here and not in the troilhan?"

"We cannot maintain the Keep's protective shield for any length of time from within."

A look of panic crossed Taaryn's face. "Ellyss has been here all this time. I know he said he could be gone for short periods of time but...please tell me you are not saying that my training time has left the Keep unprotected and vulnerable."

"Have you not noticed that every day or so, Ellyss slips away for a short time?" Phrynia asked.

Taaryn shook her head.

"Well, he has. And during that time, he ensures that his

shielding is still in place and as strong as ever."

"We plan on putting an even sturdier shield in place. One that will require both of our skills," Varlama said. "Since I have no intention of flying back and forth every day, we will just remain here. The tent will not be as luxurious as the shelter you built, but it will do."

"I would also like to propose that we make arrangements to have someone from the Keep in a position for us to communicate with them. To keep them apprised of any developments, should they arise," Phrynia said.

"So you still think Jurcheval will find and attack Hammarsh even with the shieldings?" Taaryn asked.

"I do not know, but it would be better to prepare for such a thing that never comes than to be caught off guard and defenseless if it does."

"Gantell has been working on a plan of action, should they come under attack. From what he shared with me before we left, it looked very promising," Ellyss said. "He would be the most likely candidate."

"I am not sure how Gantell will, well, how do I say this without offending you..." Taaryn said to Phrynia and Varlama.

Varlama laughed. "Just say it, girl. There is little you, or anyone else, can say that will offend us."

"I am not sure how Gantell will react to seeing you two. He says he accepts you are real but I think at some level he still does not fully believe in you."

"Yes, you are right," Ellyss said. "What about including Matteus? He seems far more open and perhaps with both of them, well..."

"Wait, how will you do that? I mean, neither of them can

mindspeak? And if you two are here and they there..." Her voice trailed off.

"There are other ways of touching one's mind," Varlama said.

"And do not be so sure the rest of your family cannot mindspeak," Phrynia added. "Perhaps they have just never tried."

"I never thought of that." Taaryn said. "Will you also communicate with my parents? I think they, too, as the Lord and Lady of the Keep, need to be informed of what is going on."

"Of course," Phrynia said.

"When will you contact them? You are not planning on just popping into their heads, are you?"

Varlama and Phrynia laughed.

"No, that would not be a good idea. We assumed before you go off to face Jurcheval, you would want to visit your family," Varlama said. "At that time, you can tell them of both the plan and us and we will contact them then."

"Sounds good."

CHAPTER THIRTY-SEVEN

"I THINK IT IS WONDERFUL that Taaryn mastered her abilities so quickly," Trebeh said.

Graeden shook his head, growled under his breath and stormed out of the house.

"I think he fears for his sister. And with all the talk of battle…" Regnaryn sighed. "I should go after him and make sure he is all right."

"No, child, leave him be for just a little while. As much as you are bound to him, he is connected to his sister in a way only they can understand. Give him some time alone to come to grips about this latest development."

Regnaryn nodded.

"Taaryn is quite amazing," Ayirak said. "Though I should not be surprised, she and Graeden are cut from the same cloth."

Both Trebeh and Regnaryn looked at him in shock.

"So, you have finally come to see what the rest of us do about the boy," Trebeh said with the slightest chuckle.

Ayirak looked at her and smiled. "I suppose I have."

For almost a full hour, they discussed both the meaning of the meeting and what needed to be done. As they left, Graeden had still not returned.

"Do not worry, dear," Trebeh said.

Regnaryn nodded. "I know. It is just he is so upset."

"He will be fine," the yekcal replied and kissed her on the forehead. "Good night, my child."

"Good night, Mama."

Regnaryn tried to keep busy while she waited for Graeden to return, first straightening up then reading a book. Finally, she went upstairs, changed into her night clothes and called to him.

:Are you alright?:

He did not immediately respond.

:Graeden, I know you can hear me. Please answer.:

:I am as well as I can be, I guess,: he replied at last.

:Come home. They are all gone now.:

:I know, I saw them leave. I am on my way.:

It was only a few moments before she heard Graeden enter through the back door and climb the stairs.

"I am sorry," he said as he entered the room. "I did not mean to act so childishly."

"You have nothing to apologize for. You reacted as any of us would under the same circumstances."

She kissed him softly on the cheek and led him over to the bed.

"Do you want to talk about it? Or do you just want to retire?"

"Sleep," he replied as he stripped off his clothes and climbed into bed. "I just do not understand."

Regnaryn was about to answer, when she realized he was not talking to her, rather, he was still trying to get his head around the situation. She turned off the lights and crawled into the bed beside him.

She lay there listening to him mumble until she drifted off to sleep.

#

:Graeden.:

Taaryn's voice came softly into his mind.

:Taaryn?:

:I wanted to make sure you are all right with this whole business. You did not say a lot earlier.:

:Of course, I am not all right with any of this. I do not want you involved. Do you have a death wish?:

:No more than you,: she replied angrily. *:Do you not think we are all worried about you going up against Jurcheval? What makes you right and me wrong?:*

:My going up against him is different.:

:Why?:

:Because, it is my duty. Because I am a...:

:Do not even think about saying because you are a man! Regnaryn is going up against him. Last I heard, she is far from being a man. As for duty, what about my duty? Do you think me helpless, or worse, hapless? Is that why you feel I should not assist in this battle?:

Graeden did not answer. He could not because somewhere within him he knew his sister was right. Still, the thought of her in such peril terrified him.

:*What? Have you no answer for me?:* Taaryn snapped. :*I may not be able to produce fireballs from my fingers, but I am not useless in a fight. And if this monster truly wants to take over the world, then if not today, then someday I will need to confront him. Is it not better to do so on our terms rather than his?:*

Graeden felt the frustration in her voice.

:*Taaryn,:* he said softly, : *you misunderstand. It is not that I feel you incapable. It is just. Oh, damn, how do I put this? The thought of you suffering even one iota of what I went through at that monster's hands absolutely terrifies me. I cannot bear the thought of you, or any of the others, experiencing such a thing.:*

He felt her mood lighten slightly.

:*Then we will just need to make sure he does not get close enough to capture any of us.:*

He could not help but laugh at her matter of fact tone.

:*Are you all right with this now?:* she asked.

:*No, but I accept the fact that it may be the only way.:*

:*Good.:*

They spoke a few more moments, then said good night.

CHAPTER THIRTY-EIGHT

:ARE YOU STAYING on the cliff?: Graeden asked.

:Yes. It keeps us from having to fly back and forth each day,: Varlama said.

:Us? You mean you,: Phrynia snorted.

:All right, me. In all honesty, there is no reason to be down there anyway. Up here is as good a place as any,: Varlama replied.

:Is it really safe up there? It has always looked so treacherous.:

Taaryn chuckled. *:It is both safe and beautiful. We can see the entire valley and beyond, and at night... well, I have no words to even describe it.:*

:This is not a social call, you two: Ayirak growled, *:We have more pressing matters to discuss.:*

:I am sorry,: Taaryn said, not hiding her embarrassment.

She looked at Ellyss.

"Do not take it personally, my love," he said. "It is just Ayirak's way. When there is a crisis, he has no time for what he considers dawdling."

:Now, down to the issue at hand—Jurcheval,: Ayirak said. *:I assume we are still of the mind that we will go to him rather than trying to draw him out to us, correct?:*

Everyone agreed.

:Good. The next thing to discuss is who will be sent to face him,: Ayirak said.

:Facing Jurcheval is not a matter of brute force, but rather one of cunning and power,: Phrynia said. *:An army is not needed here, merely a small party. Those to supply the combat skills to take on Jurcheval's guards, and those with powers to face Jurcheval himself.:*

:The magickers will be Regnaryn, of course, as well as Graeden, Taaryn, Ellyss and Romeiko,: Varlama said.

:Who do you propose for the non-magickers?: Ayirak asked.

:The drageals that take them there should be a fierce enough force—both with the element of surprise and their strength—to face anyone Jurcheval might set against them.:

:I am going, too,: Neshya interrupted, *:even if I have to sprout wings and fly myself there!:*

:Of course, Neshya, we did not mean to omit you from the list,: Phrynia said.

:Although, I must say,: Immic said, *:it would give me great joy to watch him sprout wings.:*

Everyone, including Neshya, laughed at the idea.

:That does sound like a good mix,: Ellyss said. *:How soon do we want to do this?:*

:We are ready. It is just a matter of getting everyone there,:

Ayirak said.

:*How long will that take?*: Varlama added.

:*It is a three day journey from here to where you will gather,*: Ayirak said.

:*So, you have already found a secure place to meet,*: Phrynia said.

:*Yes. We sent a small party of drageals to reconnoiter Jurcheval's palace and its surrounding areas. They found a suitable spot. It is large enough to accommodate more drageals than we are sending and it is isolated, so the chance of being seen will be minimal. This will allow them to land as soon as they arrive and not be forced to wait for the cover of darkness,*: Ayirak said.

:*That sounds perfect. How far is it Jurcheval's palace?*:

:*A few hours flight time away,*: Immic said. :*We shall not be wearied from the trip when we descend upon him.*:

:*Good thinking,*: Varlama said.

:*It will take three days for whoever is coming for Taaryn and I to arrive,*: Ellyss said. :*How far will it be from here?*:

:*Likely two days,*: Immic said.

:*I think it would be wise for those coming here to take a day or so to rest before they move on,*: Phrynia said.

:*Of course, Mother. I was thinking the same thing.*:

:*It would also be a good idea to have everyone together for at least a day, maybe two, before going after Jurcheval,*: Ayirak said.

:*Sounds good,*: Ellyss said. :*When will they depart?*:

:*The day after tomorrow,*: Immic said. :*Will that give you all enough time to prepare?*:

Ellyss looked to the others, and they nodded.

:*Yes, that will be fine.*:

:*Then it is settled, you shall all meet in about eight days from now,:* Ayirak said.

:Graeden, there is something we would like to discuss with you,: Taaryn said. *:Do you have time now?:*

:Yes, of course,: Graeden said.

:Then the rest of us will bid you farewell,: Ayirak said.

#

:Is there something wrong?: Graeden asked.

:No. We just wanted to let you know what will be happening here while Ellyss and I are gone.:

:Thank you. I was wondering about that. Are you planning on telling Mother and Father about this? Or have you already done so?: Graeden asked.

:No, we have not told them anything beyond what they learned in your letter. They are not even aware of my abilities yet.:

:They deserve to know. After all, two of their children are going off to face an enemy that may destroy them.:

:Well, I had not planned to put it that way,: Taaryn said, shaking her head. *:But we plan to tell them.:*

:Is there something else?:

:We are also going to introduce Matteus and Gantell to Phrynia and Varlama,: Ellyss said.

:You think Jurcheval may try to attack Hammarsh, even though there is no indication he even knows of it?:

:It remains a possibility,: Ellyss said.

:I would rather have them aware of us prior to an attack,: Phrynia said.

:Of course,: Graeden said and then chuckled. *:Oh, I wish I could be there when Gantell first meets Phrynia. I am sure that will be one for the ages.:*

:That is why we are including Matteus. He will be far more level-headed and accepting of all of this,: Taaryn said. *:What do you think?:*

:I am sure he will,: Graeden said. *:Give my love to Mother and Father, and I will see you soon.:*

CHAPTER THIRTY-NINE

TAARYN TOSSED AND turned that night. It was not until the meeting earlier that evening that the full gravity of the situation they faced became reality. She had, of course, always known there was a possibility that someone could get hurt, even die, but with a plan in place, it frightened her. And now, she needed to tell her parents.

"Did you sleep at all?" Ellyss emerged from the tent and approached her as she stood near the edge of the cliff and looked out over the still dark sky.

She mumbled something and put her arm around his waist. "Did I disturb you?"

He bent down and kissed her. "I am always disturbed when you are distressed."

"Good morning," Phrynia said. "Are you two ready to leave

the mountaintop?"

Taaryn and Ellyss nodded.

"I think I can carry you both in one trip. It will be a bit snug," Phrynia said and then winked, "but I do not think that will be a problem for you, now will it?"

The couple laughed.

"I will get the rigging," Ellyss said and walked away.

"What is the matter, child?" Phrynia asked when Ellyss was out of earshot.

"Nothing," Taaryn replied.

"I doubt that. Is it the fact that you have to tell your parents what is going on, or your fear of the upcoming battle?"

Taaryn stiffened. "I am not afraid."

Phrynia smiled. "If that is truly how you feel, then you are a fool. I am afraid for all of you, and I have faced many battles in my lifetime."

"Really?"

"Of course."

"That is a relief to know. I feared I was being childish or, worse yet, a coward." Taaryn sighed and relaxed her stance. "As for telling Mother and Father about all of this, that represents a whole different level of fear."

Both women laughed.

"Did I miss something?" Ellyss asked as he returned.

"No, we were just talking about family," Phrynia said. "Let us be off."

Ellyss strapped the rigging around Phrynia's neck, then helped Taaryn onto the drageal's back before climbing on himself. Once they were both secure, the drageal took to the air.

"I wish I could stay like this forever," Taaryn said as they flew down to the troilhan.

Too soon the flight concluded and they stood on the ground.

"We will contact you after we speak with Gantell and Matteus," Ellyss said.

Phrynia nodded.

"Do you or Varlama need us to bring anything back from the Keep? Food? Anything else?" Taaryn asked.

"I think we are fine. If we think of anything, we will let you know. Now, I must get back before the sun rises."

In the next moment, she was aloft and out of sight.

"It amazes me how graceful drageals are," Taaryn said.

Ellyss agreed.

#

Taaryn walked down to the water's edge, bent down and scooped up some water to splash on her face.

"We really should be leaving," Ellyss said.

She nodded and returned to his side.

"Have you decided what you are going to tell your parents?"

"Not really. To be honest, I am more concerned about what to say to Gantell."

"I will help you with Gantell, but you are going to have to deal with your parents," Ellyss said.

"I know. It is just that everything I come up with, I can hear the arguments from both of them. 'It is too dangerous.' 'You are too young.' And so on."

"That is to be expected. They are your parents, and they love you. You either tell them what is going on, or you leave them in the dark. If something should happen to us, they would never know. And that would be far worse."

She nodded. "I will tell them. I am just not sure what to say."

He put his arm around her shoulder and hugged her. "The good news is, we should arrive in time for morning meal."

She laughed. "Yes, we shall."

#

They approached the gate to the Keep just after sunrise and were met with cheerful greetings from the guards.

"It is good to have you home again, Mistress Taaryn. Sir," one said.

"It is good to be home," she replied.

They walked across the courtyard and entered the main building.

"I think it would be best if we cleaned up a bit before we make our appearance at breakfast," Taaryn said as she led Ellyss up the stairs to their room.

They entered and Taaryn almost threw herself across the room and on to the featherbed.

"Now *this* is something I have sorely missed," she said as she buried her face in the pillows.

In the next moment, they heard a knock on the door. Ellyss opened it to find one of the young servant girls with two pitchers of steaming water. She curtsied, then crossed the room and placed the pitchers beside the washing basin on the sideboard.

"Lady Prescia said she expects you both at morning meal."

Taaryn sat up and smiled. "Tell my mother we will be there."

The young girl curtsied again and quickly left the room.

"News certainly does travel fast around here," Ellyss said with a chuckle.

"It always has." She removed her shirt and then patted the

bed.

"I do not think we have time for that right now, my love."
She pouted but relented, knowing he was right.

CHAPTER FORTY

"WELL, WELL, WELL. Look who has returned," Gantell said. "So nice of you to grace us with your presence."

Taaryn smirked, crossed the room to her parents, and kissed them both. She and Ellyss found their seats at the table.

"Where have you two been all this time?" Matteus asked and then quickly added. "Never mind, it is none of my business, and I am not sure I really want to know."

The morning meal was filled with news of the goings on around the Keep during their absence.

:If they knew what we were up to,: Taaryn said to Ellyss, *:they would be shocked.:*

After the meal, as the rest of the family departed, Taaryn and Ellyss lingered.

"Mother. Father. We would like to speak to you," Taaryn said. "In private."

A look of worry crossed the faces of her parents as they both nodded.

"Of course," Emmaus said. "I have a few matters to attend to this morning. Can it wait until after that, perhaps an hour?"

Taaryn nodded.

"Good. Then we will meet in our chambers in an hour."

Taaryn and Ellyss left the dining hall only to be met by several of the younger siblings.

"Matteus may not want to know where you were," one of them said, "but we do."

The others agreed.

"We were just off on a camping trip. That is all," Taaryn said. "Nothing exciting. Sorry."

"Seriously? All that time in the wild and you were not even attacked by a wild animal?"

:Too bad you cannot tell them that you were attacked, so to speak, by a drageal and a tazzamira,: Ellyss said into her mind.

"No. Not a single attack."

The children departed, grumbling about Taaryn's boring life.

"What shall we do until it is time to meet with your parents?" Ellyss asked.

The twinkle in Taaryn's eye told him everything he needed to know.

"Woman, you are insatiable."

"I just think we should take advantage of the comforts of the featherbed while we can." She led him back to their room.

#

Taaryn knocked on her parents' door. Prescia opened it and invited them in.

"Now, what is it you need to tell us?" Prescia asked. "I fear it will not be to my liking."

"We are here to tell you of our plans to confront the Master. Jurcheval, as he is now known," Taaryn said.

"Plans?" Emmaus interrupted.

Taaryn and Ellyss told them the real reason they had gone off alone, and what had come of it.

"Are you seriously telling us that you, too, have these magical powers, like Graeden?" Prescia asked.

Ellyss nodded. "She does. Not the same, but just as impressive."

"Impressive or not, what good will that do her here?" Emmaus grumbled.

"I will not be using them here," Taaryn replied.

Both Prescia and Emmaus turned to look at her.

"We will be going to join Graeden and the others from Reissem Grove to face Jurcheval."

"Are you saying you will be directly involved?" Emmaus asked and then turned to Ellyss. "This is all your doing. First, you take Graeden away and now you wish to take my daughter, as well."

Prescia took his arm, but he shook her off.

"This whole matter is preposterous," Emmaus shouted. "I will not allow you to go."

"I mean no disrespect, Father, but I cannot abide by your wishes. The truth of the matter is, I, we, have no choice in this matter. We all must do what needs to be done."

It took a few more minutes for Emmaus to calm down enough to allow Taaryn and Ellyss to tell him and Prescia the full plan.

"I thought the reason Ellyss came here was to offer us some sort of protection," Prescia said. "If he leaves, what is to become of us?"

Taaryn crossed the room and took her mother's hand. "You will be all right."

"I was not Taaryn's only teacher," Ellyss said. "We have two allies close by that will remain here as long as they are needed."

"Allies? What allies? Where are they?" Emmaus asked, waving his hand. "I see no one."

"They are the ones who have been training Taaryn—the drageal, Phrynia, and the tazzamira, Varlama."

"A few months ago, had you said such a thing to me, I would have thought you mad, but now..." Emmaus said, shaking his head. "It is as if everything we held to be true is now debatable."

Taaryn took her father's hand, and they smiled at each other.

"Can we meet them?" Emmaus asked.

Ellyss nodded. "Of course. We would also like to have them work with Gantell and Matteus, and you, of course, Sir, to coordinate the Keep's defenses should the need arise."

"That sounds like a good idea," Emmaus said. "Shall I send for them?"

"Not just yet, we want to tell all of the family about what is going on together," Taaryn said. "We were thinking, perhaps this evening. After everyone is aware of the situation, we will meet with Gantell and Matteus to discuss what they will need to do."

"I do not wish to seem ignorant, but what is a tazzamira?" Prescia asked.

Ellyss smiled and told them all he was supposed to know of his friend.

"Where are they now?" Prescia asked.

"Atop the black cliffs."

Just as Taaryn and Graeden, her parents did not believe that was possible.

"But how did you get up there? Prescia asked.

"I flew on Phrynia's back."

The matter-of-factness in her voice left Emmaus speechless.

"Can they protect the Keep as you have?" Prescia asked.

"Far better, I am sure," Ellyss replied.

"But what of this confrontation with Jurcheval?" Emmaus asked. "I still do not like the idea of you putting yourself in such danger."

"I know, Father, but there is no other way. Regardless of the outcome, I must go and do my part, just as you must stay here and be ready to defend the Keep should we fail."

The lack of emotion in their daughter's voice surprised her parents.

What is she hiding? Prescia thought.

"Do you not have seers, like Karaleena, amongst your allies?" Prescia asked. "Surely, one of them must have some insight into what will occur. What do they see?"

Ellyss shook his head. "They see nothing."

"How convenient," Emmaus mumbled.

"When will you leave?" Prescia asked, ignoring her husband's snide remark.

"In a few days," Taaryn replied.

CHAPTER FORTY-ONE

THAT EVENING, AFTER the younger children had been sent off to bed, Emmaus gathered the rest of the family in the Great Hall.

"What is going on?" Gantell asked. "I have things to do this night."

"There will still be plenty of ale at the inn, brother," Matteus said and smirked. "If you have not yet drained them dry, no one else will in your absence."

Gantell sneered and then grinned.

"We have news of the one previously known as the Master. We have learned he is, in fact, a vile man named Jurcheval," Ellyss said.

"How have you learned this?" Gantell asked.

"We have spoken to Graeden," Taaryn replied.

She was not surprised when the room erupted in chatter and

questions.

"How is that possible? Is Graeden not still in Reissem Grove?" Matteus asked.

"Graeden and I are able to speak to each other's minds."

Again the room exploded with noise.

"Ha! Do you really expect us to believe such nonsense," Gantell said. "What kind of fools do you take us for? How can you do such a thing?"

"I do not know, it just happened," she replied. "Believe me, I was as surprised as you are. I heard Graeden speaking to me, and I just answered."

Gantell shook his head, but he said nothing more.

"As I was saying, we know where Jurcheval is, and Taaryn and I shall leave in the next few days to meet others from Reissem Grove to confront him."

"Taaryn? You are taking Taaryn into a battle?" Gantell blurted out. "Why that is as useless as trying to empty the ocean with a tea cup. If anyone should be going, it should be me."

Taaryn smiled, but she said nothing.

"Your place is here, Gantell. We have a job for both you and Matteus. And, as for Taaryn's usefulness, I do not know how much Graeden told you in the letter I gave you on my first night here, but he has awakened in himself what you might call magic," Ellyss said and saw some nodding. "The same has happened to Taaryn."

Ellyss looked at Taaryn. "Shall I go on, or do you wish to tell them?"

She nodded. He explained the real reason they had gone away and what they had done. The room fell silent, save for the occasional gasp of amazement. All listened and, more importantly, believed what he said.

"Are you saying she can throw fireballs?" Matteus asked. Before waiting for an answer, he turned to his brother. "If that is so, you had better watch out, Gant."

"Me? Why me?" Gantell asked.

His question was met with snickering.

"Do you not remember all the things you did to her when she was little? The endless teasing and everything else you made her and all of the younger ones do?" Matteus asked.

Taaryn walked to Gantell and took him by his shirt front, pulling him down towards her face. "I do. I remember every single incident, large and small."

She smiled, released him and walked away.

"It was all in fun, Taaryn. Surely you must know that," Gantell sputtered. "Just a bit of good natured teasing."

The room erupted in laughter at Gantell's groveling.

Ellyss cleared his throat. Everyone quieted to allow him to continue. When he told them what Taaryn's powers actually were, there was a distinct sigh of relief from Gantell, which made everyone in the room, including Ellyss, laugh.

"How does Graeden feel about this?" Gantell asked. "What does he think about you going into battle?"

"He has no control over what I do," Taaryn said.

"That is not what I meant," Gantell said.

"He feels the same as you do, as we all do. None of us want to have to do such a thing, but..." Ellyss said.

Gantell turned to his parents. "Are you comfortable with this?"

"Of course, not," Emmaus said. "No parent wants their child, son or daughter, to ever be put in danger. Unfortunately, that is not something we can always avoid."

"I still think I should come with you, and we should have some of our troops accompany you."

"You will be of more service to your family, and everyone else, if you remain here." Ellyss said.

"But if you fail, how are we to combat magic? We are mere men?"

"You have powerful allies nearby. They will help."

"Allies? What allies?"

Ellyss and Emmaus looked at each other and chuckled.

"That is the same thing your father asked," Ellyss said.

Ellyss told everyone about Phrynia and Varlama and that, if needed, additional drageals and the others could be summoned. The idea of drageals nearby had the room buzzing with questions, which both Ellyss and Taaryn dutifully answered.

"It is getting late," Emmaus said as he rose from his chair. "Any other questions you have can wait until tomorrow. Until then, please keep what you have heard here to yourselves."

He took Prescia's hand and the two walked toward the door. The others followed.

:Gantell. Matteus. Please stay behind a moment,: Ellyss said. *:We need to talk to you.:*

The two brothers looked around to see if anyone else had heard the voice in their heads, but it did not seem anyone did. They looked to Ellyss, who nodded at them. The brothers sat back down.

#

Gantell shook his head. "I must say, that is the oddest sensation to have someone speak into your mind."

"I agree," Matteus said.

"I know," Taaryn replied. "It took quite a while for me not to

261

jump every time it happened."

"What did you want to talk about?" Matteus asked.

"We want you, along with your father, to interact with the drageal, Phrynia, to ensure the Keep's safety should anything go wrong," Ellyss said.

"How? She may be able to speak to us, but we do not possess such a talent," Gantell said.

"We can help you," Taaryn said.

The brothers agreed and in the next moment, those in Hammarsh Keep and Phrynia spoke to each other.

:From your tone of voice, I can tell this will not be your first battle,: Gantell said.

:Sadly, it is not. Still, it has been quite some time since drageals have gone to war,: Phrynia replied.

:Will this be an all-out war?: Matteus asked.

:I hope not, but we must be prepared.:

They spent the better part of an hour discussing the resources and skills available at the Keep.

:Should we inform the nearby castles? And what of Alexandrash itself? Surely the Queen must be told of the potential threat,: Gantell said.

:Not at this time. Until we cannot contain it ourselves, I would prefer we not reveal the situation to anyone outside Hammarsh Keep.: Phrynia replied.

:Do they not have the right to know?: Matteus asked.

:Of course, they do, but do not forget how hard it was for you to believe. Can you imagine the general populace's reaction?:

:I suppose you are right.:

Ellyss snickered. *:Dear boy, you will soon come to know that Phrynia is always right.:*

:Now, Ellyss, do not go filling these boys' heads with such nonsense. I have been known to be wrong...: She paused. *:...once or twice.:*

Everyone laughed.

:Is there a chance that either of you possess the same abilities as your siblings?: Phrynia asked.

:If you mean throwing fireballs or fending off attacks with my mind, no, I doubt we can do that,: Gantell said.

:Actually, I was thinking more along the lines of mindspeaking, but the other things could also come in handy.:

:I sincerely doubt I could do that, either,: Matteus said. *:What about you, Gant?:*

:No, I doubt if I could.:

:The problem, as I see it, is that we will need to be in contact with each other and, for the time being, I cannot come to you nor you to me.:

:I had not thought of that,: Taaryn said.

:There is a solution, but it will involve you trusting me,: Phrynia said.

:Tell us,: Gantell replied.

Phrynia told him they could bind their minds together in such a fashion that they would be able to contact each other at any time.

:This is much the same thing that Ellyss did with Graeden when he helped him to escape Jurcheval's clutches. I will not be controlling any part of you, more like creating a bridge for our voices to speak mind to mind.:

Gantell and Matteus glanced at each other.

:I understand so much of this is beyond what all your conceptions of reality were. If there were any other way, I would not even

make the request to do such a thing,: Phrynia said.

:Yes, I know what you say is true, but...: Matteus said.

:Why not think about it overnight? Taaryn and Ellyss can contact me with your decision before they leave.:

:Thank you,: Gantell said in almost a whisper.

:And, as for you two, you are not to try to convince or cajole them into allowing this to happen. It must be their decision, or it will not work. Do you understand?:

All agreed.

:Good, then I will leave you for now.:

#

Gantell sat there, shaking his head. Matteus stared off into the distance. Taaryn walked over to them and put her hands on their shoulders. Each brother reached up, patted her hand, and looked at her.

"This is all so bizarre," Gantell said. "Had you told me any of this just a short time ago, I would have thought you out of your mind. And now..."

"I feel the same, and I was aware of some of this..." Matteus began.

Gantell look at him with a curious look. Matteus nodded.

"I understand," she said. "I felt the same way when Graeden first told me of all he had seen and done."

"You knew?" Gantell asked.

"Not all of it. I knew about the drageals and Reissem Grove," she said as she sat between her brothers.

"What did Phrynia mean when she said what she wants to do with us is like what you did with Graeden?" Matteus asked.

Ellyss took a deep breath, then recounted the incident at the inn and his part in Graeden's escape. He left out wiping Graeden's mind of the incident, knowing that was not something Phrynia would do. Telling them, especially Gantell, of it might color their decision.

When Ellyss finished, Gantell, who had sat in silence intently listening, put his face in his hands.

"I was not aware Graeden had suffered so. Thank you for telling me this," Gantell said as he stood. "Now, I must go and think about all that has gone on this night. I will give you my decision tomorrow."

"I, too, shall take my leave. There is much to consider," Matteus said.

#

"I am glad we decided to have both Gantell and Matteus share in this," Taaryn said. "They will need each other to make sense of so much that will happen."

Ellyss reached across the table and took Taaryn's hand in his. He looked in her eyes.

"What is the matter? You look troubled."

"It is just what you said about Graeden's ordeal."

"I thought you had heard that tale before," he said.

"Not all of it," she shook her head. "I had no idea the horrors he endured."

"I am sorry. I only spoke of it in such depth to enforce in them the necessity of my doing what I had done."

"I understand."

"Will they agree to Phrynia's request?"

"I believe they will," she said. "Despite his oft times oafishness, Gantell is a brave and honorable man who values duty above all else. As is Matteus."

"Yes, that is what I see in them, also."

She smiled at him. "I think I would like to go for a walk in the starlight. Care to join me?"

He stood and took her hand. They went out into the cool night air.

CHAPTER FORTY-TWO

TAARYN SPENT AS much time as she could with her family, making sure everyone, especially her younger siblings, received her time and attention. Too soon, it was time to go.

Taaryn and Ellyss slipped out of their room while everyone prepared for the afternoon meal, hoping they could depart unnoticed.

"You did not think we would let you leave without saying goodbye, now did you?" Prescia asked as the couple entered the courtyard.

"I guess not."

Almost immediately, the couple found themselves caught up in an onslaught of hugs, handshakes and pats on the back, as well as wishes for a safe journey and a swift return home.

"We really must be going," Ellyss said after a few moments.

Taaryn hugged her parents and siblings once more, waved to the others and joined Ellyss, Matteus and Gantell. The four walked through the gates and stopped a short distance beyond.

"Please keep in touch with Phrynia," Ellyss said.

"We have already begun doing so," Gantell replied.

Ellyss nodded. "Good. I am glad to hear it."

While Ellyss and Gantell discussed some final points of strategy, Matteus stood next to Taaryn. He put his arm around her shoulder and hugged her tightly.

"Who would have ever thought I would be the one going off to battle," she said.

"Remember, little one, this is not a child's game," Matteus said. "People get hurt or worse, so, do take care of yourself and come home to us."

"I will do my best," she said, not daring to look at him.

#

Once they moved out of sight of her brothers, Taaryn began to cry. Ellyss put his arm around her shoulder, but he said nothing. She wrapped her arm around his waist, not daring to look at him as they walked on in silence for some time.

"I told Phrynia we would be back by dusk," Ellyss finally said.

Taaryn nodded.

He pulled her closer. "I know you are sad leaving your family, but you will see them again soon. I am sure of it."

She did not respond.

They walked on for a while longer.

"Would you like to stop and have something to eat? Your mother packed some food for us."

"Why does that not surprise me?"

They sat in the grass. Ellyss opened the sack of food Prescia had handed him. He passed some to Taaryn and then took some for himself. They chatted while they ate, but avoided speaking of the obvious.

"Can we just sit here a bit longer?" Taaryn asked as they finished.

Ellyss agreed. Taaryn lay beside him, putting her head in his lap. As he stroked her hair, she smiled. He suddenly felt overcome with a sense of unexplained sorrow.

Taaryn shot up, as if sensing his emotions. She jumped to her feet. "I think it is time for us to push on. We do not want to keep Phrynia waiting, now do we?"

Ellyss was surprised by her action. Had she felt the same thing he had? He waited a moment to see if she would explain. When she did not, he said, "Yes, it is time."

#

The couple arrived at the troilhan at dusk, surprised to find both Varlama and Phrynia waiting for them. When asked, the tazzamira shrugged.

"From what I hear from Matteus," Phrynia said, "your visit went well."

"I guess so."

"Oh, come now, you totally enjoyed yourself. Especially when you had Gantell fearing you were going to scorch his hide with fireballs," Ellyss said.

Taaryn laughed. "Yes, that was a high point."

"I will say, I am quite impressed with your brothers," Phrynia said. "They both have a keen sense of strategy. I believe they will be a force to be reckoned with should the need arise."

"I agree," Ellyss said.

Taaryn scowled. "Perhaps, but please do not tell them that, especially Gant." She looked at the others and grinned. "He already has a high enough opinion of himself without additional praise."

"I will keep that in mind," Phrynia said.

"Have you had any word from Curme?" Ellyss asked.

"As a matter of fact, we did," Phrynia replied. "He said they might be here as early as tomorrow evening."

"That soon. They must be traveling at great speed."

"Youth tends to always be in a rush," Varlama said. "And since youth has long since passed me by, I think it is time for me to retire for the night."

"Yes, it is probably time we all did the same," Phrynia said. "There is a lot to do tomorrow."

CHAPTER FORTY-THREE

JURCHEVAL GREW Impatient with the lack of information about the boy. How could no one for miles around the inn have any idea of his identity?

He knew his spies would indeed do the job they were sent to do, so what was the problem? Of course, *she* was behind this. She was the reason the spies could find no trace of the boy. She was protecting him. This was all her fault.

He stormed out of the room, cursing and sending everyone unfortunate enough to be in his path scurrying for cover lest they be on the receiving end of his latest tirade.

#

The next morning, Jurcheval heard two of the spies whispering to each other about something they saw.

"What is it you are trying to keep from me?" Jurcheval bellowed through the first spy's listening stone.

Though he could not see them, he was sure they had probably nearly jumped out of their skins at the sudden interruption. That made him smile.

"Um, Sire. It is nothing."

"Tell me."

"We thought we saw something, three somethings, to be exact, flying high above us," the second spy said.

"Bah, it was likely just a flock of birds," Jurcheval said.

"At first we thought so, too, Sire, but they flew too high and seemed too large to be any bird I have ever seen or even heard of," the first spy said.

"And, Sire, they just did not look like birds."

"I see," Jurcheval said. "What do you think they were then?"

"We honestly have no idea. That is what we were trying to decide what to tell you, if anything?"

Jurcheval thought a moment. "What direction were they heading?"

"Southwest."

#

After hearing of the oddity in the sky, Jurcheval contacted Pavela and Castell, the pair of spies he knew to be southwest of the others. Once again, he savored the alarm he knew his sudden interruption created in them.

"Sire, we were not expecting to hear from you. Sadly, we have no news to report. No one in any of the villages we visited so far have any knowledge of the boy you seek," Castell said.

"So you all keep telling me," Jurcheval snapped. "I need to know if you have seen anything unusual."

"What do you mean unusual?" Castell asked.

"Are you that stupid that you need to ask such a question? Unusual…Out of place…Odd. Especially in the sky?"

"Not that we recall, Sire, but have not really been looking for anything above us," Pavela said.

"Start doing so and report back to me anything you see, even if it seems inconsequential."

The couple waited in silence for the king to explain further, but he did not.

"What do you think he wants us to look for?" Castell asked. "What would be in the sky that would be unusual?"

Pavela shook her head. "You mean besides those beasts we flew on?"

They looked at each other, almost afraid to imagine what they might next encounter.

#

After the conversation with the king, Pavela and Castell spent almost as much time looking skyward as they did to the path in front of them. On the second morning, just after sunrise, they saw high above them three spots against the clear blue sky.

"Is that what the king was talking about?" Castell asked.

"Well, they are unusual. If they are as high up as they appear to be…"

"I know, they must be massive in size. Even bigger than

273

Jurcheval's flying beasts."

Pavela nodded. "And look how quickly they are moving. We need to report this to the king immediately."

Castell had already removed the listening stone from his pocket. He held it near his mouth and whispered, "Sire. Can you hear me?"

"Have you news of the boy?" Jurcheval asked.

"No, Sire. But we did see something odd in the sky just now."

Castell went on to give the king the same vague description. Three objects that seemed too large and too high to be any bird they knew, and the fact that the things just did not look like birds. Castell added that the objects moved at a very high speed.

"Hmm," Jurcheval said. "Can you still see them?"

"No. They are already out of our sightline."

"I want you to follow them. Travel in the direction they headed. If you see them again, or if you encounter anything else out of the ordinary, inform me immediately."

"Of course, Sire."

#

With the second sighting of the odd objects in the sky, Jurcheval felt certain this was more than just a coincidence.

"Surely, those things must be drageals. What else could they be? And the only logical destination is the boy's homeland. As soon as the spies find it, I will attack. Then, the boy and, in turn, my niece will surrender and her power will at last be mine."

#

Pavela and Castell followed a path that mirrored the direction the beings in the sky flew.

"Do you think we will see them again?" Pavela asked.

Castell shook his head. "Who is to say? They seemed to be moving much faster than we can travel."

"That is what I was thinking. So what are we to do?"

"Just keep heading in this direction until we see something unusual, or we are told to go elsewhere."

The pair continued on their path with no further sightings in the sky. On the second day, the landscape changed. It went from being somewhat unremarkable to a sea of large, ancient looking trees spreading out before them.

"We should inform the king of this," Pavela said.

"Are you sure? I mean, we have yet to see anything more of the flying creatures and it could be only a forest."

"I know, but do we dare run the risk of it being more than what we see?"

"You are once again right, my love," Castell said.

#

Jurcheval sat contemplating the possibilities of what he had been told. Could the boy live in a place, a shielded place, like his niece? Is that why no one in the surrounding villages knew anything of him?

If this is so, he thought, that could dash my hopes of making both the boy and my wretched niece bend to my will. Then, he let his mind wander to the idea of what it would be like to hold sovereignty over such a place.

His thoughts were interrupted by the spy following the flying beasts again calling to him.

"What is it now?" Jurcheval growled. "Have you found something?"

"Possibly, Sire. We are now near the edge of the trees. I can see a large Keep in the distance across an open field. We do not see any of the beasts, but we are sure the Keep is large enough to hide them if they are there."

After hearing the spies' location, Jurcheval said, "Good, good. Go no further, I do not wish you to reveal yourselves."

"Of course, Sire," Castell said.

With that news, Jurcheval breathed a sigh of relief and chided himself for even thinking there was a second place like his niece's home. He smiled, thinking that even if he had to face drageals, regardless of their numbers, he could deal with them because that wretched girl would not likely be there.

"Now that our mission is completed, may we come home?" Castell said after a moment or so of silence.

"Come home?" Jurcheval laughed. "I think not."

In the next moment, all ten of the listening stones exploded and killed all of the spies.

CHAPTER FORTY-FOUR

"IT IS TOO BAD that Curme is not arriving until this evening," Taaryn said as she finished the morning meal.

The others reminded her he was already far ahead of schedule even getting there that evening.

"I know, but it would be nice to spend a bit of pleasant time with him before we have to leave."

"We will still have all day tomorrow and the next," Ellyss said.

"But three days would be so much better," she replied with a grin.

Ellyss laughed. "I think if you had your way, there would always be a drageal here."

She nodded and got back to work.

By the time everything was prepared, it was almost dusk. And

Taaryn's excitement grew to the point she could not sit still. She paced back and forth, looking toward the sky.

#

As the last rays of the sun melted away, a slight gust of air announced the arrival of three drageals at the waters' edge.

Taaryn stood in awe of the sight.

"Curme, it is good to see you again," Ellyss said.

Curme nodded. "Allow me to introduce my companions, Qhiak and Helam."

"There are three of you," Taaryn blurted out and then blushed at her statement of the obvious. "I mean, I was expecting only two."

She turned to Varlama. "Are you going with us?"

"Not unless someone knocks me out and ties me to the back of one of them!"

Everyone laughed.

"No, Taaryn, only you and Ellyss are going. Qhiak is going to travel with us about half the distance to Jurcheval's land."

Taaryn looked confused as the others nodded in agreement. "Forgive my ignorance, but could someone please tell me what is going on?"

Curme approached Taaryn and took her hand in his." My apologies. Qhiak will be stopping halfway to act as a relay. Just as one of the drageals coming from Reissem Grove will do. Need I remind you, not all of us are as adept at long-range mindspeaking as you are, dear lady. And you do not need the added burden of communicating to both Reissem Grove and Hammarsh Keep put solely on your shoulders."

"I see," Taaryn replied.

"What news have you of the Grove?" Phrynia asked.

"Speaking of manners," Varlama interrupted, "where are yours?"

Phrynia turned and glared at her old friend.

"I mean, seriously," the tazzamira continued, ignoring her friend's stare, "the poor things must be famished after such an arduous journey. Let them at least fill their bellies before you begin interrogating them."

Ellyss openly laughed as everyone else tried to stifle their reaction to the sniping of the old friends.

"Fine," Phrynia said. "And just to be clear, I was not interrogating them. I merely asked a simple question."

"Please, follow me," Taaryn said. "I hope there is enough. I was only expecting two of you."

Curme walked beside her. "Whatever you have will be fine. Drageals do not really eat that much."

Ellyss snorted. "Compared to what?"

#

After a good night's rest was had by all, the group began to discuss the plans for the upcoming encounter.

Curme spoke of the preparations that had already been made by the Reissem Grove group. "I believe once we are all together, we will be able to devise a more specific plan for when we face our enemy," he said.

"I agree," Ellyss said. "When should we leave tomorrow? Dawn or dusk?"

"It does not matter to us," Curme replied. "What do you think, Taaryn?"

"Dawn. Then I will be able to see more from the sky," she said with a smile.

"You are aware we will be flying over populated areas, so we will need to be quite high up," Helam said. "I am not sure how much you will be able to see."

"It will still be more than in the middle of the night."

The others chuckled.

"Then, dawn it is," Curme said.

CHAPTER FORTY-FIVE

"THE SPIES DID WELL," Jurcheval said.

"That is good to hear, Sire," Ilyan said. "Shall they be traveling home soon?"

Jurcheval looked at his councillor and smirked. "No."

Ilyan was about to question the king further when Undell touched his arm. Ilyan looked at the other man, who shook his head. Ilyan realized the meaning of the king's statement.

"It is time to prepare for our attack on the boy's home," Jurcheval said.

"Are you sure we have found his actual home?" Undell asked. "After all, the spies who found it neither entered nor questioned anyone nearby."

"And they did not actually see whatever was in the sky there,"

Ilyan added.

"Are you questioning my judgment?" Jurcheval snarled.

"Never, Sire," Ilyan replied. "It is just, we have so little to go on."

"We would not wish you to squander your resources on less than reliable information."

Jurcheval glared at his councillors. "I deem the information reliable. That is all you need to know."

"I do not mean to question, Sire," Undell said, "but I do not understand how destroying the boy's homeland and killing his family will make him or the girl come to you."

"The family will not be killed. They will be brought to me, alive."

"I see. You know where the boy is and if you make his family your prisoners, he will have no choice but to yield to you," Ilyan said.

"Exactly. And when the boy yields to me, so shall she."

The tone of Jurcheval's voice made the men's skin crawl.

"If there are no more questions, let us get on with the preparations. With the added weight of their passengers, it should take the sevi five days to reach their destination."

"Do you know who you will be sending?" Ilyan asked.

"I do. This time my so-called brutes, as you two previously referred to them, will be just what is needed for this mission."

The councillors looked at each other, remembering the previous conversation.

"What do you need of us?" Undell asked.

"You two will ensure there are sufficient supplies and such for their journey."

"How many are we to supply?" Ilyan asked. "And when are they to leave?"

"There will be forty-five men. The sevi can fend for themselves. They will leave tomorrow."

"Is that a large enough force to carry out such an attack?" Undell asked.

Jurcheval glared at him. "These are my men, trained and ruthless. They will be more than a match for anything that boy's family can muster."

"Will they, too, have listening stones," Ilyan asked.

"Sadly, no." Jurcheval smiled. "But the boy's family will be no match for my men."

"Of course, Sire. We will ready the supplies right away. All will be ready."

"I have no doubt," Jurcheval said.

CHAPTER FORTY-SIX

"ARE YOU AFRAID?" Neshya asked.

"Me? Bah," Immic replied with his characteristic bravado.

"Yeah, me, too."

"Do you think the others are? I mean, they possess abilities we do not."

"If they are not, they are fools," Romeiko said, emerging from the shadows.

"Why do you keep doing that, old man?" Neshya asked, not attempting to hide his annoyance.

"Doing what?" the wizard asked.

"Sneaking up on people," the yekcal replied.

"Not to mention eavesdropping," Immic added. "It is quite annoying, and downright rude."

"I did no such thing," Romeiko snapped. "Perhaps you two were just so engrossed in yourselves, you did not hear my approach. Maybe next time, I shall hail you from a distance."

Neither Immic nor Neshya liked the tone of his voice.

"Yes, please do," Neshya said.

"Is there a reason you are here?" Immic snarled.

"I was merely passing this way and saw you. I did not mean to intrude."

The trio stood glaring at each other for a few moments until the old man excused himself and departed.

"That man," Neshya said, "there is something about him that just does not seem right."

"I feel the same," Immic replied. "But my mother sensed no deceit in him."

"Yes, I know, but…"

"You do realize, it could be he is behaving perfectly fine. Other than Graeden, we really do not know any other humans."

"Regnaryn is human," Neshya said.

"She is far more like us than other humans."

"Perhaps, but I still do not trust him."

"Agreed."

#

Regnaryn's excitement at the prospect of flying was almost uncontrollable, though it helped quell, at least for the moment, her fears of what might lay ahead. After bidding farewell to friends and family, the five drageals with their four passengers were off.

"Even with all the practice flights we took," Romeiko said as the group landed at the end of the first day, "that much time in the air was taxing."

"Really?" Regnaryn asked. "I found it exhilarating."

"Why am I not surprised?" Graeden said.

She ignored him. "I actually hoped we would run into a storm or something."

Everyone, including the drageals, turned to look at her.

"Why on earth would you want that?" Neshya asked. "Do you not think there is enough danger waiting for us ahead when we reach our destination?"

"I did not want the flight to be dangerous. It is just that a storm would have made it more exciting. And fun."

"You have a strange idea of fun, sister," Neshya added. "I have no desire to be airborne on the back of a drageal, any drageal, with lightning striking all around me."

The others agreed.

"Maybe, when all of this is done, I will fly you into a storm," Immic said with a wink.

Regnaryn's face lit up. She grinned from ear to ear. "I will hold you to that."

Immic smiled. "I am sure you will."

"Now that that is settled," Graeden said, "it is time to feed our bellies and settle in for the night. I am famished."

"Me, too," Neshya added.

"So what are our plans for tomorrow?" Romeiko asked.

Neshya swallowed the last bite of food. "We fly, old man. What do you think?"

Regnaryn flashed a look at her brother.

"Obviously, boy," Romeiko hissed, not trying to hide his displeasure at the yekcal's insolence.

The yekcal growled under his breath and glared back at the old wizard.

"I was thinking we should leave early in the morning," Immic said, trying to draw the attention to him.

"Not at dawn again," Neshya and Graeden both said.

Immic and the others laughed.

"No, we do not need to leave at dawn. This area is isolated enough that we can leave at any time, so you two can sleep in a bit longer."

"Will that not delay our arrival at the meeting place?" Romeiko asked. "Do you think that wise?"

"I doubt a few hours will make much of a difference," Immic replied. "The others are not due to arrive for another day or two, so whether we arrive before sunset or after should not cause any issues."

"Unless you have a reason why you think it would," Neshya said.

Romeiko shook his head. "Nothing more than I am not a fan of flying in the darkness."

Neshya and Immic eyed the old wizard with more than a hint of suspicion. When they looked at the others, no one appeared to react similarly.

:Are we being silly suspecting the old man of ulterior motives?: Neshya asked.

:I consider it being cautious,: Immic said.

Neshya smiled. *:I like that.:*

#

As expected, the next morning both Neshya and Graeden slept far longer than anyone else.

"You know," Immic said, "I do believe if given the chance,

those two would sleep their lives away."

Regnaryn nodded.

"You used to be like that," he continued. "What changed you?"

She shrugged and smiled. "I think it was Varlama and her training. She did not allow such things."

"Well, I think it is time to rouse those two, or we will never reach our destination."

"Rouse who?" Graeden asked as he emerged from the makeshift tent. "Is that lazy yekcal still asleep?"

"Who are you calling lazy? It seems to me that you are the one who has just risen," Neshya replied.

The bantering went back and forth for the next few minutes.

"Enough! Stop this foolishness," Regnaryn said. "Both of you, get something to eat and let us be on our way."

The two friends looked at each other, laughed and did as they were told.

That evening, after another uneventful day of flying, they landed where the others from Hammarsh Keep would meet them.

"When do you think Taaryn and the others will arrive?" Regnaryn asked.

"She said they should be here before nightfall tomorrow," Graeden said.

"Good. I am really looking forward to meeting her."

"I am also," Neshya said. "I am sure she can tell us all of Graeden's deep dark secrets."

"Only you would think of that as a reason to want to meet someone," Graeden said with a wince.

"Oh, no, he is not alone," Immic said. "I, too, want to know all about your sordid past."

"As do I," Regnaryn said with a smile.

"You, my love, already know all of my secrets," Graeden said as he drew her close.

CHAPTER FORTY-SEVEN

"I HOPE WE DID not keep you waiting too long," Ellyss said as he approached those from Reissem Grove.

"Not at all," Graeden said. "You made good time, my friend."

Graeden looked around and saw Taaryn chattering away with Curme. He called to her and she looked in his direction. She held up her hand, motioning she would be there in a moment.

"That is just like her," Graeden said.

"Well, she has taken a liking to Curme, and the other drageals as well," Ellyss said.

"Oh, really?" Immic said. "Perhaps Neshya and I could use that to our advantage to find out all the things you do not want us to know about you, eh, Graeden?"

"I was thinking the same thing," Neshya said, patting

Graeden on the back. "Immic, I think you and I should go over and introduce ourselves."

"Now, just a minute," Graeden began. Before he could finish, Taaryn leapt at him and threw her arms around his neck.

He steadied himself as she kissed him on the cheek.

"Ah, Graeden, it is so good to see you again," she said, releasing her hold on him.

"Um, it is good to see you, too, Taar." He adjusted his tunic.

"Now, that is what I call a greeting," Neshya said.

Taaryn turned to the others and smiled. "Where are your manners, brother?" she asked, walking toward the yekcal and drageal standing next to Ellyss. "You have yet to introduce me to everyone."

She extended her hand to the drageal. "You must be Immic. Your mother sends her greetings."

Immic shook her hand. "It is a pleasure to meet you, Taaryn."

She turned to Neshya and studied him for a moment. "And you are Neshya, right?"

The yekcal nodded.

"Forgive my rudeness," Taaryn continued. "I did not mean to stare, but you are the first yekcal I have ever laid eyes on. I must say, my brother did you no justice in his description."

Neshya took her hand and drew her into a gentle embrace. "No apology is necessary. We are family, after all." He released her and leaned his head toward hers. "Imm and I are hoping you will tell us all Graeden's secrets, especially the embarrassing ones," he said loud enough for Graeden to hear.

"I am not sure how many secrets I know, but," she replied and winked at her brother, "we can talk later."

Graeden shook his head. "That is all I need, for you three to band together against me."

Neshya laughed. Then he and Immic pulled her in close and the three acted as if they were whispering.

"Watch out for that one," Regnaryn laughed as she teasingly pulled Taaryn away from her brother. "And since your brother has apparently completely forgotten about me, I will introduce myself."

"No introductions are necessary." Taaryn threw her arms around Regnaryn. "I am so honored to meet you, sister."

The two women shared the embrace for several moments.

"But speaking of bad manners, where are mine?" Regnaryn said as she and Taaryn separated. "All of you must be famished. Come over by the fire and have something to eat."

"Thank you, Reg," Curme said, "but Helam and I need to check on the other drageals." He paused and looked nervously at Immic. "I am sure you have been looking after them, Immic."

Immic smiled. "No worries, Curme. You are in charge, after all. I will join you after a bit, if that is all right with you."

Curme nodded, and he and Helam departed.

Regnaryn took Taaryn's arm, guided her to the fireside, and began to fill a bowl from the large pot.

"And what of us?" Neshya said. "Do we not get food?"

"You can feed yourself, brother. I am not your servant."

"Ah, so you will mistreat our other guests as you do your friends and family?" Neshya said with a wink at Ellyss.

"Oh, I am sorry." Regnaryn blushed. "Ellyss, do have something to eat." She handed a bowl to him.

"Right," Neshya continued, playfully needling his sister, "let another female come into the picture, and she forgets about everything else."

"Yes, that is how it seems," Immic added to the banter.

Graeden nodded. "Agreed, agreed. Our positions usurped by

my sister in the blink of an eye." He released a loud sigh.

Regnaryn turned toward them. She raised the spoon she had been using to fill her bowl and waved it at them.

"Watch out, she is becoming violent," Neshya cried in mock panic, running in circles as if his fear had taken over his ability to flee. "Run for your lives."

Even Regnaryn could not keep a straight face at her brother's antics. Everyone broke out in laughter.

"Enough, enough. Come, everyone, sit and eat." She finished filling her bowl and sat beside Taaryn. "But I am not serving the likes of you three. If you want to eat, serve yourselves," she continued in a not very convincing show of sternness.

"Such tomfoolery on the eve of what is to come," muttered the old man, who sat off by himself.

:Who is that?: Ellyss asked Graeden.

:Oh, I forgot you were already in Hammarsh Keep when he arrived. That is Romeiko.:

:The one who knows all Jurcheval's secrets?:

:Apparently.:

Ellyss nodded. *Hmm. Everyone, including Varlama and Phrynia, seems to accept him at face value, but I will make up my own mind about him,* he thought.

Graeden turned toward the old man. "Romeiko, come join us. You have yet to meet my sister, Taaryn, and our other comrade, Ellyss."

Romeiko joined them, politely shaking their hands. "It is good to meet you both. I hope you had a more pleasant journey than I did."

"Oh, it was wonderful. If I had my way," Taaryn gushed, "I would never come down from the sky."

The old man smiled. "Ah, to be young and reckless."

CHAPTER FORTY-EIGHT

"TAARYN," GRAEDEN SAID as the group finished their meal, "tell me of the Keep. How is everyone? And more importantly, what do Mother and Father think of all that is going on here?"

"The Keep is the Keep. You know how it is. Life goes on at its usual pace, regardless of the politics and conflicts outside its walls."

Graeden nodded. "Let us hope it remains that way."

Everyone agreed.

"As for the family," Taaryn continued, "they, too, are the same. Over the last weeks, I have seen little of them since I began training with Varlama and Phrynia."

"I knew that, but I assumed you would see them before you departed."

"We did, but it was only to bid them farewell."

"Now, Taaryn," Ellyss interrupted, "that is not entirely true."
She looked at him as if puzzled by his words.

"Your brothers, Matteus and Gantell," he said to Graeden, "are in contact with Phrynia and Varlama. And there are a handful of other people who have actually been fully apprised of the situation at hand."

"Really?"

"We thought it would be a good idea should there come a point when the Keep needs to defend itself."

"Of course," Graeden replied. "Have my brothers actually met Phrynia and Varlama? I mean, I am sure Matteus would be fine with it, but Gant? Now he is a different story."

Regnaryn shook her head. "No, but you might be surprised at Gant."

"You are not telling me he took Ellyss at face value when he first met him, are you?"

Ellyss laughed. "Hardly. He was exactly the way you said he would be, but once he realized both the truth and the depth of the situation, well..."

"Of course, having Mother and Father agree with Ellyss' every word helped," Taaryn added.

Taaryn's face brightened, and she turned to Regnaryn.

"Oh, I almost forgot. Regnaryn, it seems my mother and your mother were childhood friends. And she knew your father, as well. Is that not the oddest of coincidences?"

Regnaryn looked quite taken aback. "That is amazing. Perhaps someday she and I can talk about my parents. I have so few memories of them."

The conversation then turned to Taaryn's abilities.

"Regnaryn, you use reflective shielding, too, do you not?"

Immic asked.

Regnaryn nodded. "Yes, but from what Ellyss told us, I believe Taaryn's skills far outweigh mine. While I can be sure to reflect an attack back, I do not think I could reflect it to a specific location nor alter its intensity."

Neshya looked shocked at the response. "Wait! Is that humility I hear in your voice? I mean, I cannot be sure. I have never heard it from you, especially since your magic awoke."

Taaryn looked at the young yekcal, unsure if he was being serious or not.

"Pay no attention to them, Taaryn. Very little that comes out of that one's mouth," Graeden said, pointing to Neshya, "is ever serious toward anyone and least of all between those two. They are siblings, after all, and you and I both know how that is."

Taaryn smiled and nodded.

"So tell us more about your talent and of the training," Neshya said.

"Yes," Immic added, "I am very interested in hearing how you withstood attacks from Mother and Varlama."

"And Ellyss, too, I surmise," Graeden added.

Ellyss nodded.

Taaryn tried to make light of both her skills and the training, "Well, it was nothing really. The training was pretty much the three of them throwing things at me and me either deflecting or reflecting them."

Neshya rolled his eyes. "Oh, is that all?" he said. "Somehow, having any of those three throwing things at me is not my idea of nothing."

Graeden and Immic agreed.

"Yes, and even not knowing what you did, the short amount

of time it took you to master these skills, well, it just puts the rest of us to shame," Neshya added. "You know, girl, it is bad enough your brother here tried to show us up by coming up with this fireball thing out of the blue."

"And Regnaryn, who pretty much masters anything she puts her mind to," Immic added.

"Now, we have another one who masters not one but two techniques in less time than it took me learn to tie a knot. Geez, what is a normal yekcal to do?"

"Well," Regnaryn replied, trying to act pompous, "I guess you ordinary folk will just have to bow at our feet and give us the respect we so richly deserve. Am I correct, Taaryn?"

Taaryn tried to stifle her laughter. "Oh, yes, all the normal folk will most definitely be required to do just that." She winked at Regnaryn. "Did you say you wished to be the first, Neshya?"

Neshya looked shocked at her comeback.

"I warned you about her, did I not?" Graeden said, throwing his arms in the air.

"So you did, brother, so you did. I guess I will have to put more stock in your words in the future."

"But enough about me," Taaryn said. "What about these fireballs I have heard so much about, Graeden? What is going on there?"

"I am not sure. They just happened," Graeden replied. "I thought they were just a one-time thing, a reaction to a situation."

"And now? I heard from Phrynia and Varlama you can call them up on command. And that you control them. Is that true?"

"Yes."

Graeden seemed reticent to discuss his ability any further, so Taaryn dropped the subject.

Not long after that, Curme and the other drageals joined them. The conversation then turned to the ensuing assault upon Jurcheval's stronghold.

#

"Tell us more of Jurcheval's castle," Ellyss said.

"From what Graeden says of these kinds of places, it is not out of the ordinary. Stone walls, courtyards and inner buildings," Immic said, "is all that was seen."

"And shielding?"

"None that any of us could discern, at least not from the air."

Ellyss turned to Romeiko. "Since you seem to know the most about both Jurcheval and his land, will that hold true once we enter the grounds?"

Romeiko said, "I am not certain."

Neshya threw up his hands. Both he and Immic shook their heads, muttering words under their breath.

Romeiko glared at them. "It is as I have said all along. I do not have a clear view into either his castle or his mind. I can only surmise that, once we enter the grounds, it is highly likely we will be met with a heavy veil of evil engulfing the castle and its surrounding areas. We must be prepared for this. Our shields must be intact at all times."

"Well, that is something you have never mentioned before," Neshya snapped.

"Once we are inside," Graeden said, "what then? If it is built anything like Hammarsh, there will be defenses in place which we are not likely to see until it is too late."

"We could just burn everything to draw out Jurcheval," one of the drageals said. "Then, you magickers can take care of him."

"But what of the people?" Regnaryn asked.

"They are his people and will likely be out to kill us if given the chance," Neshya replied.

"Regnaryn is right," Romeiko said. "From what I know of Jurcheval, even when he was a child, he controls people. He manipulates them to do his will. I think there are many good people there, likely forced to do Jurcheval's bidding without even knowing they are doing it. If we just wantonly kill them, are we any better than he is?"

Ellyss said, "There will be many there of their own free will."

"Oh, great! We have to decide who we can kill and who we cannot, while all the time everyone is trying to kill us," Neshya said.

"Well, no one said it would be easy," Graeden said only half-jokingly.

"Bottom line, we really do not know what we will be facing until we actually get inside the fortress walls," Ellyss said. "We must come up with a few plans of attack for the most likely situations we may encounter."

Everyone agreed.

"At least there is one thing we will not need to concern ourselves with," Immic said.

The others looked at him, unsure of his meaning.

"The walls, people. The walls. We will be landing in the courtyard, so we need not worry about breaching the walls." Immic shook his head. "How could you forget that?"

"Do you think we will still have the element of surprise?" Taaryn asked.

"One can only hope," Ellyss replied.

The others nodded.

CHAPTER FORTY-NINE

:ELLYSS, IF YOU HAVE a moment, before you retire,: Neshya said as the group began to disperse, *:Immic and I have something we would like to discuss. Face to face. And alone.:*

:Alright, I will tell Taaryn I am going for a walk.:

Ellyss strolled toward the meeting place, uncertain what the young yekcal and drageal wanted to discuss.

"Thank you for meeting us," Immic said.

Ellyss nodded.

The three stood in silence for a few moments.

"I am sorry," Neshya said, surprising both of his companions with his humility. "But..."

"What he is trying to say," Immic interrupted, "is that we had no one else to go to for this situation."

"And since our parents consider you a trusted ally…" Neshya added.

Ellyss looked puzzled, but waited for them to continue.

"What do you think of Romeiko?" Neshya asked abruptly. "I mean, do you trust him?"

"Well, I have just this evening met the man and even that took only a brief amount of time."

"That does not answer our question," Immic insisted.

Ellyss laughed. "You are almost as direct as your mother."

"I will take that as a compliment," he replied.

"Seriously, what do you think of him?" Neshya pressed.

"You two must obviously have reservations about him, or else you would not be asking me such a thing." Ellyss watched for a reaction.

Neshya and Immic looked at each other and then back at Ellyss.

"We do. There is something about him," Immic replied.

"Something about the way he suddenly appears. How he always seems to be lurking around. I would not be surprised to have him show up here at any moment."

"I see," Ellyss said. "Is there anything else beside your guts that gives you pause about him?"

The two friends thought a moment, then went on to explain all of the things they had seen and experienced.

After listening, Ellyss shook his head.

Immic looked at him. "You feel the same. I know it. I can see it in your eyes."

Ellyss turned away, but the drageal put his hand on his shoulder.

"I have just met the man," Ellyss said.

"Still, you have your doubts, do you not?"

Ellyss nodded. "I will not deny it. I do have the sense that there is more to the man than he would like us to know, still..."

"Still?" both the yekcal and the drageal prompted.

"Still, most of us have things we prefer not to share with the rest of the world."

"I am sorry, Ellyss," Neshya said, "but we are certain there is more to the man."

Immic nodded his agreement.

"Phrynia and the other drageals do not seem to be of the same opinion," Ellyss replied.

"We know that, but..." Immic said.

"Have you thought that he seems odd to you because you have had such little contact with his kind?"

"We did, still..." Neshya replied.

Ellyss put his hand on the young yeckal's shoulder. "I will keep an eye on him."

"Thank you," the two friends said.

"Now, we should all be off. There will be much to do tomorrow, and I have had a very long day."

All agreed and went their separate ways.

#

"Where were you?" Taaryn asked as he entered their tent.

"Neshya and Immic wanted to see me alone."

"About Romeiko?"

Ellyss raised an eyebrow. "How did you know?"

"The way those two looked at the old man. Clearly, they do not trust him, even though I did not see the same reaction from any of the others."

"I see. What do you think of him?"

"The more important question, what do you think?" she replied. "You have had more experience over the years with this sort of thing. Is he that good a conjurer to be able to fool everyone but those two?"

"Well, there is something about him…"

"And?"

"To be honest, I am not sure. If it were any other situation, I would not give it a second thought. But we are dealing with Jurcheval, and we all know he is a master at mind manipulation. Is it possible he and Romeiko have been able to fool everyone?"

"I see your point, yet I still sense some conflict within you."

Ellyss smiled and kissed her cheek. "You know me so well. The man was able to get inside Reissem Grove. Whatever, however, the shieldings of that place were constructed, they would never allow an enemy inside."

"Did you remind Neshya and Immic of that?"

He shook his head.

"Please tell me you did not just dismiss their concerns."

"No. Of course, not. I merely told them I would keep an eye on the old man."

"Good. Now, it is time for both of us to get some rest."

CHAPTER FIFTY

AFTER THE MORNING meal, the group gathered once again to talk about the upcoming events.

"Romeiko, can you see more clearly now that we are closer to Jurcheval's stronghold?" Graeden asked.

The old wizard looked around the circle. "Not everything is clear, but I sense activity there. I fear he may suspect we are coming or has seen us."

"Seen us? But how?" Neshya asked.

"Who is to say? He likely has spies everywhere."

"Even so, how would he have seen us?" Immic asked, not trying to hide his suspicion of the old man.

Romeiko laughed. "Young drageal, even under the cover of a darkened sky, if one is looking in the right place at the right time, one might see the glint of moonlight off an object and realize something should not have been there."

"Well, whether he is aware of our approach or not, we still need to finalize the plans we began last night," Ellyss said.

"Agreed," the others said.

"What about the castle?" Regnaryn asked. "I must assume, since you knew where he was, you have some idea what the inside of his palace is like?"

"I do," Romeiko said.

#

That night, Regnaryn tossed and turned before falling asleep. And when she dreamed, she saw nothing but her failure, which resulted in the death and destruction of all she held dear. Suddenly her dream changed. The turmoil turned to serenity and Regnaryn saw the face of one she had sorely missed.

"Child, why do you worry yourself so over this?" asked Jucara, the emuranda who initially helped her to come to grips with her fledgling power.

"What if I falter and fail? What, then?"

"Regnaryn, you will do neither of those things. You did not do so when he attacked the Grove, and you will not do it now."

"But what if I do? Or, worse yet, what if he is stronger than me, as he has always said?"

Jucara chuckled. "We both know that is not true. He has never been stronger than you, which is why he so covets your power."

The young woman shook her head, but she said nothing.

"If you truly are concerned, there is a technique I can teach you. But I warn you, you must only use it if there is no other way and all hope is lost, for it will make the destruction wrought at the gawara cave look like the flame of a candle that even you may not survive."

"I understand," she said, not hiding the fear she felt at the thought of such a thing, "Show me."

CHAPTER FIFTY-ONE

ONCE QHIAK ACCEPTED the fact she would not be part of the offensive against Jurcheval, she decided to make the most of the situation. Her time, both day and night, would be spent soaring high overhead and exploring. She had never been very far from Reissem Grove and all of the new sights, sounds and smells fascinated her. Who knew if she would ever get the chance to come this far from home again.

The next day, after she relayed the message that Curme and the others had arrived at their meeting place, she once again took to the sky. This time, however, as she flew she saw something. Something that should not have been there. Something she had not expected.

She immediately mindcalled to both Phrynia and Curme.

:Are you sure they were not just large birds?: Curme asked.

:I know the difference between a bird and those beasts. I will never forget what they look like.: Qhiak snapped. *:Or what they did.:*

:That is not what I meant,: Curme said.

:Enough!: Phrynia said. *:What exactly did you see?:*

Qhiak told them as they listened in silence. Only when she said they carried riders, multiple riders, on their backs, did they respond.

:Are you sure? No, of course you are,: Curme said. *:Could you tell how many?:*

:I saw ten beasts and each seemed to have four or five riders on their backs.:

:And you are sure they were heading in this direction?: Phrynia asked.

:Yes, I am sure of it,: the young drageal said.

:Does that mean what I think it does?: Curme asked.

:It certainly sounds as if Jurcheval has found Graeden's home or at least the general area of where they reside,: Phrynia said before she chuckled.

Both Curme and Qhiak shook their heads in wonder at her reaction.

:I am not sure what about that idea is amusing,: Curme said.

:Oh, there is nothing amusing about his finding us. I am amused at his total disregard for the true nature of these people. Does he really think he can defeat these good people with such a small force?:

:Perhaps he thinks the sight of those beasts will paralyze them with fear,: Curme said.

Phrynia laughed. *:Well, if he does, he and his troops will indeed be in for a surprise.:*

The other drageals agreed.

:Should I return to the Keep to assist you and the others?: Qhiak asked.

:No,: Curme said, *:you need to stay where you are. Now, even more than before, we need you as our communications relay.:*

:You must keep your eyes open for anything else, land or air, heading our way,: Phrynia said. *:Curme, I think it best that you not reveal to the others what we have discussed here. We do not need Graeden and Taaryn distracted by this news.:*

:I understand,: Curme said.

:Now, I must prepare those in the Keep for what is to come,: Phrynia said. *:Curme, contact the Grove to send reinforcements here.:*

:Of course. Do those in the Keep know of us?: Curme asked.

:They will now,: Phrynia said. *:Qhiak, I will contact you as soon as there is any news from here.:*

#

"What is it?" Varlama asked.

"He has found us."

"Have you contacted the brothers to warn them to prepare?"

The drageal nodded. "We are going to meet with them now."

Before the drageal could say another word, the tazzamira grabbed the riding apparatus and motioned Phrynia to allow her to put it on.

"Where shall we meet them?" Varlama asked as they took off from the cliff top.

Phrynia laughed. "Gantell said to come right into the courtyard."

"We are not really going to do that, are we?"

"No, not yet. I think the people of the Keep will need a little bit more preparation than us just dropping out of the sky. After all, we will need them to have their wits about them in the next few days."

"So?"

"The brothers will meet us outside the troilhan."

#

Matteus and Gantell knocked on the door of their father's office and entered without waiting for an invitation. Emmaus looked up from the papers his aide was presenting to him. Without a word from them, he knew something was amiss.

"We will finish this later," Emmaus said to his aide.

The woman nodded and gathered up the papers. "As you wish, My Lord."

She smiled at the brothers as she left the room.

"I hope whatever it is you have to say warrants your poor manners," Emmaus said.

The brothers nodded, then informed their father of what Phrynia had told them. Emmaus drew in a breath and shook his head.

"This is dire news, but something we have planned for," Emmaus said. "Do you think the situation warrants bringing everyone within the confines of the Keep?"

"I am not sure," Gantell said, "but it would not be a bad idea to do so."

"Especially those living just outside the walls," Matteus said. "The farmers further out should be safe from the initial attack."

"But they should be advised of what is happening and given the choice to stay in their homes or to come here," Gantell added.

"Of course." Emmaus reached for the bell rope behind him.

In a matter of seconds, a servant appeared. "Inform the Chief Councillor I need to see her immediately. Then, find as many messengers as you can and have them assemble here in an hour."

The young man nodded and quickly departed.

"What is your plan?" Emmaus asked his sons.

"We are going to meet Phrynia and Varlama to further discuss the situation," Gantell said.

"And then we will bring them here. We thought it better if they arrive with us rather than just appearing unannounced," Matteus added.

"Bah," Gantell snickered. "I still say they should just fly into the courtyard."

Emmaus stifled a chuckle. "Why does that not surprise me?"

"From what Phrynia has told us, we have a bit of time before the enemy's arrival," Matteus said. "I think it might be best to bring them here tomorrow, in the light of day. While Taaryn had no problem meeting a drageal in the dark of night, I am not sure everyone else would feel the same."

"I agree," Emmaus replied. "And that will give your mother and I time to talk to everyone this evening. We need to help prepare them and the Keep for what is ahead of us."

The three men agreed. The brothers departed as Emmaus' Chief Councillor arrived.

CHAPTER FIFTY-TWO

"OUR YOUNG ALLIES approach." Phrynia pointed to the two horses galloping toward them.

Even from a distance, Varlama and Phrynia saw the look of amazement on the young men's faces.

The brothers dismounted and approached the drageal and tazzamira. Both looked at the two before them, at each other, then back at Phrynia.

"You are far more amazing than we were led to believe," Matteus said as he and Gantell bowed to them.

Phrynia smiled. "Let me guess, the stained-glass window in the Keep. Yes. I have heard about that. I will definitely make a point of seeing it while I am there."

The brothers nodded.

"I think we should go into the troilhan," Varlama said.

"The what?" Gantell asked.

"The place Taaryn and Ellyss ran off to for all that time. Follow me, and yes, there really is a way through the trees large enough for your horses."

"Unfortunately, not large enough for me," Phrynia said. "I will meet you inside."

Before the brothers could respond, the drageal launched into the air.

#

"It has been a bit of time since we were here," Varlama said, "so I am not sure what we can offer you in the way of food."

Matteus smiled. "That will not be a problem, we brought food, though we were not sure what either of you ate. That conversation never came up when Taaryn told me about you."

"So what do we know of this approaching enemy?" Gantell asked as the foursome sat and began to eat.

Phrynia and Varlama told them of their first encounter with Jurcheval's flying beasts and of the attack on Reissem Grove.

"How can we hope to defend against them if they killed so many of your magical folk?" Matteus asked.

"They killed our children during a sneak attack. That will not be the case here. This time, we know they are coming and we will be prepared," Phrynia said.

"They will not be facing children," Varlama added.

"You say you think they will be here within a few days. How can we prepare so quickly?" Gantell asked.

"You began preparing for this from the moment Ellyss first brought you news of Graeden and the Master. And even more so since the day we first spoke, have you not, my boy?"

"Yes, but that was for an attack by our own kind, a foe we would be evenly matched against. One we stood a chance of defeating."

"It appears they have humans with them," Varlama said. "Your people will take care of the human attackers, and we will handle the beasts"

"What if they are not humans or if they are like Graeden and Taaryn? How will we handle them?" Matteus asked.

"We have not heard that any of Jurcheval's people have magic," Phrynia said.

"And from what we know of him, if anyone did show any magical prowess, Jurcheval would dispose of them. He does not like competition," Varlama said. "Should it turn out there are some with magic, we will take care of them."

"How?" Gantell asked. "If you are dealing with the flying beasts, how will just the two of you handle so many?"

"We will be more than two." Phrynia said and then smiled at the brothers' puzzlement. "I have already sent for reinforcements from Reissem Grove."

"Reinforcements?" both brothers asked.

"Yes. Several more drageals will be here within two days. We will be able to handle the beasts, as well as any magickers that may be with them."

The brothers looked at each other in amazement.

"But how?" Matteus asked. "How did you contact them? I thought only Taaryn and Graeden were able to talk to each other across that distance."

Gantell looked at his brother. "What? How do you know that?"

"Taaryn told me."

"You are correct, Matteus, none of us can mindspeak across the distances your brother and sister can. We set up a relay system with some of our strongest mindspeaking drageals. That is how we learned of the enemy's approach."

"Very ingenious," Gantell said.

"What of your people?" Varlama asked. "Have you prepared them for our arrival so that when it comes time for the battle they will be able to keep to the task at hand in our presence?"

"My troops are always on the ready for battle," Gantell said, "and I have already prepared many of them for your arrival. Though I was not aware of the flying beasts."

"Our parents are gathering all in the Keep and those from the surrounding farms and villages to tell them of your coming," Matteus added.

"Good," Varlama said.

"We thought it best if the four of us arrive at the Keep near midday tomorrow. As we both realized earlier, even knowing you are real, seeing you for the first time in the flesh still took us aback. Adding the element of darkness to that first meeting would not help."

"I agree," Phrynia said.

"Will Varlama fly with you to the Keep?" Gantell asked.

Phrynia burst out laughing. "I sincerely doubt that."

Gantell and Matteus looked confused.

"Unlike your sister, I dislike flying," Varlama said.

"That is an understatement," Phrynia said, still laughing.

Varlama shook her head. "I will be accompanying you two. And do not worry. Even if you ride at a full gallop, I can keep up with you. Though, I would prefer you not test my speed."

"Of course, not a full gallop," Gantell said.

"Has Graeden been told of this development?" Matteus asked.

Varlama and Phrynia shook their heads.

"We thought it best he and Taaryn not have the added worry of what is going on here."

"That is what I was hoping you would say," Matteus said.

For the rest of the evening the four discussed the upcoming battle. The brothers, especially Gantell, asked many questions as to what they would be facing.

"Well, I must be going," Phrynia said. "I have been here far too long. I shall see you all in the morning. Sleep well. We have much work ahead of us."

Before the brothers could respond, Phrynia departed. They looked at Varlama, who shook her head.

"Damned drageal. Sometimes she just does not have any manners."

"Where did she go?" Matteus asked.

"Back up to the cliff top."

"Why?"

"When we are in a place like this, no one, not even Taaryn, can mindspeak to the outside world. So, while we are not expecting any news from Qhiak, the drageal who first saw the enemy, we do not wish to be out of contact with her for any great amount of time. So, Phrynia went to the cliff top where they can communicate with each other."

"Ah, I see."

"Good, now I think it is time we retire for the night. There is room enough in the shelter for all three of us, unless you wish to sleep outside."

"The shelter sounds good to me," Matteus said.

CHAPTER FIFTY-THREE

THE COURTYARD INSIDE the Keep was abuzz with curiosity over the sudden, unexpected summoning. No one, not even the messengers, who brought what was clearly more than just a pleasant invitation, seemed to know what was going on. Finally, the doors opened. Emmaus, Prescia and several members of the High Council emerged.

"I am sure you are all wondering why I called you here this day on such short notice," Emmaus began. "I assure you, I have not done so lightly. I have grave news, much of which you may find hard to believe, but every word is true."

Emmaus looked out at the confused crowd, and he smiled reassuringly.

"For a very long time, longer than all of us have been alive, we have lived in a state of peace and tranquility. Unfortunately, that is about to change and in a manner none of us, even in our wildest dreams, could have ever expected."

The crowd reacted, as he had anticipated, with shock and disbelief. He allowed them to chatter amongst themselves for a few moments before quieting them.

"We are about to face an enemy the likes of which we have never seen. An enemy that can attack from the air on beasts we never knew existed. An enemy that may even employ magic."

"Magic?" a man shouted. "Surely you joke, My Lord, there is no such thing."

Much of the crowd agreed with him.

Emmaus raised his hand, and the crowd quieted.

"Do I look like I am joking?"

Their Lord's stern tone immediately changed their laughter to fear.

"If what you say is true, how can we fight against magic?" another person cried out.

"My good people, there is no need for alarm. We have powerful allies close by who will aid us."

The crowd quieted now hushed. Many shook their heads in disbelief.

"Who and where are these allies and this strange enemy you speak of?" an old grizzled farmer, one Emmaus recognized as a retired soldier, shouted.

"One of our allies is a race I had never heard of, a tazzamira, and the other is a drageal."

The crowd again exploded with the sounds of awe and disbelief. Emmaus did not respond, he stood quietly looking out over the crowd. After several minutes, they fell silent.

"You are serious, My Lord," the old farmer said. "I can see it in your eyes."

Emmaus nodded. He looked out over the faces before him, many struggling to grasp what he was saying as truth.

"I understand your reticence to believe. I, too, did not want to accept it, but recent events have forced me to reconsider. And reminded me of what someone once told me. The world outside our sheltered walls is far more dangerous than we could ever imagine."

"Tell us more!" someone shouted.

Emmaus smiled, relieved to know his people believed him. He nodded and servants made their way through the crowd, distributing drink and tidbits of food. As they sipped and nibbled on the food, he told them what he knew. As expected, he was interrupted on more than one occasion with questions he answered to the best of his knowledge.

"So when will these allies arrive?" someone asked as Emmaus finished.

"Tomorrow. Matteus and Gantell have gone out to meet them."

"And the enemy?" the old farmer asked.

"By all accounts, they should be here in several days."

"That does not give us much time to prepare, even with a drageal and the other one."

"You are right. But we were warned such an attack might be imminent, though we were not sure who or what it might entail. Gantell and our troops have made precautionary preparations."

"Why were we not told of this possible threat before now?" someone asked.

"With the uncertainty of the warning, we chose to keep both the threat and the planning quiet, to avoid alarm."

The crowd continued to whisper and murmur amongst themselves.

#

Matteus, Gantell and Varlama prepared to leave the troilhan midmorning.

"How long will it take to get there?" Varlama asked as the brothers saddled their horses.

"At a full gallop?" Gantell asked with a twinkle in his eye.

Varlama smiled. "If you wish, but do remember who you are dealing with, dear boy."

"You have indeed met your match, brother," Matteus said with a laugh. "But seriously, at a normal pace we should arrive there in about an hour."

"Good. Phrynia will meet us there."

#

A short distance from the Keep, Phrynia joined the others.

"I thought it best if we enter together," she said.

Varlama laughed. "You never fail to amaze me. I expected you to just swoop in and land in the middle of the courtyard in a flurry of feathers."

"I did consider that," Phrynia said. "But this is not the time, nor place, to make a spectacle of myself."

Matteus chuckled. "Regardless of how you two arrive, you will create a spectacle."

"Yes, I suppose you are right," Varlama replied.

As they approached the Keep, they heard the sounds of a gathered crowd.

"I hope you are ready for this," Matteus said.

"I hope they are ready for this," Gantell said, motioning to the Keep.

"Regardless if any of us are ready," Phrynia said, "we must all face what is to come."

#

The crowd immediately quieted as the gates opened to allow entrance to the brothers and Varlama. They watched in awe as the golden drageal landed beside the other three. With the drageal and tazzamira in full view, the crowd erupted in excited chatter and exclamations of shock, surprise and disbelief at what they were seeing.

Emmaus and Prescia immediately made their way to greet their guests, though it took a moment or so before Emmaus could compose himself enough to speak.

"Forgive my rudeness," Emmaus said and bowed. "It is just the sight of you in the flesh far outweighs even my wildest imaginings of what you would be."

Varlama and Phrynia nodded to him.

"Allow me to welcome you to our home," he said.

Emmaus turned to the crowd. "My good people, may I introduce you to our honored guests and allies, the drageal, Phrynia, and the tazzamira, Varlama. Please bid them welcome."

What had been a hushed murmur, turned into shouts of excitement and greeting.

"Thank you, people of Hammarsh Keep, for your kind welcome," Phrynia said. "I only wish this meeting was under better circumstances, but the threat of violence often has a way of bringing good people together."

"While the situation is indeed unfortunate," Prescia said, "we are still honored to have you among us."

"I have informed the people of what I knew of the situation at hand," Emmaus said. "Perhaps, you could tell us more."

Phrynia nodded and related details about the approaching enemy and their master to the eagerly awaiting crowd.

"With all due respect," a voice called out, "how will we defend against so many airborne enemies, if only you are able to attack them from the sky?"

"A valid question," Gantell replied, "and one I asked, as well."

Phrynia looked out across the crowd. "As I told Gantell, I shall not be alone. As we speak, several more drageals from my homeland are in flight here to assist us."

Her reply both calmed the crowd's fears and excited them at the prospect of meeting more drageals.

"If there are no more questions," Emmaus said, "our guests, my staff and I will retire to discuss our plans." He waited a moment, then continued, "As I said last night, I want all of you to come back to the Keep prior to the start of the attack. If you have not already done so, go back to your homes, gather your things, and return here by nightfall tomorrow."

He turned to Phrynia for affirmation of the timeline, and she nodded.

The crowd acknowledged Emmaus' request. As they dispersed, they again began to chatter about all that had gone on this day and what was to come.

#

:*Does it look different than you remember?*: Varlama asked.

:*A little,*: Phrynia said as they arrived in the Great Hall.

"Ah, that must be the window I have heard so much about

from your children," Phrynia said.

Emmaus looked at the window and back at Phrynia. "Well, there is a striking resemblance."

"Funny, I cannot see it."

:You crafty old lizard,: Varlama said. *:You really are not going to tell them.:*

:Now is not the time.:

Over the next hour or so, the group discussed the preliminary plans for both the attack against the enemy and the defense of the Keep, putting off any finalization until the others arrived.

"It is wise of you to bring your people within the Keep's walls," Varlama said as the meeting disbanded. "While they may not have been in danger even had they stayed in their homes, it is better to be safe."

"Exactly what I thought," Emmaus said.

CHAPTER FIFTY-FOUR

AS MIDDAY APPROACHED, Emmaus, Phrynia and the others awaited the arrival of the drageals from Reissem Grove.

"I fear we do not have enough room to make all of you comfortable," Prescia said.

"Do not worry, my dear," Phrynia said. "The drageals will stay on the cliff."

Prescia looked relieved.

"They are almost here," Phrynia said.

As the four drageals landed, all on the ground were stunned to see they carried two passengers, the likes of which no one in the Keep had ever seen before.

"Well, this is a surprise," Phrynia said. She turned to Emmaus, Prescia and the others. "May I introduce you to the yekcals, Ayirak and Trebeh."

"It is a pleasure to meet you," Ayirak said. "We thought a little more ground support might be in order."

"And," Trebeh said as she approached Prescia, "I wanted to meet the kin of my daughter's mate."

The two women hugged as if they were old friends.

"Shall we go to the Great Hall to discuss the plans?" Emmaus asked.

#

"It has been many years since blood was shed on the fields surrounding Hammarsh Keep, or since we have had to defend against an outside threat," Emmaus said.

"It is good you did not allow your people to become fat and complacent. I have no doubt they will meet this threat bravely and emerge victorious," Ayirak said.

"Let us hope so."

"I am glad you decided not to tell Graeden and the others of this just yet. They will have more than enough on their minds facing that monster," Trebeh said.

"We thought so, too," Phrynia said.

"Tell me what you have planned," Ayirak said. "Are we going to employ a preemptive strike? Attacking them in the air, before their riders have a chance to even face those on the ground?"

"Once we realized there would be five of us that could take flight," Phrynia said, "it did become a distinct possibility."

"I do not wish to put your people in greater peril than is required," Emmaus said, "but from what Phrynia and Varlama have told us, those beasts are hardly a match for any drageal."

"It makes more sense to dispatch the enemy before they have

a chance to land and allow their passengers to disembark," Ayirak said.

"And, if any survive to the ground, our people will take care of them," Emmaus said.

"When do we expect them? I know Qhiak was the first to see them. Have we had any further word of their progress since then? Surely you are not having her track them all the way here," Ayirak said.

"Qhiak watched them for a bit, and I have been looking for them as well. As of yesterday, they were still not in the range I flew."

"Did we lose them? Or could Qhiak have been wrong?" Ayirak asked.

"Neither. They are moving quite slowly with the burden of so much weight on their backs. Jurcheval apparently has no concern for the welfare of his beasts."

"Ha!" Trebeh snorted. "That is no surprise."

Everyone agreed.

"I am certain they are still on the course they set. If they continue at the same rate of speed as when they were first seen, they should be here the day after tomorrow," Phrynia said.

"Ah, the same time the others should be facing Jurcheval," Ayirak said.

Phrynia nodded. "And hopefully, neither of our enemies are aware of our plans."

"Then, this time we will have the element of surprise," Trebeh said.

"Where will our attack take place?" Ayirak asked.

Gantell unrolled the map on the table.

"Unless they change direction, the best place would be here," Gantell said, pointing to a spot on the map. "It is open and isolated and surrounded by trees that could serve as cover, if needed."

"There is also a water source nearby should there be any issues with fire," Emmaus added.

"That looks good," Ayirak said. "Very good."

"Since we are expecting them in two days," Gantell said, "I am going to send a few of my troops there tomorrow to gather water and have it placed around the perimeter of the attack zone so we will be prepared."

"Do you think he has sent another force to attack us on a different front?" Ayirak asked.

Gantell smiled. "We seem to think alike, sir. I know that is what I would do."

"The question is, do we seek them out or just prepare for them?" Emmaus asked.

"I say we just make sure we are ready for them, should they arrive," Phrynia said. "The Keep is set in such a way that any ground attack must cross the open flatland. Your ancestors knew what they were doing when they built this place."

:*You should know*,: Varlama said into the drageal's mind.

The discussion continued, covering the details of both the attack on the flying beasts and the preparations for an assault on the Keep.

"I will be off now to meet with the other drageals," Phrynia said when their plans were complete.

"Will you and the others not be joining us for dinner?" Prescia asked.

Phrynia chuckled. "Even your amazing staff would be taxed to feed the likes of four additional drageals and two yekcal, dear lady. We will find our own meals."

CHAPTER FIFTY-FIVE

:WHAT DO YOU SEE below?: Neshya asked.

:There does not appear to be anyone in the courtyard,: Immic said.

:No one at all?:

:No.:

:Is that normal? Or do they know we are coming and are lying in wait for us?:

:I doubt they are aware of our approach,: Graeden said. *:Unless this was a day of celebration or whatever, the people are likely just going about their normal business. In fact, I would be more concerned if the courtyard was full of people.:*

:Ah, of course, just like in the Grove.:

:I am sure it will not take long for the alarm to be sounded once

we descend,: Ellyss said. *:We must be on our guard. I doubt Jurcheval will just allow us to walk in and face him without resistance.:*

#

They landed in the empty courtyard with not much more than a whoosh of wind. It took a few moments for the alarm to be sounded. Then, the courtyard immediately filled with armed men and women, some clad for battle, others with no armor at all.

"What a pleasant surprise, niece. How considerate of you to save me the trouble of coming after you," Jurcheval's voice boomed seemingly from everywhere. "I see you have brought some friends, along with your pets. I do hope they bring me some amusement before they die at the hands of my people."

The group from Reissem Grove and Hammarsh Keep reacted to neither Jurcheval's voice nor his words. Some already knew it from his attack on the Grove, and the others had been warned.

"What? None of you have the courtesy to answer me? How rude. I thought your father would have taught you better manners."

Still, no response.

"As you wish," Jurcheval said, his voice as velvety smooth as it had been during Regnaryn's first encounter with him. In the next moment, he shouted. "Bring her to me. Alive. Do as you wish with the others."

At that command, the troops surrounding them began their attack.

As the first wave attacked, Romeiko mindspoke to the others. *:Do not kill these people.:*

:What?: Neshya cried. *:They are certainly trying to kill us.:*

:It is as I told you before. Most are not acting of their own accord. Jurcheval is controlling them. Go after the heavily armed troops. They

are the ones we need to dispose of. :

:Are you sure?: Ellyss asked.

:Yes. If I can break Jurcheval's hold on the others, perhaps they will join us,: Romeiko replied.

"Watch out, Taaryn," Graeden shouted as he saw two heavily armed men attempt to descend upon her from behind. Before his warning had even left his lips, the two attackers were tossed against the stone wall across the courtyard and slid to the ground in lifeless heaps.

Two drageals maneuvered to the outer perimeter of the courtyard and began to attack the heavily armed troops who seemed to be waiting. As the drageals' fire approached, the troops fled into the courtyard, forced into the battle.

"This is doing us no good here…they just keep coming and we are no closer to our prey," Graeden said.

"Agreed," Ellyss replied.

"Then it is time for you to find Jurcheval. Find him, and end him," Neshya said. "The drageals and I will take care of things here."

"Romeiko, are you coming with us?" Ellyss asked.

"No, I can be of more help here, releasing the innocents from Jurcheval's grasp."

Regnaryn, Graeden, Ellyss and Taaryn turned and ran into the castle, easily defeating the troops who tried to stop them.

#

"How can Jurcheval have so many at his command?" Neshya called out as yet another wave of troops appeared to battle them.

"The more that come to us," Immic said, "the fewer the others will have to deal with inside."

"True, but there are still so many. Has this place always just been evil and that is what drew him to it?"

"This place was no worse than any other before he arrived," Romeiko replied. "But the people had become too comfortable in their existence. Most never even noticed the changes he brought until it was too late. The few who would not yield to him he disposed of."

"Ah, so that is why so many of them, once released from his influence, are aiding us," Immic said.

"There are still many that are not changing," Curme said. "They are now directing their attacks at the humans rather than us or are using them as shields. Cowards!"

"At least there seems to be less of them than the others," one of the other drageals said.

"Let us hope we are seeing their true numbers and not that we are just being diverted while our friends are being overwhelmed," Helam said.

"For the moment," Neshya said, "that is not the case."

"Good, but let us not dally," Immic replied.

All agreed, and they doubled their efforts.

CHAPTER FIFTY-SIX

AT DAWN, AYIRAK, Gantell, Emmaus and the drageals departed the Keep to join Gantell's troops already in place to face the aerial threat that would soon be upon them. Those left behind prepared for a ground attack they hoped would not occur.

The group arrived at the open field, noting the Keep's troops had already prepared the area with water barrels and had secured places for themselves under the cover of the trees.

"This looks very good," Emmaus said. "I doubt if those beasts will even know we are lying in wait for them."

"I agree," Ayirak said. "Your people have done a remarkable job."

"The beasts have been seen," Phrynia said. "They should be here within the hour. It is time the drageals take flight and the rest of you prepare yourselves. Good luck, my friends."

#

"We have positioned some troops within the tree line." Matteus motioned to the area across the field from the keep. "That will allow us to box the enemy in as they approach."

"That is very strategic thinking," Varlama said. "Graeden said you had a good head on your shoulders."

Matteus cleared his throat. "I am not sure about that. It is just logical to prepare an attack from more than one side."

"Do you really think we will come under attack?" Prescia asked.

"I hope not," Varlama said. "But should it come, we are prepared."

"That we are," Trebeh said. "Matteus, you and the others have done a fine job on such short notice."

"Thank you," he replied.

"Now comes the hardest part of any war or battle," Varlama said.

The others looked confused at her words.

"The waiting," she said. "The time when you know you must remain alert and not let your mind succumb to the monotony and boredom of nothing happening that tries to lull you to sleep. You wish the fight to begin, but you fear what might happen and how you will react when it does."

"I am guessing you have been in this situation before," Matteus said.

Varlama nodded. "Even once is one time too often. I wish you and your kin could have lived out your lives without having to experience it, but that is no longer an option."

"What if they have flying beasts we did not see?" Prescia asked. "How will we deal with them."

"Varlama and I have some magic that would likely counter any attack from above," Trebeh said.

"And if need be, we can have one of the drageals return to aid us," Varlama said.

Prescia nodded. "I do hope the others will be all right. The uncertainty of not knowing what is going on is maddening."

Trebeh put her arm around the woman's shoulder. "You forget, my dear sister, we can communicate with the others. Know they have arrived at the selected place and are laying their traps."

#

When the beasts were over the open field, the drageals swooped down upon them. This time it was the Reissem Grove folk who had the element of surprise on their side.

Before the beasts or their passengers could react, they found themselves engulfed in flames. Both humans and beasts screamed and shrieked as they were overcome by fire. The beasts tried to turn upward to face their attackers, but the added burden of their passengers made such a maneuver impossible.

In an attempt to save themselves, the beasts writhed and rolled until their cargo became dislodged and plummeted to the ground. Phrynia and another drageal attempted to break ranks to try to save the people, but the beasts went on the attack. Since they outnumbered the drageals, they would not forfeit life or limb of their own to save an enemy bent on killing them.

Phrynia mindcalled to Ayirak to warn them about what to expect in the next few moments.

Though outnumbered, the five drageals quickly disposed of

the beasts, sending them crashing from the sky in fiery masses.

:*How goes it on the ground?*: Phrynia asked.

:*I think we have everything under control. The fires from those beasts are not as bad as we feared, although some of Emmaus' people are quite shaken by what happened to the humans.*:

:*Sometimes, I just do not understand humans. Those people were determined to kill all of us. Which is a better death, to fall from the sky or to be burned to death?*:

Ayirak smirked. :*Ever the pragmatist, eh?*:

:*I suppose so. Since you have the situation here taken care of, we are going to check the area surrounding the Keep. They have not yet seen anything, but I think it best we make sure there really is not another attack coming. I would hate to be too hasty in presuming there is no other enemy out there only to have them take us by surprise.*:

:*Good idea. We will finish up here, and I will let you know when we are on our way back.*:

#

"We are so glad all went well today," Emmaus said as everyone gathered at the Keep.

"Yes, nary a singed wing among us," Phrynia said. "How are your people holding up after what happened to the enemy."

Emmaus shook his head. "Some better than others. I fear many will have nightmares about what they saw for a very long time. I know I will."

"While we cannot make you forget what you saw," Trebeh said, "Varlama and I may be able to help soothe your minds and help you recover and better cope with it."

"I have heard of your healing powers," Emmaus said. "Your assistance will be greatly appreciated."

"While what did happen was devastating, I am grateful there were no other attacks," Prescia said.

"I do not understand why Jurcheval did not launch a two-pronged attack. Surely he has the manpower," Gantell said.

"Ah, that is what often occurs with those blinded by their own self-importance. They can never imagine anyone being as smart or powerful as they until, thankfully for us, it is too late," Varlama said.

"Oh, I do hope that is what the others are finding," Prescia said.

All agreed.

"Speaking of them," Phrynia said, "I think it is time we contact Qhiak so she can share what transpired here."

CHAPTER FIFTY-SEVEN

REGNARYN AND THE others entered the palace and within a few moments were confronted by more of Jurcheval's troops.

"Surely those cannot be the best he has to offer," Graeden said as they easily dispatched their opponents.

"I am sure they are not," Ellyss said.

"Where is he?" Taaryn asked.

"Wherever it is, I doubt he will be hiding," Regnaryn said.

"Agreed. My guess would be in the throne room," Ellyss said.

"Well, if this place is anything like other castles I have seen, it will be in the middle of the structure. I think it would be this way," Graeden said.

"Be on your guard," Ellyss said. "We are sure to encounter his guards the closer we get to him. Mind you, they are likely far more skilled than those we have met so far."

The group warily maneuvered down each corridor, occasionally finding troops whom they dispatched without issue.

"Are we heading in the right direction?" Regnaryn asked. "This feels like a maze. It is unfortunate none of us can sense him."

"I would think that, as long as we continue to encounter resistance, we are heading the right way," Graeden said.

"Well, which way now?" Regnaryn asked as they came to a hallway that led off in both directions. "I do not see anything or anyone down either corridor."

"This way," Taaryn said and headed to the left.

"How do you know?" Ellyss asked as he followed her.

Taaryn shrugged.

Graeden chuckled. "I guess one way is as good or bad as the other."

They slowly made their way down the hall. Heavily armed guards suddenly set upon them.

"Well, it looks like you chose the right way," Graeden shouted over his shoulder as he fought off one of the guards.

"You always said I could sense trouble," Taaryn replied.

After defeating the last of the guards, Taaryn shook her head. "I guess that means we are really close to Jurcheval."

"So it would seem." Ellyss said. "Where to now?"

She looked surprised to be asked.

"Well, you got us here, so lead on," Graeden said.

"In that case, this way."

#

:I have news from Hammarsh Keep,: Qhiak said.

Graeden and Taaryn froze where they stood, shocked by the drageal's decision to contact them now. *:What do you mean?:* they asked in unison.

:*The troops and flying beasts Jurcheval sent to attack the Keep,*: the drageal continued.

:*What? An attack on Hammarsh?*: Graeden interrupted.

:*Yes. Those sent by Jurcheval have been handily defeated without a single injury to any of our people.*:

Sighs of relief escaped everyone.

:*Phrynia, Varlama, Ayirak and Trebeh all wish you the same success.*:

They glanced at each other in shock.

:*Wait,*: Graeden said. :*Are you saying Ayirak and Trebeh are also at the Keep?*:

:*Yes, they and four drageals went to the Keep after I first saw the enemy approaching.*:

:*What? You knew of this, and we were not informed?*: Graeden snapped.

:*That was a decision made by Phrynia and myself,*: Curme said. :*We thought the worry over your homeland might be too much of a distraction.*:

:*Distraction?*: Graeden shouted at Curme. :*How dare you drageals make such decisions for me?*:

:*Calm down, Graeden,*: Taaryn said.

Graeden glared at her.

:*The important thing is they are all safe. Thank you, Qhiak. Now it is time for us to get back to our task at hand,*: Taaryn said.

#

They continued through the maze of corridors until they found a hall with a large door at its end. They neared it, shocked to see it covered in writhing black snakes.

"What in all that is holy is that?" Graeden said.

"I do not know, but I am not getting any closer to it," Taaryn replied.

The four studied the door and its unwelcoming inhabitants. Ellyss took a step forward and reached toward the door.

"What are you doing?" Taaryn cried.

"Do not worry." Ellyss thrust his hand into the mass of snakes, and they suddenly disappeared. "It was nothing more than an illusion meant to intimidate. I am sure the real threat lies within this room."

All took a deep breath as Ellyss flung open the doors.

#

:This room seems empty,: Taaryn said as they ventured into the dark room. *:Could we be in the wrong place?:*

:No,: Ellyss replied. *:This is just another of his games.:*

:I agree,: Regnaryn said. *:I am sure he will appear at any moment to try to take us by surprise.:*

They crept deeper into the room and, once again, they encountered Jurcheval's guards. Guards who appeared out of thin air, a trick that would indeed rattle most other foes. As the last of the guards were dispensed, a bright flash lighted up the entire room.

"At last you have come to me," Jurcheval said, his voice almost a cackle.

Graeden and the others were taken aback by Jurcheval's tone more than his words.

"Sevich, brother of my father, I bring you nothing but your own demise."

"So, you know who I am. Then surely you know I shed the skin of that weakling long ago, although not before I destroyed both

341

your father and his pitiful excuse for a mate." He laughed.

Though she had suspected her uncle was the culprit, hearing his admission along with the memory of that laugh, sent a cold chill down her spine and momentarily shook her. She regained her composure and steeled herself for more of his mind games.

"You cannot rattle me, Sevich," she purred.

"I told you, I rid myself of both that name and existence long ago after I was reborn from the ashes!" He rambled incoherently for several minutes about the differences between his former and current selves.

:Is this an act, or is he truly a raving madman?: Graeden asked the others.

:Have we ever thought him to be sane?: Ellyss replied.

:Sane or not, we must stop him,: Regnaryn said.

The others agreed, though all silently worried about what he might do.

"Jurcheval or Sevich. The name does not matter. Today will be your end," Graeden said.

"Ah, the boy with the fireballs that killed my sevi. I, too, like to play with fire, but I can conjure far more than fireballs." The fireplaces around the room strained to keep their flames contained and then returned to normal. "And who are you two?" he asked, directing his attention to Ellyss and Taaryn. "I was led to believe Regnaryn and the boy were the only humans in that wretched place. Are you the ones from the south? His family, I presume. Wonderful. It is so fulfilling to kill others in front of their family, so much more raw emotion and life force for me to assimilate."

No one responded.

Jurcheval turned his attention back to Graeden. "It may interest you to know that, at this very moment, my troops are decimating your homeland. They were instructed to make sure everyone in that place suffers greatly before they die."

Graeden smiled.

Jurcheval looked confused, momentarily fearing he had sent his troops to the wrong location.

"Are you trying to tell me you have no emotional attachment to that place? To your kin?" He shook his head. "And they say I am heartless."

Graeden laughed. "There is nothing to be emotional over. Your forces were easily routed without a single casualty to my people."

"Your troops were defeated at Hammarsh Keep. But that is not all. Surely, you feel your grip, your hold, over this place and its people slipping away. Soon, you will be alone to suffer defeat," Regnaryn added.

Jurcheval's arrogance faltered as rage overcame him. He cursed at all who stood before him. In the next moment, he regained control. "You are wrong, girl. None of the others matter. You have always been the prize I sought and one I will soon possess. What to do with the rest of you? I have never had a drageal at my beck and call, and now you have brought me so many. Ah, the possibilities..."

:He is truly a madman,: Taaryn said.

:A madman or a genius trying to make us think he is mad,: Ellyss said. *:We must not let down our guard.:*

"Your minds are strong," he said, as if knowing their thoughts. "I have beaten ones far stronger. As for you, dear, dear niece. I shall leave you until last. I shall not end you until you have watched me destroy all you hold dear. A fitting end for all the trouble you have caused me."

Regnaryn shook her head and smiled. "You have said that many times, Sevich." She watched him bristle at her continued use of his former name. "Somehow, you have yet to come close to doing any such thing."

"So, you had no feelings for those I destroyed outside that wretched place you call home? Did that not show what I am capable of?"

Regnaryn swallowed the sorrow that welled up at the memory of those who had perished. "You murdered helpless children. That is not power. It is cowardice."

Jurcheval clenched his fists and glared at her.

"My father was right," she continued. "Even now, you are nothing more than a spoiled child throwing a tantrum."

"Enough talk," Graeden said.

Jurcheval turned toward Graeden. "Have you forgotten the pain I inflicted upon you at the inn, boy? Perhaps you need a reminder."

Graeden felt Jurcheval try to breach his shielding and laughed. "Ha! You forget I am no longer the vulnerable innocent I was then. You can no longer hurt me like that."

Jurcheval seethed. "If I cannot breach your mind, I will destroy your body."

In the next moment, Graeden cried out as he was engulfed in flames that seemingly came from nowhere. Taaryn and Ellyss ran to his side and extinguished the flames with their cloaks before Graeden could be injured.

The sight of Graeden distracted Regnaryn. For a brief moment, her focus slipped.

Jurcheval made his move. He took a step toward her and spoke ancient words only Ellyss understood. As the words left his lips, Regnaryn felt as if something was holding her. She tried to break free, but she could not move.

"Now, at last, I shall have your power," Jurcheval said.

Regnaryn began to convulse as her uncle's spell took a greater hold on her.

"No, you shall not," Taaryn said and stepped toward Regnaryn.

She took Regnaryn's hand.

"Come, sister, together we shall defeat him."

Regnaryn nodded as she broke free from the spell.

Jurcheval laughed. "You cannot stop me, girl. Get in my way, and I will destroy both of you where you stand."

Neither woman responded.

Jurcheval smiled. Then, he realized something was wrong.

"What are you doing to me?"

"What you intended to do to me," Regnaryn said.

"No!" he shouted and collapsed to the floor, too weak to move. "This cannot be happening! I was resurrected by the demon god Jurcena himself. He could not have meant my existence to end at the hands of the likes of you," he wailed.

CHAPTER FIFTY-EIGHT

THE STENCH INFORMED Jurcheval he no longer stood in his throne room. "Where am I?" he shouted as he opened his eyes.

"Do you not recognize this place?"

The unfamiliar voice, soft yet menacing, filled Jurcheval with unfamiliar emotions—dread and fear. He took a breath to calm himself.

"Or have you never visited where you have sent so many of your victims?" the voice continued.

Jurcheval looked toward the voice, but he saw nothing more than a dark shadow.

"Who are you, and why have you brought me here?" Jurcheval demanded, his voice cracking just enough to display his fear.

"You invoke my name, speak the ancient tongue, yet do not

recognize me?"

"Jurcena? My Lord," Jurcheval bowed his head in reverence.

The sulfur stench intensified as the shadow expanded.

"I am not your lord. The thought of something as weak and inconsequential as you daring to say I had anything to do with any part of your existence disgusts me."

Jurcheval trembled. "I do not understand. I have patterned my life after you. Everything I have done has been to honor you and your memory."

"Ha! Do not lie. Everything you have done, every heinous act of torture or murder, you did for your own satisfaction. There was no thought in your mind of me or any other god or demon. You are pitiful."

Jurcheval sneered. "If that is truly how you feel, then I reject you and all the others."

Jurcena laughed. "As if your fealty ever meant anything to us. Now, begone and face your fate at the hands of your betters."

As Jurcheval looked toward it, the shadow changed into the shape of a man. A somewhat familiar man, but not one he could immediately identify.

#

In the next moment, the voices of Regnaryn and the others let him know he was again in his throne room.

"What are we to do with him now?" Graeden asked.

"If you ask me..." Neshya said as he and Romeiko entered the throne room.

"Leave him be," Taaryn interrupted. "His power is gone. He will never be able to gain any of it back. He cannot harm anyone ever again. Living like that, with no power, will be a far greater punishment than anything else we could do to him."

She turned and walked toward Ellyss.

Jurcheval drew up all the physical strength he had left, picked up the sword that lay on the ground next to him and threw it at her, hitting her squarely in the back. She immediately dropped to the ground.

"Not all my power, girl!" he shouted. He looked at the others and laughed

As Taaryn fell, Regnaryn raced toward Jurcheval.

He looked at her and smirked. "And what are you going to do? Kill me like you did my gawara and sevi?"

She glared at him.

"Well, do it. Kill me. Fulfill the deepest desire in your heart. Achieve your revenge for what I did to your weakling of a father. Do it. Strike me down with blade or fire."

Regnaryn felt the desire to incinerate him as she had done to the gawara rise within her.

The others watched in horror as she stood before him. They called to her, but she did not respond.

As Jurcheval continued to taunt her, the desire to annihilate him grew. She closed her eyes, feeling the heat of a thousand flames within her. Just one thought, and he would be gone. She opened her eyes. Jurcheval stood there, grinning at her.

She shook her head. "No."

"Ha, I knew you did not have the stomach for such things. I know how you suffered and mewled like a babe each time you had to kill something. You will not strike me down, especially now that I am weak and powerless. If you did, your worst fear would come to be. You would be just like me." He laughed.

"I will never be like you." She turned to the others. "I am

sorry. I just cannot kill him. Not this way."

Jurcheval laughed. "Ah, I so love the morality of others. It makes it so easy to control and destroy them."

Jurcheval turned to leave only to have his path blocked by Ellyss.

"You!" Jurcheval cried, recognizing him as the shadow figure.

Ellyss nodded. "It is your bad luck that I am not bound by morality and have no qualms over ridding the world of the likes of you, regardless of the state you are in," Ellyss said and thrust his blade deep into Jurcheval's chest.

Jurcheval looked in disbelief first at the sword and then at the man who put it there. "But, I served no one but you, My Lord..." he said as he dropped to the floor dead.

#

As soon as he released his grip on the sword in Jurcheval's chest, Ellyss ran to Taaryn's side. He pulled the blade from her body and turned her towards him. She smiled and brushed away the tears that had begun to stream down his face.

"It is all right, my love, this was the outcome I knew was to be. This is what I was shown. Be happy, my beloved, we have won. We have defeated Jurcheval. And, more importantly, you are free from the burden you have borne for so many eons."

"Why? Why did you turn your back on him?" Regnaryn screamed in anguish as she and the others approached. "How could you be so reckless?"

Graeden, tears streaming down his face, took Regnaryn in his arms to console her.

Taaryn smiled at them. "It was not reckless. It was foretold...foreseen...chosen."

"By whom? When? How?" Ellyss cried, unable to stop the flow of tears.

Taaryn just smiled at him. "Regnaryn, you were the one who needed to survive. You and Graeden. The rest of us are minor players in the scheme of things. But you two have a great legacy to build together. You have a destiny to fulfill that will, indeed, change the world forever."

"This is his doing. He coerced you."

"No, my love, there was no coercion. I did this of my own free will."

Ellyss looked up and screamed. "Do not do this! I beg of you, do not let her die. I will do anything, anything at all...forsake everything, even her, if you will only let her live. She is not the one who deserves to pay the ultimate price, I am. Condemn me to the fires of a thousand volcanoes for a million lifetimes or more. I beg of you."

The others looked at each other in confusion, struggling to understand the meaning of Ellyss' words. He vehemently pleaded, but with whom?

Taaryn motioned to Ellyss. He leaned in, and she softly kissed his lips.

"My love, you have already paid the ultimate price over countless ages. It is now your turn to be free, to live as a normal man. That is the bargain that I freely struck with Xanchad."

"No! No! I will not allow it," he screamed, pulling her to his chest.

She stroked his face, pushing the hair from his eyes as she smiled. "This time, you have no say in the outcome, but know this, I will be waiting for you when your journey ends."

She pulled his face to hers and kissed him again. "Be happy, my love. That is my final wish."

She closed her eyes and was gone. Ellyss held her close to him as he wailed.

CHAPTER FIFTY-NINE

A LARGE COLUMN of red smoke appeared, shocking everyone. It stopped in front of a kneeling Ellyss as he clutched Taaryn to his chest. The red smoke transformed itself into the shape of a man.

Ellyss tearfully looked up. He rocked back and forth, still cradling Taaryn in his arms.

"Xanchad! I know you put her up to this, compelled her into agreeing to it."

"No. This time I did not. Before I even had a chance to suggest such a bargain, she freely offered her life in order to free you from your punishment. All I did was show her how this conflict would play out, thus revealing to her how and when her sacrifice would be accepted."

"Why would you accept such an offer? Surely, she did not

fully understand what she was doing."

The red smoke figure shook his head. "She knew exactly what she was doing. As a matter of fact, I had no desire to free you from your torment, but she was quite persuasive. I see why, after all these ages, you gave your heart away."

"Please, I beg of you, bring her back. I will gladly spend the rest of time in whatever hell you desire. As an insect stepped on and painfully smashed over and over for eternity, or whatever else you wish if you will just bring her back."

Xanchad laughed. "Ah, while both that suggestion and your offer of burning in a volcano, sounds tempting, you know that is not how this works. Have you forgotten the rules? If an innocent freely offers to give their life in another's name, they are released. I will admit that I, and the others, never expected such a thing to happen in your case, but it has. She has done this. You are free. The bargain with the young woman is binding."

"Surely there is a way out. Something I can offer you in exchange," he begged.

Xanchad shook his head and put his hand on Ellyss' shoulder. "You are mortal now. As such, you have nothing to offer. Is not your mortality what you desired? What you have pled with us to grant you through the ages, Jurcena?"

"Yes, that is what I wanted all these many years, but this price is too high. This cost is too dear. I am not worth it."

The others, still in shock over Taaryn's death and the appearance of the red smoke, looked at each other in disbelief at the name the smoke figure called Ellyss and how he so casually answered to it.

Ellyss raised his head and faced Xanchad. "I realize my crimes were unforgivable, and I have accepted my punishment as it was laid down before me, only occasionally over the ages praying for it to end. I again implore you, negate the contract this innocent has made with you and let things go back to what they were before—I in eternal servitude to you and the others, and she once again vibrant and alive. I beg of you."

Xanchad laughed. "Jurcena, is not taking her from you, even if it is only for a human's lifetime, a much harsher punishment than anything else I could devise?"

"But, by allowing her to die this way," Ellyss continued, "you are not only punishing me but her family and all others who know and love her. Look at her brother, see how he suffers already. And what of her parents? Are they to endure this pain for the rest of their lives also? I swear to you, Xanchad, bring her back and I will leave her thereby carrying that additional punishment with me until the end of time."

Ellyss shook his head and sobbed. There was no more he could do, no more he could say. If Xanchad refused to listen, refused to bring Taaryn back...

"I do not know who you are or what this man's crimes were," Regnaryn said, stepping forward, "and it is true I have only known him a short time. But, in that time, I have seen a man who is honorable, loyal and loving. You say he deserves to suffer. That may be true, but to what end?"

Xanchad turned to Regnaryn and hissed, "You have no right to speak to me, mortal."

"Perhaps, but it is you who has chosen to appear before us and allow us to hear your words. So I will give you mine." Regnaryn continued, ignoring the fact Xanchad had changed his form from that of a human to a cloud of smoke that now enveloped her and obscured her from the view of the others. "If your only purpose for punishing

Ellyss is to cause him pain then there is nothing more to say. But if the purpose of his punishment was to show him the errors of his ways, to make him repent his sins, is this the right course for you to take?"

"You do not fear me?" Xanchad asked.

"I do," she replied.

Xanchad reformed himself into the shape of a man, stood before her, and then laughed. "Ah, of course, now I recognize you. You are Regnaryn. We know of you."

Regnaryn shrugged, surprised by his words. "I am of little consequence."

"I think we both know that is not true. You are the one so many have been waiting for."

Regnaryn did not respond.

"So," Xanchad continued, "you feel my actions are unjust. I do have a contract with the girl. She freely offered her life to free Jurcena, or Ellyss, as you call him. Why should I break that contract?"

"Because of the pain it will cause so many others. She offered herself out of love for Ellyss. That was perhaps not the wisest thing she ever did in her young life. Yet her motives were unselfish and noble. Perhaps in your world those things have no meaning, but they do in this one. And I know with every fiber of my being that letting her die, and letting Ellyss and the others suffer over losing her, is not right."

Xanchad did not respond.

Regnaryn shook her head. "You must do what you feel necessary. We both know I have no means to force you to my way of thinking. Whoever you are, whatever you are, you must at some level know that what you are doing here is wrong."

Xanchad turned to Ellyss. "This is quite surprising and unexpected, Jurcena. In all the years you have walked this world, you have never had others that were so willing to stand up for you, to the point as this one did to sacrifice her life. It does seem, with all who are willing to stand by you, that you have indeed learned the lesson your punishment was meant to teach you, a lesson that I and the others seem to have lost sight of through the ages."

Ellyss, with tears still running down his face, looked at Xanchad. "I care nothing about myself...of what I have or have not learned. All I desire is that you revive Taaryn, then I care not what you do with me."

Xanchad looked at Ellyss. "Yes, I do believe that is the truth. Something that, up until this time, you would never have suggested. It has taken this long for you to be willing to sacrifice yourself, your entire existence, for another. Yes, you have come a long way in this journey. I do believe the time has come for it to end."

Ellyss was not sure what Xanchad's words meant, but he did not care as long as they meant Taaryn would be saved.

#

The next instant Taaryn coughed and opened her eyes. Ellyss' tears flowed but now with joy. He embraced her and she him. She saw Xanchad and broke free from Ellyss' embrace.

"What is happening here? You cannot renege on our contract. You must set Ellyss free. That was our bargain."

"Now, now, girl, I have already done so. At the moment of your death, his punishment was lifted," Xanchad said.

"At the moment of my death, but if I am dead," she looked around to see the others, "why are they here? They cannot be dead, that was not part of our agreement. This cannot be," she cried. "This was not part of the bargain."

Xanchad laughed. "You were dead, and now you are not.

None of you are dead, at least not yet."

He watched in amusement as Taaryn grasped his meaning. He continued, "I have, in fact, allowed both of you to have your heart's greatest desire. You wanted him to be free of his curse. It is done. He wanted you to be alive. That, too, is done."

"You are serious," Ellyss said joyfully. More cautiously, he added, "No, there must be something more. You are not the kind to do such a thing without other consequences."

"True, true. You know me well, Jurcena. Yes, there are conditions to be met before these things will come to pass."

Ellyss' heart plummeted.

"Neither of you will have magic or power, none whatsoever. Not even the ability to speak mind to mind. You will both be ordinary mortals with all the pains and sorrow and eventually death that go along with that existence. Do you understand?"

The couple nodded.

"And you both agree to these conditions?"

"We do," they said in unison.

Xanchad nodded and then turned to Regnaryn. "I will be keeping my eye on you. It will be interesting to see if you..." He stopped. "Ah, I will say no more, some things are best left unstated. We will all just have to wait and see how things transpire with you."

He let out a final laugh and then disappeared as quickly as he had originally appeared.

Ellyss and Taaryn did not seem to notice. They held each other tightly, murmuring words only they could hear.

CHAPTER SIXTY

"WHO WAS THAT and what was all that talk of eternal punishment and life sacrifices?" Neshya asked.

"I think the only ones who could tell us that is those two," Romeiko replied.

"Is it not best to leave these matters as they are? I do not think we really need to know," Regnaryn said. "We have both of them, and they are happy."

The others nodded.

"But where did Jurcheval's power go?" Neshya asked as the group left the throne room to join the others outside.

"I dissipated it into the air," Taaryn said as she and Ellyss walked up behind the others. "I could not be certain how any of us would react with that level of evil power being thrust upon us. I would hope that none would turn, but…"

She looked at the others, hoping no one took offense at her words. She was glad to see that they all nodded in agreement.

As they reached the drageals, Immic approached. "We have sent word to both Reissem Grove and Hammarsh Keep about the victory here."

"And of Taaryn?" Regnaryn asked.

"We said nothing other than all were safe and the evil one dead," Curme added.

"I guess with the news of our victory, Phrynia, Varlama and the others will be returning to Reissem Grove," Taaryn said. "I had hoped to see them again."

Immic put his wing around her. "You will, dear one. Mother said they would wait for your return."

Taaryn smiled.

"As for this place," Ellyss said, his arm still wrapped around Taaryn's waist, "what will happen here now that the evil taint is gone?"

Romeiko turned and motioned to one of the men they had previously fought. "I believe we have found someone to take charge."

The man stood next to the old wizard and looked embarrassed. "I apologize for my, for our," he said, pointing to some of the others, "inability to better defend ourselves from that man's influence. And for what he made us do."

Regnaryn took his hand. "Do not apologize, good sir, we understand."

The man kissed her hand. "Please stay with us awhile, all of you," he said. "Allow us to thank you for freeing us."

"While we appreciate the offer," Graeden said, "we must be going."

Romeiko stepped forward. "If it is all right with these good people, and all of you, I would like to remain here. This seems a good place to live out the rest of my days."

"If that is your wish, Romeiko," Regnaryn said.

The old man nodded.

"Then, we wish you the best and offer our gratitude for all you did to help us. And know you are always welcome in Reissem Grove."

She hugged him and then kissed his cheek. And, for the first time since she met him, the old wizard looked flustered.

#

That evening, the humans, yekcal and drageals regrouped at their previous camp.

"Graeden, will you and Regnaryn return to Reissem Grove?" Taaryn asked.

Graeden looked surprised. "I had not really given it much thought," he said.

"You cannot possibly still have the doubts over how Regnaryn would be received nor how she would react to those at Hammarsh Keep, can you?" Taaryn asked.

Graeden shook his head and looked at Regnaryn, remembering those bitter memories that led to their previous separation.

"No, Regnaryn can handle anything. And we neither seek nor require the acceptance of anyone else. It is just that, well," Graeden continued, "I just have not given any thought to going home. I guess I assumed Regnaryn and I would just stay in Reissem Grove."

Taaryn looked hurt. "And never come back? Are you saying this is the last time I will see you...that Mother and the others will never see you again."

She turned away before he could see the tears welling in her eyes. Graeden put his hand on her shoulder.

"You know, no matter how many times we tell Mother you are all right, she will not fully believe us until she sees you with her own eyes," Taaryn said. "And everyone would love to meet Regnaryn."

"I think it is a wonderful idea," Regnaryn said. "I would so love to meet the rest of your family."

"Curme and I were just discussing our departure plans," Ellyss said. "And we think perhaps we should all go to Hammarsh Keep."

"Really? Everyone?" Taaryn and Graeden asked as one.

Ellyss chuckled. "Just a few short days ago, I would have said that would have been an implausible thing to suggest, but after what has gone on there, I see no reason not to."

"Yes, after all, everyone in the Keep has already seen drageals and yekcal, so it will not be a shock to see a few more," Taaryn said.

"Oh, I so wish I could have seen Cook's face when she saw them for the first time," Graeden said.

"I wonder if she has been fattening them up to the point the drageals will no longer be able to fly?" Taaryn said with a chuckle.

Taaryn scrunched down to about half her height, wrapped her arms around Neshya and did a little dance that both Ellyss and Graeden recognized as a good imitation of Cook. The others laughed, imagining the tiny woman they all had heard so much about.

"Good, then it is settled," Ellyss said.

"We really should get word back to Reissem Grove of our

plans," Graeden said.

"It has already been done," Immic said.

"We will, of course, need to maintain the relay system now that..." Curme began and stopped.

Taaryn smiled at him. "Do not fear, dear Curme, I do not mourn the loss of my abilities. I received something far more precious in return." She clasped Ellyss' hand before he drew her closer.

Curme nodded. "I understand."

"Oh, I am so excited about this," Regnaryn said. "How long do you think we will stay?"

Graeden shrugged.

"You all will be welcome for as long as you wish," Taaryn said. "Now that the drageals are known to those in Hammarsh Keep, you can visit as often as you wish."

"And perhaps, little sister," Neshya said, "we can get you to visit Reissem Grove."

Taaryn was thrilled with the idea but then her face darkened. "What if it will not let me in? What if I am not one of those chosen by it?"

"That is possible," Ellyss said, "but highly unlikely. That place knows good people and you, my love, are very good people."

"And perhaps on our return trip, Graeden, you and I could travel on horseback," Regnaryn said, wrapping her arm around him.

Graeden looked at her with surprise

She smiled and continued. "I have seen very little of the world outside Reissem Grove. Perhaps it is time for me to do so."

Graeden smiled, up until that moment he had not been sure Regnaryn really wanted to visit Hammarsh Keep.

Neshya shook his head. "You know, after this, everything will change."

"It already has," Regnaryn said.

***

Also by Dot Caffrey

The World of Drejon Series
The Power Trilogy

AWAKENED: Book One
CURSED: Book Two
CONQUEST: Book Three

About the Author

I was born and raised in New York, mostly on Long Island not "The City". After high school, I moved to California and then did a three-year stint in the Navy before going to college and getting a Microbiology/Medical Technologist degree.

According to my Dad, I've been a storyteller from the time I began talking (which was at a very young age). But, it wasn't until a few years ago that I decided to take my passion for writing and my love for all things magical or mythical seriously and set out to write fantasy novels.

When I'm not at my day job or writing, I enjoy creating and wearing costumes (cosplay), playing video games (though, I'm not very good at it) and watching NHL hockey and assorted other things many of which are merely time wasters. Of course, hanging out with my friends and my cats also pleasantly fills my time.

I invite you to join my mailing list by visiting my website
http://dotcaffrey.com

You can also "Like" me on Facebook
http://facebook.com/DotCaffreyFantasyAuthor